P9-BIW-641

ARMY WITHOUT BANNERS

Other Spectra titles

Between the Red and the Rockies, Grant MacEwan
In Western Canada Before the War, Elizabeth B. Mitchell
Red Lights on the Prairies, James H. Gray
Mice in the Beer, Norman Ward
The New North, Agnes Deans Cameron
Trooper in the Far North-West, John G. Donkin

ARMY WITHOUT BANNERS

JOHN BEAMES

Foreword to the Spectra edition
by Dick Harrison

Western Producer Prairie Books
Saskatoon, Saskatchewan

This Spectra edition copyright © 1988 by the estate of John
    Beames
Foreword to Spectra edition copyright © 1988 by Dick Harrison

Western Producer Prairie Books
Saskatoon, Saskatchewan

All rights reserved. No part of this publication may be
reproduced, stored in a retrieval system, or transmitted, in any
form or by any means, electronic, mechanical, photocopying,
recording, or otherwise, without the prior written permission
of the publisher.

Originally published by Ernest Benn Limited, London,
    England, 1931

Cover illustration courtesy Public Archives Canada C 82970
Cover design by John Luckhurst/GDL
Printed and bound in Canada

Western Producer Prairie Books is a unique publishing venture
located in the middle of western Canada and owned by a group
of prairie farmers who are members of Saskatchewan Wheat
Pool. From the first book in 1954, a reprint of a serial originally
carried in the weekly newspaper *The Western Producer,*
to the book before you now, the tradition of providing enjoyable
and informative reading for all Canadians is continued.

The publisher wishes to acknowledge the assistance provided
by the Canada Council for this publication.

Dick Harrison would like to acknowledge the assistance of
John Beames's family, particularly Mrs. Amy Ward, in the
preparation of the foreword to this new edition.

Canadian Cataloguing in Publication Data
Beames, John, b. 1889.
    Army without banners

    (Spectra)
    First published: Toronto: McClelland, 1930.
    ISBN 0-88833-262-9

I. Title. II. Series: Spectra series.

PS8503.E25A75 1988   C813'.52   C88-098016-8
PR9199.2.B42A75 1988

Foreword to the Spectra Edition

After reading this thoroughly engaging story, readers may wonder why *Army Without Banners* took more than half a century to find its way into a popular reprint. In addition to its historical value as one of the few authentic fictional accounts of pioneering in northern Saskatchewan, it is also a pleasure to read, enlivened as it is by humour and deepened by John Beames's honest assessment of the pioneer experience.

Descriptions in the novel have the ring of authenticity because Beames was himself a pioneer farmer. Born in 1889 in India, where his father served in the British Army, he attended a public school in England, and at the age of fourteen moved with his family to a homestead north of Prince Albert. Major Beames seems to have been one of the feckless dreamers who are often drawn to a frontier, and his sons were obliged to run the family farm. John also "worked out" as a lumberjack, mill hand, and trapper, and hauled freight with dog teams and horses on winter trails like those he describes in *Army Without Banners*. He made his way off the farm by becoming a bookkeeper and part-time writer, publishing stories in various pulp magazines. In 1928 his agent persuaded him to move to Toronto and devote himself full time to writing. Soon the Depression threatened his livelihood, closing down many of the magazines that published his stories, but two more novels did appear after *Army Without Banners* (1930). *Gateway* (1932) and *Duke* (1933) are both set in a town evidently modelled on Prince Albert. They extend his chronicle of pioneering with an ironic treatment of small-town business and social life. No collection of John Beames's stories has been published; his novels were neglected during his life and all but forgotten after his death. It is a fate he does not deserve.

CAMROSE LUTHERAN COLLEGE LIBRARY

The neglect of Beames's work is partly explained by the general collapse of the Canadian popular fiction industry that coincided roughly with the publication of his novels. In the three previous decades, sentimental and didactic romances of pioneering, such as those of Ralph Connor and Nellie McClung, had been enormously popular, Connor's with sales in the millions. By the 1930s they had faded with the British imperial ideals that inspired them, though a few established favourites were kept sporadically in print. Later writers in the popular vein, including such westerners as John Patrick Gillese and Ross Annette, published mainly in American magazines and remained virtually unknown at home. With the loss of the popular tradition, Canadian publishers have tended to revive novels of "literary" rather than popular interest, like the work of Frederick Philip Grove and Sinclair Ross, reprinted primarily for academic markets.

Beames not only published at an unfortunate time, but he was also not writing the kind of sentimental romance that had been popular. *Army Without Banners* is realistic, not in that tradition of prairie realism rooted in a tragic sense of man's spiritual alienation from the land, but with a variety of unsophisticated realism that has never been common in Canadian fiction. Beames's nearest ancestor among well-known prairie novelists would probably be R. J. C. Stead.

Beames's descriptions of the beauties and hardships of the northern bush are unusually vivid and precise. The fortunes of his pioneers follow logically from their strengths and weaknesses, tested by the primitive conditions of homesteading. The pioneer character he views sympathetically but unsentimentally. His main figures, Billy and Maggie Clovelly, are admirable for their hardihood and basic goodness of heart, but they are not given any implausible graces of mind or manner. Billy has the savvy to carve a living out of the bush, but he is vain and foolish enough to be taken in by an implement salesman. He is loving and generous, but often selfish and insensitive towards his wife. Neither introspective nor articulate, the Clovellys are

CAMROSE LUTHERAN COLLEGE

presented mainly through the visible externals of speech, manner, and action, and thus distanced enough for comedy of a stringently ironic tone.

Beames's particular strength is his sureness of touch in depicting his pioneers. They speak a language familiar to us from people of that time and place, confirmed by typical turns of phrase: "get a move on," "damned if I know," "What in Sam Hill's eatin' you?" He also captures their attitudes in the local idiom, as in Billy's rude expression of western alienation: "You take them yaps in Ottawa. . . . Do they care what happens to a homesteader? . . . No sir, a homesteader can't look for no help from man, an' God ain't got this far yet." And Beames sees both sides of the pioneer spirit. He sums it up in a reflection on Clovelly's ill-planned and hastily dug well:

> One of the outstanding characteristics of the pioneer is that he is usually satisfied with "plenty good enough." He will suffer great hardships with cheerful fortitude; the vicissitudes of the wild cause him no anxiety; he is supremely resourceful in emergencies and quite fearless in the face of danger. He is capable of magnificent endurance and heroic exertions when the need is urgent, but once the need is met he lapses. He never does a thorough job, and long-continued, unhasting toil bores him to desperation.

There is an ironic balance here. Beames can humorously deflate the illusions of pioneering without losing his admiration or sympathy. He clearly shares many of his pioneers' attitudes—present-day readers may be uncomfortable with his acceptance of racial and sexual prejudices—yet he judges his characters frankly on their own terms. *Army Without Banners* is a refreshing change from nostalgic reminiscences and sentimental romances of pioneering.

DICK HARRISON

To

EDWARD WEEKS

A Man of Understanding

CHAPTER I

" GET up, there. Sam—Jimmy ! "

The willing little bay team plunged into the foaming creek, brimful of snow water, proceeded a little way, hock deep, sank suddenly to the withers, and struggled up on the other side.

The heavily laden wagon followed. Down went the front wheels. A frantic effort by the horses. Up came the front wheels, and down went the big hind wheels. There they stuck fast while the waters of the creek creamed around them.

" Damn, stuck again," said Billy Clovelly with philosophic resignation. " Get out, Maggie."

His young wife, inured to such occurrences, for they had already stuck in three flooded creeks in a fifteen-mile haul, gathered her skirts together and climbed over the front of the wagon box. She worked her way along the pole between the horses, and leaped to dry land. Billy pulled out the pin that fastened the double-trees to the pole, and Maggie led the horses away.

He unloaded the wagon, grunting a little and dropping a casual curse now and then. Piece by piece he had to carry their bedding, their tent, sheet-iron stove, boxes of groceries and utensils, sacks of sugar, flour, and oatmeal, tools, and all the hundred and one things necessary for starting life in an unsettled country, through water above his knees.

When all the vehicle contained was a breaker plough and some pieces of lumber, he sat down and pulled off his boots to let the water run out of them.

"That water's cold," he grumbled. "My feet's like chunks of ice. This is a hell of a road."

He got out his logging chain, that indispensable aid to travel in a new country, hooked one end to the wagon pole and hitched the horses to the other end. A short hard pull and the wagon stood once more on dry ground.

"Goin' to camp here," he announced. "Be damned if I'll load that wagon again to-day. There's wood an' water."

He unharnessed the horses, hobbled them, and turned them loose to graze. Then he cut dry wood and built a fire. While Maggie sliced salt pork and boiled the billy, he pitched the tent.

They ate fried salt pork, bread and butter, and drank black tea without milk. And because they were young and healthy and wholly unused to luxuries, they enjoyed every mouthful.

A pale, ovoid sun was setting in the midst of light clouds tinted violet and purple and crimson. Not a breath of air stirred the crisp dry brown grass. Only the faint cries of some water birds came from the slough that fed the creek until a coyote lifted his voice in undying lamentation and was answered by another mourner on a distant hill.

Billy busily whittled a plug of tobacco with his knife and filled his pipe. The day's worries dropped from his shoulders and he smiled across the dancing flames at his wife.

" Not so bad, all this, eh, kid ? " he said, with a wide gesture.

She nodded and smiled in return, not because she felt the magic of the unknown that was beating in his veins, but because he was happy and she loved him.

" It's fine, honey," she said.

Vega and the wide-winged Swan came out high overhead ; Spica winked on the horizon. All the sky was full of brilliant stars, and little wisps of pale green flame came and went between them like ghosts. Presently the little flames would grow into broad bands of changing light whirling in revel rout from horizon to horizon. But the pair were sound asleep long before that, huddled close together for warmth, for a keen north wind had come up with the dark.

And in this way the vanguard of the Army Without Banners, a mighty host, without sound of trumpet or drum, came into the beloved land to possess it.

Both the Clovellys were of the blood of pioneers. Billy, though unaware of his pedigree and caring nothing about it, was of the most ancient white lineage on the continent, the first of his house having settled near Boston in the seventeenth century. Succeeding generations, ever restless and mirage-led, had passed west and north until, in due time, Billy came to be born on the banks of the Red River in Manitoba.

At the age of twenty-two, with his bride of a month by his side, he had followed the call of his blood, westward and northward still, into Saskatchewan, across the noble river of that name, into virgin country.

Maggie, just nineteen, was a descendant of one of Lord Selkirk's Red River colonists. Intrepid and enduring, cheerful, resourceful and industrious, none could be better equipped for the heavy task before her.

Morning, and a meadow lark whistling gaily, the stiff purple crocuses, first flowers of spring, opening to salute the rising sun, and Billy crawled out of the tent into the sparkling air of the great upland, crisp with frost.

" Daylight in the swamp, old woman ! " he shouted, and fell furiously at work with his axe to warm himself. " Roll out an' make breakfast while I go look for the horses."

By the time he had brought the horses back to the wagon and given them their morning oats the meal was ready.

Maggie had waked with an imp of mischief in her. She mocked him across the fire as he ate.

" Old sour-face, what're you lookin' so cranky for ? "

" Why, I ain't cranky."

" You are too. Bawlin' at me like that."

Billy's lean face creased in a slow grin. " You're lookin' for trouble, that's what's the matter with you. Well, now, I'm goin' to maul the daylights out of you."

He rolled her on the ground in sheer animal spirits, and she screamed and giggled, and sat up to pull bits of grass and sticks out of her hair and scold with tears of mirth in her eyes.

Billy jumped into the air, clapped his heels nimbly together, and sent a war whoop ringing across the low ridges.

" I'll learn you. Now will you be good ? "

" You're an old bear," she pouted. " Old sorehead."

" Want some more ? " he threatened.

" No, I'll be good," she squealed. " I'll take it all back. Oh, Billy, quit ticklin'. Now quit."

He sat back on his heels panting and laughing. " Well, now, let's be done foolin'. Best hitch up and get goin'."

She helped him reload the wagon and hitch up the horses, for she could do such things almost as well as he.

They went on, roughly north by west, for there was no road. Billy was a trail-maker by inheritance. Only half-consciously, his eye took in every detail of the landscape, choosing the most direct route by the easiest grades and the driest land.

The faint track of his wagon wheels on the dry grass that day would be in time beaten into a trail and become a main artery of traffic because it was the best possible route and could not be improved upon.

The way led over low, rounded hills, patched with clumps of willow, hazel, and poplar, with long narrow belts of spruce and tamarack in the lowlands, by stream and slough. And sloughs and streams abounded.

In the dialect of the Canadian Northwest, a slough is any body of water not big enough to be called a lake, small woods are bluffs, bogs are muskegs, and all watercourses are creeks.

In time, and after they had crossed a couple of runways, where the overflow water from some slough sought lower levels, they came in sight of a hill, rising somewhat abruptly from a wide level.

" There you are, kid," said Billy, " that's home. That there hill's right on the homestead. Come on, come on, Sam, Jimmy ! "

The horses pricked their ears and mended their pace. The rattling wagon trundled along the crest of a ridge, dipped into a damp hollow, climbed another ridge, skirted a poplar bluff, and halted on the shores of a reedy slough some fifty acres in extent.

" We're home," announced Billy.

They pitched their tent and set the sheet-iron stove up in front of it. There was dry wood in plenty along the margin of the slough, and Billy came staggering up the slope with one long pole after another on his shoulder while Maggie prepared dinner.

Afterwards, hand in hand like two children, they set out to explore their land. It was a beautiful and a fertile land, but lonely, for the buffalo were gone for ever and the white man's cattle had not penetrated so far. The deer, still plentiful, kept to the coverts and were seldom seen in the open.

The railroad halted at Riverton, fifty-five miles to the south-west; their nearest neighbour was eight miles away as the crow flies, and ten by the only practicable trail—that which they had just made. Over all that their eyes surveyed they were supreme.

Billy had been there once before, when land hunting. But the snow had been still on the ground then, and the sight that greeted his eyes from the top of the hill was almost as new to him as to Maggie.

There was no sign of human life, no houses, no fences, no cattle, no roads. But of animal life there was plenty. Gophers, like little brown posts, sat bolt upright and watched them with beady eyes; small birds fluttered and chirped all about them; a big hawk or two sailed lazily by on wide wings. On the slough there were wild ducks, moor hens, and grey and white terns, filling the air with their strange and haunting cries.

" Looks peaceful, don't it ? " said Billy with deep satisfaction. " Real, wild, new country—that's what I like. Fences give me a pain in the neck."

" Well, but you got to have fences," said the practical Maggie.

" Aw, I know, I know. But I don't like the looks of the dern things. Well, anyway, there won't be many fences around here for a while."

They wandered happily about until Maggie had picked out the place where she wished her home to be. She chose the site wisely. It lay on a gentle slope, with the bulk of the big hill shutting off the north and north-west winds, direst tribulations of the Canadian winter. A thick poplar bluff provided more protection on the west and, as Maggie pointed out, would form a good windbreak for the winter cattle corral.

Southward the land trended toward the slough, on the edge of which they would dig their well. It was was characteristic that it troubled neither of them that the drainage from byre and stye, kitchen midden and barn, would all flow in the direction of the well. Sanitation was a thing neither had heard off, and a lesson they were fated to learn in tears.

In the morning they moved their tent to the new site, and real work began. The well was the first thing, for while the slough water was good enough still for the horses, the decaying vegetation it contained gave it an unpleasant taste.

Billy got a sufficiency of good water at a depth of four feet in stiff clay and, as the sides of the well showed no signs of caving in, he was satisfied to do no more to it, and promptly turned his attention to other things.

One of the outstanding characteristics of the pioneer is that he is usually satisfied with " plenty good enough." He will suffer great hardships with cheerful fortitude ; the vicissitudes of the wild cause him no anxiety ; he is supremely resourceful in emergencies and quite fearless in the face of danger. He is capable of magnificent endurance and heroic exertions when the need is urgent, but once the need is met he lapses. He never does a thorough job, and long-continued, unhasting toil bores him to desperation.

Billy had dug his well and got enough water. He had toiled like a madman digging it, and he came out caked with clay and too exhausted to do anything but lie on the grass for the rest of the day. It never occurred to him, or to Maggie, that the well was nearly a hundred yards from where the house would be, and that the time wasted in going to and fro with buckets of water would mount up in the aggregate to many hundreds of hours more than it would have taken to dig a deeper well close to the house. No, they had their well and they were satisfied.

The next thing was the house. There were plenty of good, sound poplar logs, not too big, in the bluff. Billy took his four-pound axe, and Maggie her little two-and-a-half-pound blade. He felled the trees and she lopped and topped them. They worked hard but merrily.

" Guess we got enough," said Billy a few days later. " Let's lay off for to-day, an' start snakin' 'em to-morrow."

Maggie was for barking the logs too, which would make them last all the longer. But for Billy it was another case of " plenty good enough," and the logs went unbarked. He hitched the team to them, one by one, and dragged them out of the bluff.

He whetted his axe once more to a razor-like keenness, and began to notch them into place. He disdained the clumsy " squaw notch," where one log sits simply in a shallow groove cut in the one below, and fitted them neatly into place with the " saddle notch," a triangular ridge cut to fit closely into a deep V in the log above. One grade higher is the dovetail, or " square corner," but that takes time and requires a good axeman at each end of the log.

It was easy enough to lift the lower logs into place, for Billy's lean, six-foot frame was a mass of wiry muscles and sinews, and Maggie, for all her youthful slenderness, was surprisingly strong.

But when the walls were breast high the struggle to lift the logs became severe. There were no friendly neighbours to form bees and help them, so they rolled the heavy green timbers painfully up inclined poles, straining and heaving until their eyes started from their heads and their hearts were like to burst.

They might have used the team, but a coil of rope was one of the things they had forgotten to bring with them, and the logging chain was too short.

But a day came when the last and lightest wall log was in place on a level with Billy's head.

He drew his forearm across his forehead and wiped away the sweat. " Begad, I'm glad that's done," he said.

Maggie sat down suddenly on the ground, leaning limply against the wall, and began to cry.

He dropped on his knees beside her and took her in his arms.

"Poor kid, poor kid. You done fine. You're a great little woman, you sure are," he said sympathetically.

She smiled, but it was two days before she was able to help him again.

CHAPTER II

THE weather had been fine and warm and the country had dried out rapidly under the strong rays of the sun. It was the time of prairie fires. All day long columns of white smoke were to be seen in the distance, and at night the horizon was ringed with patches of dull crimson light. Particles of feathery white ash floated in the air, and the winds were tainted with the acrid reek of burning.

One of the greatest perils a settler in a new country has to face is the prairie fire, and it has been the cause of many a tragedy. The wise settler always protects his belongings with a ploughed fireguard.

" Say, Billy, hadn't you best take the team an' run a few furrows ? " suggested Maggie one evening, gazing eastward, where a long line of flame glowed like a belt of blood on the skyline. " That fire is too close to suit me."

" Aw, that won't bother us—wind's against it," said Billy easily. " Plenty of time, anyhow—do it sometime —want to get the roof on the old shack first."

He spent the next day searching for suitable rafters. He found at last some fire-killed trees, light and sound, and dragged them home. Then he made some rough trestles and, with their aid and Maggie's, got the rafters into place.

Next he cut out the door and two small windows. This

was the only part of the entire building into which iron entered, for nails were precious.

For window casings, door, and door jamb he used the lumber that had formed the bed of his load. The doorway, when completed, was very low, and he had to stoop to enter. But, as he said, they could dig out a few inches of the floor and so make head-room within.

The day they finished the door they went early to bed, worn out with their labours. The evening had been calm, but it came on to blow with steadily increasing strength from the north-west. The little tent, sheltered though it was, began to flap and strain.

"Hope this wind don't bring a fire down on us," mumbled Billy, only half awake. "Ought to have ploughed that fireguard—do it in the mornin'."

He fell promptly asleep again, but Maggie was more wakeful. She thought she smelt smoke and snuffed anxiously. Once she got up and peered out. There was smoke certainly, but no fire to be seen, for the hill and the bluff shut off the view to north and west.

Billy missed her presence in his sleep and called out drowsily, "Aw, come back here an' lay down."

"But I'm scared there's fire comin', Billy."

"The devil with the fire—let her come. You come an' lay down."

She obeyed uneasily.

The wind lulled and presently she fell asleep. She woke an hour or so later smothered in smoke and fighting for breath. She sprang up and ran out. The sky was filled with a lurid light, and a hoarse roaring, hissing, and crackling met her ears. Waves of blinding smoke eddied about her and tortured her lungs. The whole

crest of the hill was on fire and the flames were racing
down the slope.

" Billy ! " she screamed. " Billy ! Fire, fire, fire ! "

He was beside her in a bound, gave one look, and
dashed back into the tent. " Get your shoes on," he
shouted, struggling with his boots.

" But the fire . . ."

" Get your shoes on. Do you want your feet burnt
off ? " he roared, tying his own laces in frantic haste.

She was in shift and petticoat only, her legs and feet
bare. She ran in and thrust her feet into her shoes, and
rushed out again.

The fire was within a hundred yards, and but that
the hill broke the force of the wind would have been
upon them ere now.

Billy flung her a couple of empty sacks. " Hustle
down to the slough and wet these," he ordered. " I'll
have to backfire. It's our only chance. Run like hell."

While she raced down to the slough, he ran forward
and began striking matches, setting fire to the dry grass
at ten-foot intervals across the face of the oncoming wall
of flame. As the patches of flame spread to meet each
other, he stamped them out on the inward or tent side.

When she came panting back with the dripping sacks
there were two opposing lines of fire, with bare and
blackened ground behind each. Swinging the sacks
in frenzied haste, they beat out the flames on the inner
side of a wide arc, working outward from a common
centre.

The two lines of fire, offensive and defensive, met
and roared upward ten feet in a mad embrace, roared
upward and sank away into darkness.

But on either side of the burnt-out area the flames rushed on with almost sentient malignance, striving to outflank them, darting out quivering, hungry tongues at the tent and the half-finished shanty.

"You take that side and I'll take this," coughed Billy. "Run it down into the slough."

Half blind, smarting with burns, choking in the stifling smoke and heat, they fought on. Step by step, ever watchful that the smouldering grass did not treacherously burst into flame again behind them, they beat down their terrible foe. Once a spark set light to a tuft of grass in the heart of the enclosure, but Billy raced back and beat it out.

"There," he gasped. "Take that, damn you."

The fire was curving inward lower down, and he had to run again and fling himself upon it like a madman. At last the flames on his wing died down in a prolonged hissing among the wet reeds of the slough.

He ran across to where Maggie, the tears coursing down her face, alternately attacked the flames with feeble sweeps of her failing arms and battled with the sparks that, falling upon the thick masses of her brown hair, threatened to set her head on fire.

"Quit," he shouted to her. "I can handle her now. Go an' set down."

On that side too the fire was vanquished. To westward it had burnt itself out among the damp dead leaves along the edge of the poplar bluff, but a sheet of living flame coursed and bounded in great flaring leaps over the wide level to the eastward.

The shack and all their poor belongings were saved. The horses, prairie born and bred, had wisely taken refuge in the waters of the slough, and stood unscathed.

The man and woman were in far worse plight. Billy, in shirt and trousers, with a hat on his head, had suffered only singed eyebrows and a few burns, but Maggie's unprotected legs were a mass of scorched flesh from ankle to knee, and her hair was in many places frizzled to the scalp.

When he hastened back to her she was lying on the ground sobbing with pain and weakness.

" There, there, there, honey girl," he crooned over her. " You're the bravest kid in the whole world— the best little woman a man ever had."

She tried to smile as he lifted her, but the effort was too much, and she suddenly became limp in his arms.

He lifted her and staggered with her to the tent and laid her on the blankets, kissing her again and again and begging her wildly to speak to him.

" Oh, Billy," she moaned, " it hurts awful. I'm 'fraid my both legs is burnt off."

" No, no," he assured her. " They'll be all right ; I'll fix 'em." He dabbed around in the darkness. " Where's that damn butter went to ? "

" It's down the well," she told him. " I put it there to keep cool."

A liberal application of their precious butter to both legs, and bandages made from strips torn from her petticoat, and she presently declared that the pain had lessened, and so fell into a feverish, groaning sleep. Billy watched tenderly over her until his own pain and weariness overcame him and he fell asleep beside her.

The morning was far advanced when they woke,

and looked upon a new world. The day before everything had been a dull brown, save for the sapphire eyes of the sloughs. To-day the face of the land was black, a waste of cinders and ashes that blew in clouds before the wind and begrimed everything.

All they had contrived to save from the flames was a patch an acre or so in extent, stretching from the tent to the slough, and on this the horses grazed hungrily until they had nibbled the ground bare. Poor beasts, there was nothing else for them to eat.

Maggie's legs were blistered and swollen and more than half her hair came away when she combed it. Another application from the butter crock helped her legs, but all that could be done for her hair was to let it grow again.

" I look awful," she said sadly, surveying her face in a tiny mirror. " I'm glad there's nobody to see me."

" Well," said Billy, philosophically surveying the desolation, " that fire saved me the trouble of ploughin' a fireguard, anyway."

" Yes, but it didn't save my legs," grumbled Maggie.

" Never mind your legs," mocked Billy. " They don't hurt me."

" You dirty, mean thing. You didn't talk that way last night."

" Oh, well, last night I was kinder rattled an' said more'n I meant maybe."

" I don't believe you care for me a bit," she pouted.

" Not a nickel's worth," he assured her with an impish grin. But, seeing that the tears had come into her eyes, he kissed her and began to rumple her hair.

"Quit, be-have," she said pettishly. "Go on an' do some work now, you big loafer."

"Just as you say, old woman," he rejoined equably, and bent to kiss her again.

But she averted her face. He shrugged his shoulders and picked up his axe. He glanced back as he went into the bluff, and saw her face smiling at him from the tent. He waved his hand with a sigh of relief, and went to work.

What he required now was thin straight poles for the roof of the shanty, and he was busy selecting and cutting them down for the next two days.

Then the fine weather broke. Beginning with a cold north-east wind that brought a smart flurry of snow with it, it changed to a steady downpour of icy rain. Life outside was impossible.

They huddled together in the tent, shivering under their blankets, with everything around them damp and clammy. They were very crowded in there, for the groceries had to be kept dry, and they took the sack of flour to bed with them. The tent dripped at intervals and the stove at the door hissed and crackled dismally.

When the rain slackened temporarily Billy went out to cut wood, but a fresh squall would blow up and he would return to the tent, wet and shivering and cursing.

The wretched horses, with hardly anything but their morning and evening feed of oats to eat, stood motionless for hours, tails to the wind, with the rain sluicing down their flanks.

Maggie, what with the cold and discomfort, and the pain of her scorched legs, wept frequently and longed audibly for the home she had recently left. Billy turned sour and sulky and prone to swear furiously about the merest trifles.

They ran out of bread and the new batch Maggie kneaded refused to rise, even in the bed between them under the blankets. When baked it came out in ugly little lumps, heavy as lead, hard on the outside and raw dough within. Maggie wept inconsolably for two hours over the failure.

Billy, looking at her glumly, told himself that a man who got married was a fool.

On the fourth day the wind changed, swinging slowly from east to south to south-west.

Billy, waking in the night, lay listening for the woefully familiar drumming of rain on the canvas over him. But all was silent. He got up and looked out. A few stars glimmered faintly through the thinning clouds, and the misty east was grey with the coming dawn. With a grunt of satisfaction he returned to his blankets, glancing with a softer expression at the peacefully slumbering Maggie.

CHAPTER III

THE landscape changed again. During the rain tiny green spikes had sprung up in the blackened earth. The willows were in full bloom, laden with silver and gold pods, and among the catkins the buds showed a tip of green. Feathery silver catkins waved on the white poplars, and presently changed to clouds of soft white down floating in the air, for the thrifty poplar sows its seed before the leaves come. The sticky brown buds of the balm of Gilead swelled almost visibly, and minute crimson blossoms were to be found in the hazel brush.

The real bird migration from the south began. Flocks upon flocks of juncos, song sparrows, red-winged blackbirds, grackles, cowbirds, robins, thrashers, sapsuckers, and many species of tiny finches and warblers, made their appearance. The crow had been there almost before the snow was off the ground, and the meadow lark had followed him close. But now only the insect eaters were to come, and they would not be long delayed.

The dawn chorus of birds was almost deafening, and sleep was impossible after sunrise.

A few days of strong, bright sunshine, and all the trees seemed to burst into leaf at once. In a week the transformation was complete. Wild flowers of every hue spangled the new grass, and the pin cherry, the choke cherry, and the saskatoon berry were masses of fragrant snowy bloom over which hovered innumerable butterflies.

But there was another side to all this beauty and luxuriance. Up from their breeding places, the innumerable sloughs, rose clouds of mosquitoes, insatiably greedy for blood. During the day, if the wind blew, they were merely a passing nuisance to those who, like Billy and Maggie, had been salted to mosquitoes from infancy. But when the wind went down with the sun, they came down in their hungry armies and set their poisoned needles in every inch of unprotected flesh.

Smudges of green wood and leaves are some mitigation, but Billy, coughing in the acrid smoke, did not think so.

" I'd as lief be eat alive as choked to death," he growled. " This is a hell of a country for flies."

He pushed the completion of the shack, for on the heels of the mosquitoes would come the sand flies, tiny atoms, but with a bite like a red-hot needle. And then there would be the beelike bulldog flies, leaving a spot of blood behind them at every bite. Sand flies and bulldogs torment live stock, sometimes even to the death, but they have one redeeming trait; they will not enter a building, though they will swarm and buzz and crawl and bite viciously in a tent. Billy hastened to roof the shack with poles on which he would lay sods.

Thus the first sod was turned in the new land.

The Clovellys did not sentimentalize about it; the thought never entered their heads that they were bringing into subjection to the plough land that had lain untouched through all the ages by the hand of man. They wanted sods to roof a house and a patch of land to plant potatoes in, and they went and got them.

Billy set up a stick in the open land east of the house for a guidepost. Maggie took the reins while he guided the plough. The sharp-pointed snout of the breaker dug into the chocolate loam as the horses laid themselves into the collar, and the mouldboard flung aside a long narrow ribbon of tough sod.

They broke up half an acre or so, and then began to cut the sod into squares with a spade. These they loaded on the wagon, and Maggie handed them up one at a time to Billy, who laid them in their places on the roof, packing the joints with loose earth, with a double row along the ridgepole.

In the West, where heavy rains are infrequent, such a roof will give protection under most circumstances. The sod will absorb a great deal of water, and it is not until it reaches the saturation point that it begins to leak. But woe to them who dwell under sod roofs if the rain continue for more than two days.

That night they slept in the shack, filled with a home-like feeling of security, untroubled by the uneasy fear that a gust of wind might blow their tent away or a late fall of snow flatten it upon them.

In the morning Billy brought in the stove and set it up, packing wet clay around the stovepipe, where it went through the roof as a precaution against fire. Next he put in the two little windows they had brought with them, and knocked together a door out of the remains of the lumber.

At last they had a real home. Civilization might sneer at it, but on such early homes is all civilization founded. The inside dimensions were twelve by fourteen feet, six feet from floor to eaves, and only three more to the ridgepole, the floor of natural earth, the roof of poles and sod, a window in each end twelve by eighteen inches, a door only five feet six inches high.

But Maggie was in love with it. It was the first home of her own and precious beyond words. She demanded a shelf here, an empty packing box there, nailed to the wall to form a cupboard, wooden pegs to hang things on, and called loudly for a table, chairs, and a bed.

Billy ran up a bunk of poles in a corner, with tough willow sticks for springs, and an armful or two of coarse slough grass for a mattress. Two empty boxes had to serve as chairs, but there was no lumber left to make a table of.

Food was running low. Ducks and rabbits in unlimited quantities were to be had for the shooting, but the flour sack was very limp and the butter had been eaten long since. More important still, carefully as Billy had rationed them out, the oats for the horses were nearly done, and the pioneer must care for his beasts before he thinks of himself.

" Well, guess we'll hit for town in the mornin'," said Billy.

" What about plantin' the spuds first ? " demurred Maggie.

" Aw, the devil, can't they wait a little ? "

" Must be around the twenty-fourth of May," said

Maggie. " Potatoes planted later than that never come to nothin'."

" 'Tain't the twenty-fourth yet," said Billy.

They argued about the date, Maggie maintaining stubbornly that it was a Tuesday and Billy with great vehemence that it was a Thursday. Actually it was a Wednesday.

The discussion covered a lot of ground, though the potatoes and the date remained the focal point. Relations became exceedingly strained, and there were uncomplimentary references to the relatives of the respective parties. Weariness stilled their voices without a decision having been arrived at.

Billy was the first to wake in the morning. A bright idea came into his head as he looked at the still slumbering Maggie. He shook her by the shoulder.

" Goin' to lay in bed all day ? How about gettin' them spuds planted ? I tell you I ain't goin' to town till I do."

Maggie stared sleepily at him until he had repeated his brazen remark. A hot retort sprang to her lips, but she checked it diplomatically.

" Have it your own way," she said. " I'll get up."

They planted the potatoes that day, and set out next morning for Riverton.

The shack was left just as it stood : locks and bars were unknown in the country in that day. You might leave your property scattered over fifty square miles of territory, go away and forget about it for a year, and come back to find it just where you left it unless it was perishable and the elements or the coyotes had harmed it.

They went back by the way they had come, and so the first faint marks of the wagon wheels on the inward journey were pressed a little deeper into the sod and became a trail. The water was lower now in runway and creek, but their bottoms, hard frozen on the way in, had thawed out. The result was often an almost bottomless morass, but they were travelling light and they wallowed through somehow.

In time they came to beaten trails, and at last to something like a real road with bits of grading here and there and an occasional culvert.

At noon on the second day they reached Riverton, in that day only a few dirty streets, deeply rutted, a huddle of wooden stores with high, false fronts, a bank or two, a few small churches and schools and hotels, a railway station, an elevator, and a sprinkling of scattered houses. Tethered cows grazed on vacant lots, chickens pecked in the dust, and dogs and ragged children abounded.

The Clovellys stayed in the place just twenty-four hours, buying lumber and groceries and miscellaneous goods they had forgotten, or been too heavily loaded to bring, on the first trip. In fact, they spent all their money and came away at last without a number of things they wanted.

From now on they would be thrown absolutely on their own resources. What they could not make money enough to buy they would have to do without. But how to do without is the first secret of life in the wilderness, and both had served their apprenticeship in the school of privation.

Both were glad to be once more on the out trail. Even the few odd hundred population of Riverton seemed a crowd to them and they felt cramped in the streets.

" I must say I'm glad to be goin' home again," said Maggie with a contented sigh, as the cluster of hideous frame buildings were hidden by the trees.

" Me too," agreed Billy fervently. " Can't understand why anybody would want to live in a town. No neighbours in mine."

" Oh, but a few good neighbours is nice," said Maggie.

" I like my neighbours far enough away so I can't see 'em," grunted Billy.

CHAPTER IV

THE return trip was a hard one. Five times Billy unloaded the wagon and drew it out of the clinging mud with a logging chain. They welcomed the sight of the little shack nestling under its hill with the joy of returned travellers who have been a very long journey.

Now began the serious business of breaking land for next year's crop before the summer heats toughened the sod too much. Billy laid out a six-hundred-yard furrow on the big level east of the house. Maggie drove the team along the guide lines while he held the plough, and then went back to her housekeeping.

Billy did his breaking as he did everything else, taking the easiest way. When he came to a big clump of bushes he ploughed round it, intending at some indefinite future date to cut it down and grub out the roots. But years later little islands of poplar and willow rose above the green waves of the sown grain in his field.

Maggie was busy all day long. The highest praise a pioneer can give to a woman is that she is a " good worker." Maggie was a good worker, and with the meagre resources at her disposal she did wonders. Single-handed she lowered and levelled the earth floor, chinked the holes in the walls with bits of wood and plastered them over with puddled clay, cut out the pictures from a couple of illustrated papers and pasted them inside, hung up a gaudy calendar or two, and kept the whole as clean as the nature of the place would permit. And still she found time to help Billy in the field from time to time.

The days lengthened ; dawn trod close on the heels of dusk ; the noondays blazed with fierce heat ; the short-lived growth of the prairie struggled fiercely to attain full maturity before the killing frosts of autumn.

Occasionally it rained, and when it rained too heavily streams of muddy water trickled down the walls and made everything damp and dirty and wretched. Mosquitoes were still a nuisance, though an abating one, but the sand flies were diabolical in the open.

One day there occurred that most notable event in the lonely life of the pioneer, the arrival of visitors. One was Webb Ginnery, an old-timer from the settlement, who had located Billy in the spring. In the old buckboard at his side sat a tall, loose-limbed, slow-moving stranger in clothing of rough tweed and the most peculiar headdress Billy had ever seen. It was a cap with a peak back and front, and flaps that were tied up on the crown with strings. The man had a heavy reddish moustache, at which he tugged thoughtfully while conversing.

" Make you 'quainted with Billy Clovelly, Mr. Kent," said the genial Webb.

" Pleased to meet you," said Billy, cordially, holding out his hand.

The stranger grasped it with a murmured " How d'y' do ? "

" Just in time for dinner," said Billy. " Come an'
set."

It must not be thought that because everybody calls
everybody else by a first name or a nickname, and asks
the most searching questions of total strangers, that
there is no etiquette in the backwoods. On the con-
trary, it is as easy to make a grave *faux pas* in the wilderness as in the most formal society. The stranger made
such a social error at the very beginning.

Maggie had been hovering in the background, the
correct thing to do until called by her husband. Then
she came forward, nodded casually to Webb, who nodded
as casually back, and was about to shake hands with
Kent, who had by now disentangled his long legs and
reached the ground.

But he, bred to different conventions, took off his
weird cap and made her a stiff bow. To the other three
it was almost an insult, equivalent to a refusal to shake
hands. Maggie coloured angrily and, with an indignant
whisk of her skirts, hurried indoors.

Blissfully unaware of what he had done, Kent turned
to Billy. " Must be rather lonely for your wife out
here—ah—Clovelly," he said in a deep, throaty voice.

The tone was meant to be conversational, but to
Billy, used to the harsh, sub-nasal speech of the North-
west, it sounded affected or condescending. And,
moreover, you call a man " mister " in the backwoods
if you wish to be excessively formal or hostile ; otherwise you use his first name. It is not customary to use
the surname alone.

For a second Billy was really angry, but he caught

Webb's eye gleaming impishly at him over Kent's shoulder, and the truth burst upon him. The man was an Englishman, a green Englishman, and naturally he could not be expected to know how to behave.

"No, sir," he replied courteously, "she ain't lonesome—don't have no time to get lonesome—too busy. But come on in an' set down."

In the shack he took occasion to murmur to the still deeply offended Maggie, "Don't pay no 'tention to him ; he's English ; he don't mean no harm."

"He'd ought to know how to be-have himself even if he is English," pouted Maggie.

But she saw the force of his argument and her resentment was blunted.

She set before them the inevitable fried salt pork, bread and butter, and milkless tea, with the equally inevitable formula of frontier hospitality.

"Ain't much," she said, "but you're welcome to all there is. Eat hearty." A formula, but no empty one.

Kent seemed finicky about his food and ate with extraordinary deliberation. While the others bolted their food in great chunks, noisily gulping tea between mouthfuls, he eschewed the really useful broad-bladed, blunt knife, and pinned his faith to the totally inadequate three-pronged fork.

He was still eating long after the rest had finished and were loading their pipes. Not that he ate more —indeed, rather less ; but, as Maggie said afterwards, "he chewed an' chewed an' chewed, till I come to think he was never goin' to swaller."

Lonely pioneer people, however little they may talk

at other times, make up for it when they meet. Settlement news is exchanged ; all that has happened within
a radius of thirty or forty miles is discussed ; and
every little event grows by repetition to amazing pro-
portions.

Strangers, particularly, are expected to give an account
of themselves. But Kent maintained his taciturnity,
tugging at his big moustache and puffing at his pipe.
His presence made them feel irritable.

" I figure on locatin' Mr. Kent on the north-west of
eight, just across the slough," said Webb. " It's just
about as good a quarter as I know of."

" That so ? " said Billy, not at all pleased.

" You'll be near neighbours," continued Webb,
" an' you'll be able to put him wise to things. He's
new in the country."

Kent cleared his throat as if about to say something,
and took his pipe out of his mouth. But he thought
better of it, and put the pipe back.

During a conversation of over an hour he made only
one remark, and that seemed to his hearers a peculiarly
foolish one.

They were discussing roads, with particular refer-
ence to the abounding mudholes, when he said slowly,
" I wish these—ah—muskrats were a little bigger ;
one might break them in and use them. Horses are
not sufficiently—ah—amphibious."

Billy blinked and Maggie stared. " Amphibious "
was a new word and might have an improper meaning.
But Webb, though he understood what was said no
better than they did, passed off an awkward moment
with an uneasy laugh.

When they rose to go, Kent put his hand in his pocket in a hesitating way, but Webb dragged him out before he had the opportunity to put a final affront upon his hosts by offering them money.

" Well, I sure do hope that English guy don't locate over across the slough," said Maggie with decision, gazing resentfully after the buckboard. " A little more of him an' I'd thrown something."

" He sure ain't got much sense," agreed Billy. " What the devil word was that he used ? "

" Don't ask me. I wouldn't use a word like that if I was paid for it," said Maggie.

But on the evening of the eleventh day thereafter they heard the long-carrying rattle of approaching wagon wheels. In the sunset hush the prairie becomes a vast sounding board, and the roll of a wagon can be heard at extraordinary distances.

Darkness had come before the first of three wagons crept round the base of the hill and drew up before the shack.

Kent drove it, a woman on the seat beside him and two small boys perched precariously on the billowing load behind. The wagon was new and shiny, and the team, as Billy noted at the first glance, a noble pair of greys. They were splashed with mud to the withers, and their hanging heads and the caked wheels showed how hard a day's journey they had made.

The other two wagons were worn outfits belonging to farmers from the old settlement, and were heavily loaded with lumber and farm implements. It was plain at once that Kent was a man of means.

Whatever their prejudices might be, the tradition

of the country insisted that the strangers be made welcome. Billy was beside them in a moment, while Maggie
ran into the shack to prepare a meal.

"Good evening, Clovelly," said Kent. "D'you
mind if we stay here to-night? There's another bad
mudhole to cross to get to my homestead and the horses
are about knocked up."

"Why, sure, sure," said Billy. "You got to stop
—couldn't let you go by. Come on down : my woman'll
have supper for you right away."

Tired Mrs. Kent, aching all over from the unaccustomed jolting, was assisted down, and the even
more weary small boys, half asleep, were carried by
Kent and Billy into the shack.

Maggie bustled about, lavishing their slender means
as though she had ample in reserve to feed an army.
The horses being looked to, everybody was somehow
fed, and then Kent was for pitching a tent.

"What for?" said Billy. "Your woman an' the
kids can sleep in the shack. It's clean—you won't find
a louse in it—an' it won't hurt me an' you a particle
to sleep out under the wagon."

"Oh, but I say," said Kent, quite visibly affected.
"That is good of you. I—ah—really don't know how
I can thank you. I'm sure they couldn't be in a better
place."

Which display of human feeling almost reconciled
Billy to his new neighbour then and there.

CHAPTER V

" WELL, what d'you think of 'em ? " asked Billy next morning, the Kents being faintly visible across the slough erecting a tent.

" She ain't so bad," said Maggie. " But it's mighty difficult to get anythin' out of her. An' smooth—say, I didn't know until I come to figure up that she hadn't told me anything I couldn't have found out for myself."

" Well, I don't know whether to laugh or swear when I think of him," said Billy. " It sure beats all how little some people knows. It'd make a wooden monkey weep to look at that guy aholt of a axe. But I'll say this for him : he ain't too bad with the lines—handles his team pretty nice an' looks to know how they ought to be took care of."

Meanwhile, the tent being up, the three wagons unloaded, and the settlers on the way home, the Kents had time also to discuss their neighbours.

Mrs. Kent was a small woman, very erect, with a long, pointed chin, fearless light-grey eyes, and fluffy pale hair. She was talkative, positive, swift to like or dislike, and given to gossip.

" Most extraordinary people, Tom," she said in her musical English voice. " But the very soul of hospitality. And so poor, so terribly poor. We're millionaires in comparison—fancy ! But she brought out everything they had for us. I never saw anything so spontaneous and ungrudging in my life. But she was so terribly inquisitive—I'm sure she didn't realize for a moment how ill-bred she was—but she asked the most pointed questions. It took all my tact to evade them without hurting her feelings. I wouldn't have done that for the world. She's such a child. And all alone in the wilds—so plucky."

"I like Clovelly too," said Kent with his slow smile. "Even if he isn't quite sure in his own mind whether I'm a raving lunatic or merely imbecile."

"Oh, Tom, how can you say such things ? I'm sure there's nothing ridiculous about us. You're trying to be funny, and you know I can never see your silly jokes."

Kent's eyes twinkled. "Anyhow," he said, "he's a useful man to have about, and he can teach me a lot of things. I understand he was born to this kind of—ah—palaeolithic existence. I don't suppose he'll object to earning a little money."

Across the slough, Billy and Maggie were discussing that very point.

"Why don't you go over an' see if he'll give you some work ?" asked Maggie. "He looks to be just loaded with dough, an' he ain't fit to look after himself accordin' to your say-so. If he gives you work you could put up a few loads of hay for the horses an' stay here all winter. That'd be a whole lot better than you goin' off to the bush an' leavin' me work for some slave-drivin' old farm woman all winter."

"That's all right," said Billy. "I'm willin' enough to work for him if he wants me. But if I go over there lookin' for a job, they'd get the notion, maybe, we wanted to bum on 'em. They can see we ain't any too well fixed."

" Oh, allright," pouted Maggie. " If you'd just as soon be separated from me all winter, an' don't care what I've got to put up with workin' for some old hell cat, go to it. They all said back home that you wasn't the kind that'd make a woman happy, an' now I guess maybe they're right."

" Your damn mother said that," growled Billy. " An' you're growin' to have a p'isen tongue like she has." ,

" Don't you call my mother names," flared Maggie. " An' your brother Dick never sober a day in his life ! "

" What the devil's your mother an' my brother got to do in this ? " demanded Billy.

" Well, you brought it up. You can't say I did. An' I won't stand here an' be bawled at by you, neither. See. I'm goin' in."

She flounced back into the shack, leaving Billy to rub his ear and swear. He had been married long enough to realize that he was being made the victim of a little feminine strategy. And, after all, he had to admit that she was right : it did seem an unfeeling thing to leave her and go away into the woods for six months just because he was too proud to ask for a job.

But he could not acknowledge to Maggie that he was in the wrong : in the unending struggle between every well-mated couple neither side can afford to concede even the smallest point.

He rose and picked up his axe. Maggie, watching covertly from the window, saw him lounge into the bluff. She heard him chopping and the occasional crash of a falling tree, but soon there was silence. She stole out. He was going down the slope toward the Kent homestead. With an enigmatic smile she returned to her work.

With the firm determination in his mind not to ask for a job, but merely to inquire in a friendly way how his new neighbour was getting on, Billy went down to where a way had been cut through a willow thicket that fringed a shallow runway joining two sloughs.

It was a typical mid-July day in the North-west, with the temperature at ninety in the shade. A dry, fierce heat without humidity, burning but not oppressive. Rich grass, matted with the purple pea-vine, and jewelled with goldenrod, aster, sunflower, and crimson tiger-lilies, stood waist high, and the whole fertile, hospitable, beautiful land distilled a heady perfume. Billy, dumb poet, lifted his head with a happy smile and snuffed.

" Gosh, it smells good," he murmured.

Though little water trickled down the runway, the ground was very soft, and the wagon wheels had already cut deep gashes in the fat black ooze, giving promise of a glorious and bottomless mudhole there after a little more traffic. But as all the trails in the country passed at frequent intervals through just such bogs, Billy hardly noticed it.

It was far otherwise with Kent. Billy found him a little on the hither side of the tent, in his shirt-sleeves, wielding vigorously though clumsily a spade, and busily filling a damp hollow with earth.

Billy stopped and regarded him pityingly. " Say
he suggested, " if you was to cut down them two poplars there, you could go around that soft place."

Kent nodded. " But you see," he explained, ". I
don't want to go round. I want to make a good
road."

". Uh," said Billy, his opinion of Kent's intelligence
dropping another point.

Kent wiped the sweat from his forehead. " Devilish
hot, isn't it ? Afraid I haven't quite got the hang
of this—ah—agricultural implement."

" Well," drawled Billy, " you do seem to be workin'
a lot harder'n you're goin'."

Kent looked at him sidelong in silence for five seconds,
and then his whole solemn face broke up into a myriad
pleasant wrinkles. He laughed a short, deep " Ha,
ha," and his face settled back at once into its usual
impassivity.

From that moment Billy began to entertain grave
doubts as to whether this Englishman was altogether
such a fool as he seemed. Of his ignorance and
clumsiness there could be no doubt, but was that allied
also with idiocy or not ?

Suddenly Kent became loquacious. " I say, Clovelly, I've been thinking about you. I don't want to—
ah—pry into your private concerns, but possibly you
could spare time to teach me the ropes, you know.
You may have noticed that I have—ah—something to
learn."

Billy grinned and nodded.

" Ah, you have ! Well, do you think we could work
together on some equitable footing ? Pardon me if

I put it a little bluntly, but possibly you have more experience than—ah—money, and I have more money than experience. Couldn't we arrange some kind of—ah—co-operation on that basis ? "

The unaccustomed phrasing took a few seconds to filter through to Billy's comprehension, but when it did he laughed joyously.

" Say, d'you know, matter of fact, I just come over to see couldn't you an' me come to some kind of deal like that. It's a fact I got no money, not a nickel, an' Maggie an' me was figurin', as soon as we got our six months' residence in on the homestead for this year, I'd go to the bush for the winter an' she'd hire out to some farm. But if you an' me could make a dicker, why, we'd put up hay for the horses, an' do a little fall breakin', and trap a few rats in the winter, an' scramble through that way."

Details were not long in being settled after that : an informal partnership was quickly formed, Kent furnishing money and Billy experience.

"' And just to start with," said Kent, " we'll make some kind of road across that confounded mudhole. I shall have a lot of stuff coming out from Riverton, and I don't want to have every load bogged there."

" Well, it's your funeral," said Billy with a grin. " You sure do have a love for fillin' mudholes, but if you keep on the way you're goin' you'll have damn little time for anything else."

" But one of these days all the mudholes will have to be filled up."

" Maybe so, but that'll be a long time from now. I ain't sayin' nothin' against the country, mind : it's a good country, but I never see so many mudholes in my life before."

" Well, we'll do what we can to help the good work along," said Kent. " When can you begin ? "

" Right away," said Billy. " I'll go get my axe."

For the rest of that day and all the next day—for Kent insisted upon a good road—they cut willows for a roadbed and laid upon them a corduroy of poplar poles, making a small culvert in the centre to carry off the water.

" And now," said Kent, " we'll go and bridge the brook."

" Hell," protested Billy, " you mean the creek. Why, it's five miles from here anyway, an' the whole dern country'll be usin' our bridge."

" Let them," said Kent placidly. " But we'll lose more time loading and unloading wagons at that cursed creek than it would take to build two bridges. We had a devil of a time there yesterday."

The two settlers came along with their second loads just after the bridge was begun, and Kent made them camp on the far side and help. There was plenty of timber available, Kent had some slight engineering knowledge, and, the other three being expert axemen, they were not long in erecting a very substantial bridge. It endured with minor repairs for some years, and was always known as Kent's bridge, and the creek as Kent's creek.

The sun had baked the sod brick-hard, so that it was too late to break more land, but there remained more than enough to do. Hay had to be put up for the long winter and barns needed to be built.

Kent employed a couple of Riverton carpenters to build him a frame house. He intended to have them build him also a barn, but Billy pointed out that this was a needless extravagance with the woods abounding in excellent building timber.

When they had completed a comfortable four-roomed cottage, with a wide verandah, the carpenters were allowed to return to Riverton.

Kent and Billy cut their hay around the margins of the sloughs, where the grass stood man-high. Kent remained almost incredibly awkward, but he was a very willing worker and contrived to get a great deal done. He never seemed to be in a hurry, but, on the other hand, he never got bored with his job, as Billy so often did.

Being a big man and muscular, when his thews hardened and the blisters on his hands thickened into callouses he was soon able to do a very creditable day's work.

Meanwhile, Maggie and Mrs. Kent improved their acquaintance, though, from the nature of things, they did not see as much of each other as their husbands did.

They agreed quite well in the main, and Maggie took a strong fancy to the Kent boys, Harry aged eight, and Ted, five and a half. They were sturdy youngsters, and charmed with the new land. They were disappointed that wild Indians and buffalos no longer roamed at large, but Harry, with a small rifle, roamed about, half hoping and half fearing to meet a moose or a bear, and Ted followed him like a shadow.

More than once they lost themselves, but Ted, who

had a stronger sense of direction than his brother, brought them home safely, except upon the memorable day when they strayed as far as the creek, and Kent and Billy galloped their horses nearly to death searching for them.

CHAPTER VI

THE Kents were invincibly determined to be what
they called comfortable. Mrs. Kent would say with
great satisfaction over any achievement, " There now,
that'll make us a little more comfortable."

This was quite incomprehensible to the Clovelleys :
their standards were naturally more modest, but they
were also different in kind. When they indulged in
vague dreams of future wealth, they thought of wide
lands, enormous herds, and stupendous red barns. But
for actual, practical, everyday purposes, enough to
eat, a few clothes, and a more or less weather-tight
roof were all they needed.

Maggie envied Mrs. Kent her cottage to some extent,
though she did not feel at home in it herself, but
it left Billy absolutely cold. He saw no necessity
whatever for separate rooms to eat and sleep and
cook in.

He was much more interested in the log barn he
and Kent were constructing of spruce logs from a near-
by muskeg. It was an imposing building, eighteen
by twenty-four feet. Kent went up several degrees
in his estimation by rigging an ingenious crane for
lifting the heavy logs into place. They were both very
proud of it when it was completed.

The Kents bought a couple of milch cows, and Maggie taught Mrs. Kent how to milk. The cows were named Lily and Lightfoot.

Lily was a large, slow-moving, light roan, with a placid disposition. She was not a heavy milker, but her milk was rich and she gave it easily. She was affectionate, too, in an undemonstrative way, and would turn her head to blow damply in Mrs. Kent's ear when being milked.

Lightfoot was a mustard-coloured, sharp-horned, pop-eyed, long-legged brute, with a dash of Jersey and a very strong spice of the devil in her. She was perverse and wrong-headed ; a heavy milker, but given to holding her milk. On occasion she kicked, and she was also " hooky," as country folk call a cow given to using her horns.

She kicked Mrs. Kent's shiny new pail into a ruin without warning at the third milking. Mrs. Kent shed angry tears and then slapped the cow and hurt her hand. Then she demanded that the beast's hind legs be tied.

" I'm going to milk her," she declared with her pointed chin quivering and a red spot in either cheek. " I'm going to milk her if it takes me all day."

It was a protracted struggle, but Mrs. Kent won, and Lightfoot came in time to regard her with great respect, though it was never safe to leave her heels untied.

Kent refused to learn to milk. It was one of his whims, and he was an immovable person. In general he seemed to give way to the views of his talkative and energetic spouse, but when he had made up his mind to

something her loudly expressed wishes were calmly
ignored.

" Yes, my dear, you are probably quite right, but
still I think I'll try my way and see what happens,"
he would murmur with his slow smile.

" Tom, you're the most obstinate and exasperating
man on earth. I could shake you."

" Go to it, as Clovelly says, my dear, if it'll relieve
your feelings."

The argument would end by Kent quietly leaving
the house. By the time he poked an inquiring head in
at the door again her ruffled plumage would have had
time to smooth itself. Hers was not a sullen or vindictive
disposition.

Billy said he would not buy a cow until he had somewhere to keep her. Besides, cows would be cheaper
in the fall.

Maggie flew into a furious and unaccountable rage
at this. It was not the first hint he had had that she
was not herself. She had grown listless of late, whimpered
that she was homesick, and complained bitterly about
her food.

Billy was first puzzled, then irritated, and when
the matter of the cow came up, and she accused him
of not caring for her any longer and never doing anything
to please her, he lost his temper.

" Say, what in Sam Hill's eatin' you ? " he demanded.
" You're crazy as a bedbug."

" That's right," she screamed hysterically, " abuse
me, call me dirty names. Why don't you hit me ? "
She burst into violent and uncontrolled sobbing.

The astounded Billy worked over her for an hour,

petting her, telling her he loved her, and begging her
to stop crying and tell him what the matter was. At last
she kissed him with wet lips and fell suddenly asleep.

He had been working hard all day and he had only
time to wonder vaguely what it was all about when
sleep fell upon him also. She was still asleep when
he rose in the morning and lit the stove. The noise
woke her and she sat up and smiled at him affectionately.

" Well, how d'you feel the mornin' after the night
before ? " he queried.

" Fine an' dandy."

He grinned and shook his head. " Well, it's lucky
it don't last long when you do get that way," he said.
" Last night you was goin' to wreck the country an'
me too."

" Oh, well, I wasn't feelin' so good."

" Huh. Say, just let me know next time when you
begin to feel real bad. I'll get ready to pull my freight
right away. I can't stand only just so much of that
stuff."

At intervals through the day he caught himself mar-
velling what had come over his usually sunny-tempered
and active wife, but the puzzle was not solved until
after supper.

Sitting on a box by the door, enjoying his pipe and
the warm, scented twilight, he found her beside him.
He put an arm around her and gave her a squeeze,
and she turned and kissed him on the ear.

She said casually, " Say, Billy, d'you know I'm that
way ? "

" Wh-a-t ? What way ? O-oh—you mean. . . ? "

" Uh-huh."

"Well, I be damned." He began to puff hard at
his pipe.

"I was hopin' it wouldn't be quite so soon," she
went on placidly. "But I guess it can't be helped
now."

"Well, what are we goin' to do? How about a
doctor?"

"Don't need no doctor—got no use for doctors.
My mother never had no doctor, an' she had nine,
an' eight of 'em still livin'. Your mother never had
no doctor, neither, an' there's seven of you, ain't
there?"

"No, eight, an' there was two died before I come."

"Well, then, what would I need a doctor for? I
told Mrs. Kent, an' she said she'd come over an' 'tend
to me."

"That's good, anyway. When's it goin' to be?"

"Oh, long about the end of March, I figure."

"Well, that's not so bad," he said musingly. "You
know, Mag, I believe I would like a little skeezix around
here."

"Would you, Billy, would you now? Won't you
give me a little hug, Billy, an' say you love your wife
just a little bit, eh?"

This put a different complexion on the matter of the
cow. Kent's barn being now completed, they proceeded to put up one for Billy. It was a small building
of unbarked poplar logs, with room in it for four head
of live stock.

He bought a quiet brown cow, called Daisy, due
to freshen in the early spring, and meanwhile they
got their milk from the Kents' overflowing abundance.

In early September the first real frost descended and froze Maggie's carefully tended potatoes. The tops turned black at the first touch of the sun.

They dug the potatoes and stored them in a hole in the floor of the shack. Billy also got some rough boards and made a wooden floor, much to Maggie's delight. Many old-timers in the settlement were still living in houses with earth floors, though they had been ten years or more in the country.

CHAPTER VII

THE change from summer into winter was accomplished almost as rapidly as that from winter into summer. In the Northwest spring and autumn, or fall, are hardly more than courtesy terms.

The white poplars turned to silver columns supporting broad fans of pale gold, the hazels turned a rich brown, the wild cherries crimson, and the kinnikinnick blood-red. The landscape became a palette splashed with fifty different tints, and over all arched the cloudless sky of pale turquoise.

V-shaped flocks of honking geese went by high up, and whirring drifts of wild ducks. Now and again small flocks of great white birds, moving in wide spiral sweeps, floated across the zenith with a wild, strange trumpeting. They were cranes, a beautiful bird daily growing rarer.

In ten days from the first yellowing the leaves had gone. When September was born every tree wore its green garment intact. At the death of the golden month they doffed their robes in mourning, and stood naked to the snarling north wind. Only the sombre spruces in the muskegs kept their ever-green needles; the tamaracks were already yellow-clad, and would soon be bare.

Morning was crisp with frost, noonday bright and

warm ; dusk brought a swift chill. The glowing colours of the countryside faded slowly to a uniform dull brown.

The barns were finished and weather-tight. The settlers hitched their four horses to Kent's big breaker plough. They turned over some fourteen acres before the breaker was found frozen in the furrow one morning and was with difficulty pulled out.

" Freeze-up," said Billy. " You'll do no more ploughing till April, maybe May."

That was on November 3. That night the fine weather broke. Keen and hard blew the north wind when day dawned, the temperature was at zero, and little pellets of ice rattled briskly on the frozen ground. The sloughs stiffened in a few hours into ice strong enough to bear a team of horses.

A day or two of bright sunshine with a deceptive promise of moderating weather, and then the wind went into the east and the heavy grey snow clouds came rolling up from Hudson's Bay. All that day and all night it snowed. The sun rose next morning on a white world that sparkled with prismatic colours, a world so dazzling that the eye involuntarily cloaked itself against the glitter.

" Six good inches of snow," said Billy with satisfaction. " Make dandy sleighin'. Well, we got nothin' to kick about : good tight shack an' barn, lots of spuds in the cellar, hay up, an' plenty wood for the cuttin'. Looks to me like we struck it lucky."

Maggie began to laugh. " I was just thinkin' about how we didn't think much of Tom Kent first time we seen him," she said in answer to Billy's stare.

He grinned back. " A feller can't always sometimes tell how far a cat can jump, eh ? "

Kent took advantage of the snow to make his first
trip to Riverton on sleighs, and Billy commissioned
him to buy three dozen steel rat traps. The sloughs
nearby swarmed with muskrat houses, or dams, as the
settlers call them—domes of reeds and flags rising several
feet above the ice.

The method of trapping muskrats is simplicity itself. All that it is necessary to do is to cut into the
side of the dam until the central chamber is reached.
There the trap is set, the opening tightly plugged to
keep the frost out, and the chain of the trap anchored
to a stick outside.

Twice a day Billy walked his line of traps ; the rest
of the time he spent skinning his catch and stretching
the pelts on shaped boards. He caught from ten to
twenty rats a day, and by the time the sloughs in the
vicinity were trapped out he had over four hundred
good pelts.

Rats were worth little enough in those days—ten cents
apiece was a good average price—but other things
were relatively cheap too. Billy traded his catch for
sufficient groceries to last him all winter.

The days were mostly sunny, though the fanged
north wind struck ruthlessly. At night the skies blazed
with the northern lights and the owls hooted mournfully to
the wailing coyotes. A little snow fell from time to time.

Christmas Day was wild and blowy, with a lowering grey sky and a temperature of twenty below zero
—the worst day of the winter so far.

Kent came over in the morning to wish them a Merry Christmas and invite them to dinner. He also presented Billy with a briar pipe from himself, and Maggie with a mysterious parcel from Mrs. Kent. The parcel contained Lilliputian garments over which Maggie gurgled with delight.

A path had been made across the slough that separated the two houses, reducing the distance to about five hundred yards. After some discussion they agreed to walk over.

Your Westerner will invariably harness a team to go more than half a mile. Walking for the pleasure of it he regards as an infallible indication of a weak mind.

The Kent living-room was brilliantly lit by two oil lamps. The table was laid with white linen, silver, and cut glass. There was even a snowy napkin at each plate. The furniture was simple but good, the Clovellys had never seen so many books in their lives as were collected in the substantial bookcase, and the flowered-chintz curtains that shut out the dark seemed to Maggie the last word in ultra-refinement.

The Clovellys were uncomfortable, Billy especially— for Maggie, for all her ignorance, had a woman's instinct for society. They were kitchen dwellers by inheritance. They could understand wealthy people who wanted to "put on dog" having a "parlour," but it was always understood that a parlour was for show purposes only. However, they remembered that these benighted English people had much to learn about right living, and they generously forgave them.

The Kents displayed tact. Mrs. Kent had thoughtfully

CAMROSE LUTHERAN COLLEGE
LIBRARY

provided Billy with a silver dessert knife so that he should not cut his mouth. He found it rather short and narrow, but he did his best with it.

They had roast beef and Yorkshire pudding, for the turkey and the goose are birds of civilization. Billy shied a little at the Yorkshire pudding, but found it quite palatable when he ventured upon it.

There was a small dish of olives on the table. Curiosity overcame Billy. He tried one. A look of sorrow overspread his face as his teeth sank into it. He abstracted it carefully with finger and thumb, gazed at it curiously, sighed, and dropped it furtively under the table.

The skin of Mrs. Kent's face became suddenly tight and little quivers ran silently up and down her slender throat. Kent slowly and carefully wiped his moustache with his table napkin and his ears burned a dull red.

Billy's next great experience was with the plum pudding, which Mrs. Kent brought in blazing from the kitchen, amid the plaudits of her small sons.

"Will you have some of this, Mr. Clovelly?" she asked brightly.

Billy sighed again. "Well, I've tried a lot of things to-night," he said bravely. "But ain't a feller liable to have his stummick burnt out with that stuff?"

She assured him he would not, and he ventured upon a piece.

"Why," he said, "it's good, it's real good. Mrs. Kent, you certainly can sling the chuck. I ain't on to your Old Country cookin' yet, and I believe I'd pretty near just as soon eat after you as Maggie."

"Thanks very much for the compliment, Mr. Clovelly," she laughed.

The crown of the feast for the Clovellys was a bowl-ful of big red apples. Neither of them had tasted an apple for over a year and they beamed with de-light.

There were also some nuts, but Billy waved them away. " I never was much on squirrel food," he ex-plained.

After dinner Kent produced cigars. " I likes to whittle my own," said Billy, pulling out plug and knife. " Them things always gets tangled up in my mouth an' taste like a cow's tail."

They sat around the stove, the only un-English thing in the room, and ate apples and nuts and talked until nine o'clock.

" They're good people," said Billy on the road home. " They mean well, but they got funny notions about grub. That green thing like to killed me."

They had still plenty of potatoes, flour, tea, sugar, and butter, but no meat. Maggie voiced a craving for fresh meat, and said peevishly that she was starving to death.

" Guess I'll go see can I get a deer," said Billy. " There's lots of tracks every place around the bush."

He loaded four shotgun shells with buckshot, and set out for a big muskeg to the northward. Though he had seen plenty of tracks, he had been too busy with his trapping to follow any of them.

When he did follow them, of course, not a deer was to be found. After a long and fruitless day of tramping through deep snow, he returned home along after dark with nothing larger than a spruce partridge.

He found Maggie in tears, having persuaded herself that he had met with an accident.

She kissed him and clung to him. Then her mood changed.

"You don't care about me," she scolded. "Go runnin' around all day, amusin' yourself, just amusin' yourself. You don't care how I am. Then you come home with a measly little bunch of feathers. You're a fine hunter."

"I'll take another trip to-morrow—might have better luck," said Billy patiently.

"Billy Clovelly, you don't take that gun out of this house again. How do I know what you'll do to yourself with it? It's all right with you—you don't care if you blow your head off—but what'll happen me? You never think of it. You don't care."

"All right, then, I won't," he said.

She sniffed. "An' I suppose I got to eat bread and spuds. I'm sick of the stuff. I'll go crazy if I don't have some fresh meat."

He was reduced to silence, brooding darkly on woman's inconsistency.

But in the morning she had regained her serenity.

"Go along," she said. "I know you're just wild to go. But don't be late."

"No, I won't be late."

But it was a promise impossible of fulfilment. The days were only seven hours long, and it is slow work ploughing through twelve or fourteen inches of dry powdery snow.

He followed more trails until he was on the verge of exhaustion. All he saw was a few white rabbits, and

no dweller in the Northwest will eat rabbits until actual
starvation is upon him.

Empty-handed again, tired and irritable, he turned
homeward as the sun was sinking cloudlessly into the
south-west.

" Now I'll catch hell," he mused. " Dern that
woman. Does she expect them deer to come right up
for me to shoot at ? "

His way led him past a haystack less than a mile
from the shack. As he approached, three vague grey
forms suddenly bounded up out of the snow. He flung
up his gun and loosed both barrels at a venture. The
creatures scattered, but one, after giving a few con-
vulsive leaps, dropped and lay still. He ran up eagerly,
to find a fine young buck crimsoning the snow with
its lifeblood.

He arrived home half an hour later, dragging his
kill by the heels, and so tired he could scarcely stand.
He found Maggie, in a state bordering on dementia,
preparing to come in search of him.

It was midnight before he had quieted her.

Billy took a haunch over to the Kents and felt that
he had requited their hospitality. But Kent shot a
deer himself soon after almost in his own yard, and both
families had a sufficiency of the somewhat tasteless
meat for the rest of the season.

Billy went up to the settlement, eighteen miles, to
get the mail. Not that there was any for him, but the
Kents invariably received a big roll of English periodicals
and usually several letters.

Aaron Smith's post office was the big clearing house
of district news. There you could learn who had married

whom, what horses had been traded by whom to whom, who was sick, or dead, or in trouble, what new settlers had arrived and where they had taken up land.

Billy returned with an important piece of news.

"Say, Tom, there's an outfit goin' to run a sawmill on Bone Creek this summer. It's about ten mile east of here. How about gettin' out some logs? It costs like the devil bringing lumber from Riverton. I figure to get me a few logs sawed anyway."

Kent caught eagerly at the suggestion. "By Jove, I'm glad of that. I've been wondering where I'd get the money for all the lumber I need."

They turned lumberjacks. Kent had by this time learned to use an axe after a fashion, but he had every vice known to sawyers. He was for ever riding the saw or binding it in the cut. He never acquired an eye for timber, but that is something that only comes with long practice. Billy found him very exasperating at times.

"For Pete's sake, Tom, think I'm takin' you a sleigh ride? Let up on that saw; let her run. All you got to do is pull her: she'll do the work. When you get through pullin', let me do a little. I don't need nobody pushin' on the other end."

The six-foot blade stopped with a vibrating twang. Billy rolled his eyes to heaven.

"Bet you pulled six teeth out of her that jerk. Take it easy, man. I never see such a man to tear his guts out on a job."

Kent grinned behind the mask of icicles on his big moustache, for the temperature was thirty below zero. "Sorry, old man."

Billy carefully loosened the jammed saw, and shook his head over a turned tooth. He put it right with a few strokes of the file.

" Now, ease her in. Pull easy. Take her your way a little ; I want her to clear that poplar. Stand by to snatch her when she goes."

The tall spruce nodded and groaned. Billy, with one eye aloft, took a short quick pull at the saw. There was a sharp pistol-like cracking.

" Snatch her," snapped Billy.

They jerked the saw out of the cut before the grinding butt had time to snap it in two, for steel is brittle in very cold weather.

The spruce bowed like a stately old dame, hung an instant, the last fibres cracked, and it began a swiftly accelerating descent. But a little puff of wind swung it out of alignment. The poplar Billy had hoped to clear received the trunk in its main fork. Frozen twigs, brittle as glass, whizzed through the air like javelins.

" Well, hell," grumbled Billy. " Hung up, an' I got to get under and cut that cursed poplar down. Stand back, Tom ; this is a one-man job. Never know what'll happen with a lodged tree."

He walked all round the prop, kicked away the snow, set himself, and delivered a full-power blow. The axe rang sharply on the frozen wood. Billy crouched, looking up. The poplar vibrated, but did not break. He took a deep breath and swung his axe again.

With a loud report the poplar split half its length. The big spruce came whistling down, only to hang up in a little sapling. In his eagerness to help, Kent sprang forward and aimed a blow at the sapling.

It broke off short, swinging its burden in the direction of the flying Billy. A sweeping branch flung him on his face and the spruce trunk pinned him to the ground across the loins. Had the full weight of the tree fallen upon him his back had been broken then and there, but the branches held it clear of the ground.

He clawed the snow out of his eyes and turned his head towards the conscience-stricken Kent.

" Clovelly, Clovelly, are you hurt ? "

Billy achieved a twisted grin. " Tell you later. Hustle now an' cut a handspike an' pry this damn log off of me ; it's squeezin' my liver out."

Kent slashed at the nearest sapling, cut himself a pole, drove it under the end of the big log, and heaved until his muscles cracked. Billy scrabbled at the snow, clawed his way free, and got upon his feet, rubbing his back ruefully.

" Gosh, old-timer, the old woman come pretty near bein' a widder that trip," he said.

Kent sat down weakly on the stump, the sweat pouring down his face. " If you feel like kicking me," he said contritely, " go ahead. I deserve it."

" It's all right," said Billy. " No harm done. Little things like that's always happenin' in the bush. I seen a man get killed once by a chaser just like that. But, say, don't tell your woman ; I wouldn't like Maggie to know. I ain't goin' to tell her myself ; she'd raise the devil with me, an' likely have it in for you too."

Kent had been married long enough to learn the extreme inadvisability of telling a woman anything she does not need to know. He nodded understandingly.

Billy did no more work that day, but huddled over a fire and directed Kent. On his return home he told Maggie that he had had a hard day and was worn out, and she was so interested in her own sensations that he had no difficulty in keeping the truth from her. He was very stiff and sore for a couple of days, but managed to get through a certain amount of work, and Kent became less of a trial as he picked up the rudiments.

The weather remained cold ; once the temperature fell to fifty below ; once a powerful wind blew from the north-east under a cloudy sky for three days with a temperature of thirty below, and life became a torment in the open. But, on the whole, it was a mild winter, and the cold spell only lasted three weeks. It may last for three months.

The men suffered the usual frostbites : Kent's big nose was raw and peeling, and the lobe of one of Billy's ears swelled to the size of a marble. At noon, under a bright sun, the temperature rose sometimes above zero, but afternoon brought a swift drop, and it was coldest at about eight in the morning.

They worked steadily on. When the logs had been cut, they pulled them out of the bush with their teams and piled them on a skidway ready for loading and hauling to the mill.

On an early February morning Billy heard a new note in the wind that hummed around the shack. He got out of bed in a hopeful frame of mind, lit the stove, dressed, and stepped out of doors to feed the stock.

He was met by a blast of warm air from the south-west.

The thrice-blessed Chinook, beloved of winter-bound folk of the Northwest, was blowing. There was a delicious languor in the air. Everyone was sleepily happy. A great weight seemed to have been lifted from their shoulders, and the universal desire was to sit idly in the rays of a sun that had suddenly become warm and genial, instead of a pale, heatless yellow ball.

The Chinook held for two days, and the gritty snow, heaped into knife-edged drifts by the north wind, softened and took on rounded contours. Sleighs slipped easily along, no longer whining and groaning like beasts in pain, and the sleigh bells chimed mellowly instead of ringing sharply.

Kent and Billy, with light loads of logs, broke trail to the mill through snow now two feet deep. By the time the trail was well packed the respite ended. From then until the end of March intermittent blizzards swept the land; the temperature swung from thirty below to thirty above in the space of a few days; but milder weather predominated.

Time after time the trails blew in, until, as they were broken and packed afresh each time, they came to stand up like ridges above the surrounding snow. To step off was to flounder waist deep, and to attempt to break a new trail incredible labour.

But all the logs were hauled to the little portable mill, and sawn, and the lumber hauled home again.

The work was finished none too soon, for the days were growing longer and the high-ridged trails began to cut down as the snow softened under the powerful rays of the March sun. Twice their loads skidded off the trail and overturned. That meant reloading in wet sticky snow that soaked them to the skin, and much hard and picturesque swearing, in which Billy was an adept, as most pioneers are.

CHAPTER VIII

It was now getting near Maggie's time and Billy was afraid to leave her for long. The weather hovered, as it were, in suspense. A day of bright skies and melting snow would be followed by one of overcast skies and raw winds. Winter was unwillingly loosening his grip upon the land, but the sun was a mighty enemy.

Black patches appeared here and there on the breaking, and spread slowly. But the wind swung from east to west and back again by way of the north, and deliverance could come only from the south.

And then on a night, about two in the morning, Maggie began to cry aloud, and Billy knew by a sort of instinct that her hour had struck.

She would not believe it herself. As he scrambled into his clothes, she whispered at him, " It's all right, it's all right, Billy. It won't be this time—I had just as bad pains before. Don't go away from me, Billy ; I'm scared. Oh, Billy, I'm scared."

" No, I got to go," he insisted. " You never been this bad before. I'll be right back."

" Well, maybe you best. But don't be long, Billy, because I'm awful scared. Kiss me, Billy, and hurry back."

He kissed her. She clung to him and wept, and he

had to break her hold and run. He could hear her wailing after him as he raced across the slough.

The Kents' big black retriever, Cus (short for Marcus Aurelius), came bounding to meet him, baying.

" Down, Cus, down," he panted, and hammered on the door.

He was answered by a sleepy masculine growl, and cried, " It's Maggie, Mrs. Kent, it's Maggie. Can you come quick ? "

Mrs. Kent's clear high voice answered him, " Yes, Mr. Clovelly, I'll be over immediately. Run home again, my good man, and get lots of hot water ready."

He whirled and fled back the way he had come. Maggie was moaning and seemed hardly to recognize him.

" Don't go away, Billy. Billy, I'm scared. Don't go away," she repeated over and over.

Wild-eyed and breathing short, he bent over her.

" I'm here, honey, I'm here. I won't go away again, an' Mrs. Kent's comin' over right away. She said for me to get some hot water."

He began to charge aimlessly about the shack. He stumbled with a full pail of water and upset it all over the floor. Cursing under his breath, he grabbed a sack and began to mop it up, remembered suddenly that he had to get lots of hot water, and with a groan caught up the pail and fled out to the well.

With the stove full of wood and wide open, so that it roared like a blast furnace, and with the kettle and every available thing that would hold water piled on top of it, he went back to mopping the floor, jumping up every second to see if Mrs. Kent was coming.

He saw her coming, moving with maddening deliberation. He would have run to meet her, but Maggie
lifted a sudden, shrill, long-drawn shriek that turned
his heart to water and sent him plunging to her side.

" Oh, Maggie, what is it ? "

To his stupefied amazement, she smiled at him.

" When I yell like that it makes it easier," she explained.

" For God's sake ! " gasped Billy, and went back to
the door.

" Now don't go away," she cried imperiously. " Come
back here. I'll yell if I want to."

Mrs. Kent came in bearing a big bundle. She was
a little out of breath with her load and the haste she had
made, but she wore a calm and smiling expression.
Maggie chose that moment to send forth another of her
harrowing cries.

Mrs. Kent nodded at her brightly. " Scream all
you want to, young lady, if it does you any good."

Her keen eye took in the array of pots on the raging
stove, the wet floor, and Billy's staring eyes and dis-
hevelled hair.

" The best thing you can do, my man," she said,
" is to go outside and cool off. You'll only be in my way
here. I'll call you when I want you. Don't go far."

The distraught Billy wandered out into the night,
glad in spite of himself to escape from the ringing
shrieks that Maggie was now sending out at regularly
decreasing intervals.

It was the first really mild night of the year. The
wind had at last hauled into the south and breathed
warmly upon the sinking drifts. A gibbous moon,

close to her setting, veiled her face from time to time
in thin clouds. The landscape, in soft tones of silver
and grey, was of an indescribably tender loveliness.

Billy saw nothing of it. Mechanically he whittled
his plug and filled his pipe, lit it, and forgot to puff,
came to a moment later as another of Maggie's cries
shivered to the stars, lit another match, burnt his fingers
and cast it way with a muttered curse.

One scream succeeded another. He sat down limply
on the woodpile and clapped his hands over his ears.

" Clovelly, Clovelly, I want you."

He got up, gulped, and with pale face and trembling
limbs followed Mrs. Kent into the house.

It was over.

Billy, with an ashen face and twitching limbs, sat
beside the stove in a state of collapse. Mrs. Kent, pale
and shaken, but keeping herself sternly under control,
was busy with a tiny, red, squirming creature, which
was making a surprising amount of noise for its
size.

The person who appeared least affected was Maggie.
There was sweat on her face and a drawn look about
the mouth and eyes, but childbirth was to her no such
ordeal as to pulpy, degenerate townswomen.

She lifted herself on one elbow. " What is it, Mrs.
Kent ? " she inquired in a strong voice.

" It's a girl, my dear—a beautiful little girl."

" Aw, pshaw ! An' I hoped it was goin' to be a boy."

" Don't talk nonsense," said Mrs. Kent sharply.
" I only wish I had a little girl."

This was not true, for Mrs. Kent prided herself on
being the mother of sons, but Maggie sank back rebuked.

Dawn had broken, and the lamp, its oil burnt out, sent up a thin wisp of foul black smoke.

"Put that smelly thing out, Clovelly," commanded Mrs. Kent. "And get me another bucket of water."

Billy was glad to have something to do. As he returned from the well he met Kent, bearing a pail of milk.

"Well, old man?"

"Girl," said Billy hoarsely. "Girl."

"Congratulations. And your wife?"

"Claims to be feelin' fine—I don't know. Gad, it was awful." He shuddered.

Mrs. Kent came to the door. "That you, Tom? Did you bring the milk and the flannel?"

"Got the milk. Clean forgot the bally flannel."

"Then go back at once and get it. Here, give me the milk before you go, you great big silly."

Kent winked gravely at the still bemused Billy and went off.

"Well, when can I get up?" inquired Maggie.

"Not till I permit you, young woman," said Mrs. Kent sharply.

"Aw, but I don't want to lie in bed; there's so many things to do. Can I get up to-morrow?"

"No, of course not. You must stay in bed for nine days."

"I'll go crazy," said Maggie with conviction.

However, on the following day she was not feeling so well and Billy threatened her with dire penalties if she attempted to move. By the third day she was becoming very restless and irritable. Her remarks on Billy's housekeeping were scathing.

Next morning she rose in spite of all he could say, but hopped into bed again at Mrs. Kent's approach. The day following she threw off all disguise, and once more took the management of her house into her own hands.

Billy, used to frontier women, saw nothing unnatural in that, but Mrs. Kent was gravely perturbed until she found no ill came of it.

The new arrival was named Lucy in compliment to Mrs. Kent, and Maggie found in the atom beauties undiscernible to Billy. He felt that he ought to love and admire his own child, but he could not conceal from himself that the creature was ugly, helpless, and imbecile, and caused an amount of trouble out of all proportion to its size and apparent value. But he realized that no good end would be served by revealing his thoughts to Maggie.

Daisy, the brown cow, very obligingly calved two days after the baby was born.

CHAPTER IX

THE day Lucy arrived was the twenty-ninth of March and the first of the break-up. The Chinook roared across the prairie for a week, and soon there arose everywhere the murmur of running water, mere whispers at first under the snow. Soon, though, sparkling rivulets danced on every hillside, and every hollow was a pool of azure water.

The Chinook died down, the wind veered to the north, and it froze hard again. But the break-up had definitely come, and leaf and flower were now only a matter of days.

The first crocuses appeared, and on a calm night Billy heard the whistle of wings and a subdued " quack quack," and knew the ducks had arrived. But spring is not really come until the frogs begin.

It had been raining a little, and a most delicious smell rose from the earth, doubly delightful because the winter frost kills all scents. The clouds cleared just before sunset and the wind dropped.

Billy lit his after-supper pipe and went and sat on the sawbuck. Suddenly he called, " Maggie ! Oh, Maggie ! "

" Well, what ? " she asked tolerantly, for she knew that he was likely to be mildly insane every spring.

" Listen."

Faintly from the borders of the slough, " Croak-craak, croak-craak." And the answer on a higher key, " Churr-churr-churr."

" Why, it's only the frogs," said Maggie.

Billy stood up. There were tears in his eyes, and he was quivering all over with strange, sad, confused emotions and longings. He heard spirit voices.

" Yes, it's the frogs," he said softly. " Kid, I got spring fever. I'm runnin' wild to-night."

Maggie withdrew quietly to the baby. She was glad spring had come, but she had more important things to attend to. She did not in the least understand Billy's emotion, but she knew he was insane for the time being, and best left alone.

Billy was in the grip of the pioneer's longing. Somewhere, just over on the other side of the next hill perhaps, there lay the Desirable Land. No human foot has ever pressed its soil, no human eye has ever looked upon it. But all pioneers dream of it, and even stay-at-home men, poor grey grubs in office or factory, receive spirit messages from it in the spring.

No Clovelly had ever been able to resist its spell. It was part of Billy's very being. He had sought it in the body, as his fathers had sought it before him, as his sons would seek it until the world has no more frontiers. And when that day comes, when all the earth is polluted by man, then the pioneer will set flight for the stars and seek the Desirable Land in the depths beyond the Milky Way.

Billy took a few steps and broke into a run. There was a belt of trees before him. Perhaps he would find what he sought just beyond it. He knew he would not, but the hope would not down. He would find something, surely he would find something.

The branches slashed him in the face and tore at his clothes, but he burst through. There was a dim field before him. Mysterious thickets crouched to right and left. Beyond was the gleam of water. The air was full of the maddening perfume of spring, and a moorhen lifted its shuddering cry. And then a loon, that lonely mysterious wanderer, spoke that word which is the password to the Desirable Land if only a man can understand its meaning.

Billy started like a wild broncho and raced down to the slough. The icy water splashed about his knees, and the loon, silver and black on the steel-grey water, reiterated his mystic formula.

Billy skirted the slough and headed westward, following the Sun, who alone has seen that country.

There were more ghostly fields and gloomy thickets and pale calm waters, and the northern lights were at play among the stars. All things were strange and unfamiliar and steeped in magic.

Billy ran on and on, and sometimes he laughed, and sometimes he sang, and sometimes he set his teeth and crept silently through screening woodland to pounce upon what lay beyond.

At about two in the morning he came to himself, lying spent on the crest of a sandy hill, chilled to the marrow.

Wearily he dragged himself home, with hanging head, and a grief in his heart too deep for words. He had failed in his quest, and the yoke of toil, that galling, grinding, monotonous yoke, settled firmly upon his rebellious shoulders once more.

The cycle was complete. Once more the night was vocal with uncounted frogs, the buds swelled, the birds returned, and the sullen smoke of prairie fires hung in the air.

The frost was out of the topsoil. Kent and Billy cut up their new-broken land with disc harrows and sowed it to oats broadcasted by hand. Then it was necessary to fence the fields to keep the cattle out.

Kent bought two more cows, and Daisy Clovelly herded with them. Harry and Ted Kent, with Cus, the black retriever, watched over them.

There was new land to break after the fencing was done, and new buildings to put up. There was, in fact, always a great deal more to do than time to do it in.

Most of the work was done on Kent's place, but Billy contrived to turn over five acres of new sod on his own place. He helped Maggie plant the garden, though she looked after it alone thenceforward. He also put a better floor in the shack with his new lumber.

In June the supply of oats for the horses ran out. There was a shortage of oats in the old settlement that year, but Kent learned that there were possibly oats to be had at an indefinite distance to the south.

Billy was the logical man to go in search of them, for the intervening country was totally unsettled and there were no trails. He set out one bright morning with Sam and Jimmy, delighted to escape from the monotony of following the plough.

The new country was similar to his own : low ridges, small poplar bluffs, multitudinous sloughs and muskegs with their thin belts of spruce and tamarack. Then he came into a country of bolder hills, with scattered spruces growing here and there on their summits, fewer and larger sloughs, and a thin grass that showed a sandier soil.

Skirting the largest of the hills, he saw before him a wide, willow-grown flat, out of which rose a knoll on which perched a white spot. He recognized it at once for a tent. Evidently a new settler.

Proceeding, he came in a little while to a pile of logs. From them a well-beaten path led in one direction to a spruce bluff and in the other toward the tent. He was puzzled to account for the logs, for they had evidently not been dragged along the ground, nor were there any wheel tracks.

His curiosity turned to amazement when there walked out of the bluff a man bearing upon his shoulder a green spruce log some sixteen feet long and several inches in diameter. Such a stick would make a heavy load for any two men.

But the man plodded steadily up, dropped his burden on the pile, straightened his back with a deep breath, and wiped the sweat from his eyes.

He was hardly of middle height, but of enormous solidity of body, and his short legs were like trees. He was bareheaded and his close-cropped hair, very thin on top, was iron-grey. He had fierce little eyes of a bright blue colour and a heavy dark moustache, pointed like the horns of a bull.

" Good day, sir," said Billy.

" Mornin'," returned the stranger shortly.

" You sure must like hard work," said Billy with a grin.

" Ah," agreed the stranger.

"Take two men to heft one of them logs," said Billy.

The strong man thawed visibly. "Bit for*mid*able, ain't I?" he remarked complacently.

"Why don't you get a team?"

"Can't afford it yet. Don't need 'em any'ow—not till I'ave to plough, I don't."

"My name's Clovelly—Billy Clovelly; live about five mile north-east of you."

"Mine's Darke—Arthur Darke, late sergeant, time-expired, Second Cloamshires," said the strong man crisply. "Pleased to make your acquaintance." He reached up a hand like a ham.

"Say," suggested Billy, "how'd it be if we was to load them logs on my wagon—save you a few trips, eh?"

"It would that," agreed the sergeant. "Much obliged, I'm sure. An' you'll come an' take a bite with me an' my missus."

They removed the wagon box and began to load the logs. Sinewy as he was, Billy found that lifting his end of each over the wheel was all the exertion he cared for, but Darke handled the other end as if it were a straw.

They drew the logs up to the vicinity of the tent, dumped them, and returned for more.

The horses being unhitched and fed, Billy was presented in form to Mrs. Darke, a small, faded, subdued-looking woman of thirty-odd. She stood evidently in great awe of her husband, who treated her as if she were a private soldier who was not quite as smart as he should be.

Their tent was pitched with military precision, exactly

upright, the guy ropes exactly spaced and taut, and everything about the camp was a miracle of orderly cleanliness.

Mrs. Darke was dressed in a dark blouse and skirt, cut with the severity of a field uniform ; her hair was drawn smooth and tight and parted exactly in the centre.

The meal was served on a well-scrubbed table before the tent, and the tin cups and plates had been scoured until they shone. Billy was about to commence eating at once, but was stayed by the formidable man's uplifted hand. The ex-sergeant said a short grace in an impressive voice, while the amazed Billy rolled an incredulous eye at him.

Mrs. Darke did not open her mouth, but her husband was gravely conversational.

Billy asked the inevitable question, " Well, how do you like the country, Mr. Darke ? "

" I think it's a good country," said the sergeant judicially. " It's a 'ealthy country, but the mosquitoes is worse than what they was in Injia."

This led to a short disquisition on India, of which Billy's ignorance was absolute. The sergeant's statements were so incredible to Billy that he was forced to the conclusion that his host might be religious but had little regard for accuracy of statement. Wherein he did the honest sergeant injustice.

Returning to subjects nearer home, Darke inquired, " Family man, Mr. Clovelly ? "

" Uh-huh, one kid."

" Boy or girl, might I ask ? "

" Girl."

" Ah. But even girls is better than nothin'. Your good lady will prob'ly do better with a little experience."

His stern glance fell upon his shrinking wife. " She 'as at least tried to do 'er duty. I 'ave been married twelve years an' I 'ave no children, boy or girl."

Billy looked up to see an expression of dumb suffering on Mrs. Darke's face. He felt himself upon dangerous ground and hastened to change the subject.

" I wouldn't think as a man what'd been soldierin' as long as what you have would get much farmin' experience," he said.

" Ah, Mr. Clovelly, but I was brought up on a farm, you see. I always meant to 'ave a farm of my own when my time was up. But farmin' in England don't pay, so I came out 'ere. I 'ave kept my eyes open, pickin' up 'ints 'ere an' there, in Injia an' East Africa an' Egypt. Of course, farmin' is different in different parts, but, if I may say so, the basic principles is the same everywhere. I 'ave no doubt I shall learn the ropes 'ere."

" I bet you do," said Billy encouragingly.

" Thank you, Mr. Clovelly, I 'ope to justify your good opinion."

Continuing south for seven miles through a still unpeopled country, Billy arrived at the place of Squatter Banks, a quite extensive collection of corrals and log buildings. The squatter had entered the country previous to its being surveyed, and was the prosperous owner of several hundred head of cattle.

He was an extraordinarily gaunt man with a tightly curling grey beard, and dressed in beaded buckskin shirt and moccasins.

"Banks is my name, sir—Leander Banks. I come here from Ohio thirty-seven years ago—yes sir. I fit Injuns right on the ground where I'm standin' right now. I seen the buffalo goin' by in the thousands. There's been changes since I come, sir, you can believe me."

Billy wagged his head. "I bet there has, Mr. Banks. Uh-huh, I bet. What I come to see, Mr. Banks, have you got any oats to sell?"

The Ohian's easy, jovial manner dropped from him at once. "Them'll be fifty cents a bushel."

Billy winced. The price was extortionate, but the squatter knew he possessed the only oats within thirty miles.

"Well, I guess I'll take twenty bushel," said Billy reluctantly, tendering a ten-dollar bill.

Banks pocketed it promptly, and his manner changed again.

"Business is business, sir. I don't figure to do business for my health. Maybe you think I soaked you. Maybe I did. That's your funeral, eh? Now unhitch them horses and come an' eat."

Billy found himself sitting at a table loaded with Western delicacies and waited on by a brown lady, whom he suspected to be Mrs. Banks, by courtesy at least, though the original settlers were somewhat casual in their marital relations.

There were several young breeds in the house, who treated Banks with the greatest deference, and were given curt orders.

After supper Banks filled a large pipe with raw leaf tobacco of the rankest flavour, and discoursed at large on old days.

" That's the best woman I ever had," he remarked casually with a jerk of the pipestem in the direction of the brown lady. " A feller don't get on to how to handle 'em until he's had two or three." He puffed meditatively for a few minutes, and added, " Yes sir, yes sir, they take some handlin'."

Billy had brought sacks enough with him to hold thirty bushels of oats. Banks gave orders that they were all to be filled.

" Business is business," he said, forestalling Billy's protest. " But what's a few bushel of oats among friends ? You come an' see me again next time you're around this way."

On his return journey Billy stopped for a short chat with Darke, who was building his log house on a new plan, driving stout posts at each corner and laying the logs flat between them.

It was not the traditional method, and Billy, who was as intensely conservative in such matters as pioneers usually are, at once doubted its value.

But Darke was one of those men who will succeed in their own way or not at all. He quietly disregarded Billy's hints and suggestions.

" One of them bullheaded damned Englishmen you can't learn nothin' to," Billy decided mentally, and drove on.

CHAPTER X

PEOPLE began to trickle into the country that summer. A family of Minnesota Swedes took up land on Kent's creek. A young couple from the old settlement, where land was getting scarce, set up housekeeping three miles north-east. Darke was still the outpost of the settlement creeping up from the south-west, but he had two neighbours before the end of the year.

One warm September noon a team of oxen came creeping along the trail toward Billy's place, their driver prodding them with a long goad and shouting in a queer mixture of French and English. Beside him, sitting bolt upright, was a large woman with a heavy face of startling pallour and big, melancholy dark eyes. The man himself was short and very solidly built, with a black spade beard and sparkling grey eyes.

He drew up before the shack and took off his hat with a flourish to Maggie, who had come to the door on hearing the rattle of the wagon.

" *B' jour, M'dame*," he said. " I can 'ave vataire for me, mine vife, an' mine beefs, not ? "

" Good day," replied Maggie staring uncomprehendingly.

" Vataire," repeated the man, throwing back his head and drinking from an imaginary cup.

" Oh, sure, sure," said Maggie, ashamed to have seemed remiss in hospitality, and ran into the house for the water pail and dipper.

The man sprang down from the wagon, relieved her of the bucket with a deep bow, filled the dipper, and handed it up to the woman, who took it with a low murmur and a bow to Maggie and drank.

" The well's down there," said Maggie, pointing. " Soon as you get your bulls unhitched, come on in the house—dinner'll be ready right away."

" *Mille remerciements, m' dame,*" said the Frenchman with a grateful bow, and spoke volubly to the woman on the wagon, who climbed slowly down and followed Maggie into the house.

Billy drove up a few minutes later to find the stranger trying to give an account of himself to the blank-faced and uncomprehending Maggie, while the Frenchwoman sat erect in one corner, her hands folded in her lap, preserving a sphinxlike silence and immobility.

Billy had a few French words and a man's greater natural aptitude for intercourse with people of diverse tongues.

He gathered that the man's name was Pierre Normandin, that he and his wife were lately from France, and that he had taken up a homestead on the advice of another man, and did not even know exactly where it lay. He begged Billy to find it for him.

His volubility, his vivacity, and his merry infectious laughter appealed strongly to Billy's natural melancholy. Maggie laughed till she wept at his curious English, without offending him in the least.

" Me, I do not speak de English good, hahn ? I

am not . . ." He tapped his head. " No. But I learn
me, hahn ? "

Madame said nothing whatever until she rose to go,
and then she bent over little Lucy, who was having
her dinner, too, in her mother's arms. She touched
the little fluffy head with gentle fingers, smiling faintly
and murmuring something in French.

Maggie smiled up at her cordially. " You be sure
an' come an' see me any time you're lonesome," she
said.

" *Merci*," replied the Frenchwoman hesitatingly. " I
—I sall com'."

Billy mounted to the seat beside Pierre, and Madame
took hers behind on the load. Pierre erupted like a
volcano.

" *En avant* ! " he roared, prodding the lazier ox of
the two. " Gett opp ! "

The oxen surged forward and shouldered along,
blowing through their nostrils and rolling their heavy
heads languidly.

" Ah, zese beefs, zese beefs," lamented Pierre. " Zey
arre so slow. Ah, *sacré cochon*, zis is no place to sleep.
Gett opp, I say. *Mille tonnerres*, what a man do wiz
zese damns ? "

" Got no use for bulls myself," said Billy. " Why
don't you get a team of horses ? "

Pierre shrugged his shoulders and spread his hands.
" But 'orses are so expensif. I am not reech, me. I
buy de ox—zey arre good to plough. I plough, I sow,
I get de crop. Good crop, I sell mine beefs, get 'orses,
hahn ? "

Crossing the runway the oxen showed considerable

distrust of the corduroy, stopping, despite Pierre's frantic objurgations, to snuff at the poles before venturing forward.

Farther on it was necessary to turn northward off the trail that led to the Kent place, and the new direction brought them presently to a steep descent. Here, through Pierre's ignorance of the correct way of harnessing oxen, the neckyoke came off the end of the wagon pole, which promptly buried itself deep in the ground.

The wagon stopped with so sudden a jerk that Pierre and Billy were flung forward upon the backs of the oxen, while the unfortunate Madame Normandin described an ungraceful parabola and came down heavily in a sitting posture, her too solid legs conspicuously displayed.

The oxen, fortunately, behaved like oxen and stood still.

Pierre rushed to his wife's side, clasped her in his arms, and burst into a torrent of expressions of affection and alarm delivered in rolling French. He cursed himself for having brought harm upon his angelic Felice.

She calmed him with a few words, and, smiling bravely, let him assist her to her feet. Between them they hoisted her back upon the wagon, chocked the wheels, dug out the pole, and readjusted the neckyoke straps.

They then got safely down the slope, and Billy pointed out a better road to follow in future. They passed through a narrow belt of poplar, where Billy had to cut a road with his axe, crossed an open ridge, and halted on the edge of a spruce muskeg. In such a spot you may always be sure of finding good water and plenty of wood, a settler's two prime requisites.

"This here's on your place," said Billy. "I don't

just know how the lines run, but I think you got a good quarter all right. You can camp here, anyways, until you figure out where you're goin' to build."

Madame was assisted down from the wagon. She limped upon being set on her feet, but protested earnestly that she was only a little shaken. She commenced to unload the wagon while Pierre and Billy pitched the tent.

Overwhelmed with thanks by Pierre, who waved his hat and shouted after him until he was out of sight, Billy decided to drop in and tell Mrs. Kent about her new neighbour.

"Oh, poor woman," said Mrs. Kent, sympathy and curiosity in equal measure aroused at once. "I hope she isn't badly hurt. I'll go over and see her at once. French, you say?"

"Uh-huh, don't believe she speaks a word of English; an' you can't hardly understand the half of what he says, neither. Funny pair."

"I'll go at once. I used to be rather a dab at French. Harry, tell your father when he comes in I've gone over to see some new neighbours. Put the kettle on at five if I'm not home, and don't let Ted get at the sugar. Don't play with matches. I'll be back as soon as I can, but don't wait tea for me if I'm not here. Where's my old Zulu hat? Ah, here it is. All right, Mr. Clovelly, come along and show me where they are."

The oats had done well on the new land and now stood four feet high, their heavy silver heads rustling musically in the wind. Kent went to town and returned with a binder. They had fine weather for the harvesting, and the sheaves were soon neatly stacked, awaiting the threshing outfit, which would arrive when it should please fate and the owner to be propitious. Meanwhile the horses were fed oat sheaves.

Pierre Normandin came and lent a hand at harvesting in return for assistance in getting out logs and building a shack. He was inexperienced, but quick to learn, and a perfect volcano of energy, singing all day at his work.

Kent understood him quite well and spoke a halting French himself, but this Pierre would not permit, saying that he had to learn English and the sooner he did the better.

He was a never-ending joy to Maggie, who never understood a word he said, but laughed unweariedly at and with him. Billy found his keen pleasure in living a tonic for his own gloomy moods.

Mrs. Kent penetrated further into the heart of the enigmatic Madame Normandin than anyone. Maggie was half afraid of her dark and tragic eyes and melancholy smile ; Billy and Kent were polite but distant, realizing early that Pierre was fiercely jealous. In all the years she dwelt in the settlement Madame made no real friends save Mrs. Kent, nor ever learned to speak more than a few words of English.

Aided by an unusually open fall, they ploughed their land ready for seeding in the spring, and Pierre wrestled mightily with his oxen at breaking. Madame assisted him. They toiled from dawn to dark. The big French-woman, with her skirts kilted above her knees and her big brown arms bare to the shoulder, drove the oxen or tugged and hacked at tough willow roots.

And yet she found time to keep her tiny shack scoured

to the bone. The place was almost miraculously clean, but appallingly stuffy, for they had all the superstitious horror of their race of fresh air.

She was, too, a devout Catholic, and spent time daily in prayer, beads in hand, before a small crucifix. She appeared never to sleep at all.

Pierre was an avowed atheist, but that seemed not to affect in the least the affection between them.

" For why should I pray ? " asked Pierre. " *Ma femme*, she pray for two."

Kent had been talking of getting out more logs for building purposes, putting up a couple of big barns, and buying a band of cattle and some land.

Billy and Maggie talked it over one evening, while Kent was making a trip to the post office, where mail had been accumulating for three weeks.

" Well, we struck it pretty lucky," said Billy. " I figure to get some logs out for a big barn. We'd ought to buy a few head of young cattle in the spring. Get a herd started an' they'll keep us. To hell with ploughin' ."

" Best get out logs for a new house too," said Maggie.

" What the deuce do you want of a house ? Ain't this good enough ? "

" Well, I'd like it a little bigger, so we could have two rooms into it. The bunk don't look so good, an' I'd like some different roof than sods."

" Huh, you got big notions, ain't you ? Well, I don't know ; maybe we could do with a better house."

His imagination gradually took fire. " By gosh, why not, eh ? " Rapidly he began to sketch out plans, grandiose and far-reaching.

Maggie listened, smiling. She had obtained her point :

he was committed to a new house. Even if the rest of the rosy plan fell through, as inevitably most of it must, she would hold him grimly to his promise. She counted herself one up in the game of wits.

She held up a hand presently for silence. " That'll be Kent ; I know his wagon. Wonder if he got them buttons for me at the store."

The rattle approached and stopped without.

Maggie flung open the door and cried, " Come on in, stranger, an' thaw out before you get home."

Kent entered, looking more than usually serious. He had not even a smile for little Lucy. He had a letter for Maggie from her parents in Manitoba, and had discharged her commission at the store, and brought Billy three plugs of tobacco.

" What's the trouble, old-timer ? " asked Billy, catching sight of his face. " Bad news ? "

" Yes," said Kent, tugging at his moustache. " Yes, the pater—my father—is dead. Died very suddenly a month ago."

" Tck-tck, too bad, too bad," murmured Billy sympathetically.

" It is—in more ways than one," agreed Kent quietly. " I must get home and tell my wife. Good night."

The Clovellys thought little more of it, but Kent was very silent and abstracted for some time, and spoke no more of projected improvements on his farm.

CHAPTER XI

In the second week of November, after the first light snowfall, the threshing outfit arrived. It was an ancient and rickety hand-fed outfit, for which the motive power was supplied by a team of spindle-shanked mules on a treadmill. The whole was the property of a lean and grey-headed American negro of the name of Washington Blue.

There is no prejudice against negroes in the Canadian Northwest except among a few of the American settlers, and Blue was received everywhere on an equal footing.

Nor was there any reason why this should not be so, for he was better educated than the majority of the settlers, and possessor of a stately courtesy that would have graced a duke. Mrs. Kent, who had more than a touch of the grand manner herself, found him quite charming.

His crew consisted of a young Hollander and the mules aforesaid. Mules were a novelty in the country then, and the team aroused much interest.

" Mewls an' coons always does go together," explained Blue with a deep chuckle. " An' I got a real houn' dog to home—yes, ma'am."

The Hollander looked after the mules, Blue cut bands and fed the machine, Kent pitched the sheaves, Pierre forked the straw away at the other end, and Billy hauled grain.

When the aged separator had ceased its frenzied rattling and the cloud of dust had settled, Billy found himself with nearly six hundred bushels of sound plump oats, and Kent with eleven hundred bushels.

Blue took a courteous and cordial farewell of Mrs. Kent, hitched up his mules, and creaked south to thresh for Squatter Banks.

The potatoes were all dug and stored, they had plenty of hay, and a year's supply of oats for the horses, with some over.

Fresh meat was the only thing required, and so Lightfoot's hour struck. The Kents were weary of the iniquities of the mustard-coloured cow. In addition to being a kicker and hooky, she was breachy and no fence was proof against her. She battened on crops and gardens all summer long, and autumn found her fat enough to invite her fate. Her hide made an excellent lap robe.

Brown Daisy Clovelly was rapidly going dry, and milk was required for little Lucy. Billy traded oats with the Minnesota Swede on Kent's creek for a cow due to freshen in December.

There was now nothing wanting at the Clovellys but money for groceries. Billy had created such havoc among the near-by muskrats during the preceding winter that the sloughs were half empty, and a couple of Indian families had pitched their tepees by the big swamp and were already busy trapping.

"Don't know what's come over Tom," said Billy in a worried voice. "Ain't said a word yet about gettin'

out logs. If he don't have any work for me—gosh,
I don't know but what I'll have to hit for the woods this
winter."

" Maybe if I'd ask Mrs. Kent ? " suggested Maggie.

Billy shook his head. " You leave 'em be. Likely
they know their own business best. I got a notion maybe
things ain't goin' so well with them neither. But I'd
like to know what the hell we're goin' to do."

A trip to the post office provided him with a
solution.

Many of the less prosperous settlers were in the
habit regularly every winter of hauling freight for the
Hudson's Bay Company from Riverton to its northern
posts.

The work involved privation, hardship, and peril,
but the returns were relatively high, and the time between
trips could be spent at home.

Maggie was not enthusiastic, but agreed that it would
be better than a whole winter spent in the bush away
from her.

" Well, Tom, guess I'll have to hit the freight trail
this winter," said Billy as if casually. " Got no money
for groceries."

" The freight trail—what's that ? " inquired Kent.

Billy explained.

" Jove, you don't say. Tell you what, Clovelly,
I believe I'll come too."

" Hell, Tom, you don't need to go freightin'. I tell
you it won't be no snap layin' out in the snow with it
forty below. They tell me there ain't no stoppin' places
only halfway. I'm only goin' because I'm broke an' need
the money."

Kent smiled. "Exactly my own case, old man," he said blandly.

"The devil, Tom, you don't mean it!"

"I do. When the poor old pater died the money stopped. To put it plainly, Clovelly, I'm—ah—stony broke, and we've been wondering a lot how we were going to keep alive. So, unless you have any rooted objection, I'll come along too."

"Well, that's fine, Tom. It would be kind of tough tacklin' her alone first trip."

Kent appeared to be seized suddenly with a desire to unburden his soul.

"You know, Clovelly, it's only lately I've begun to realize that homesteading in this country isn't all skittles. You can rub along while you have a little money, but there's the devil to pay when the money's all gone."

Billy grinned and repeated the grim old Western joke.

"That's it—the Government bets you ten bucks against a hundred an' sixty acres you can't live on the damn place three years without starvin' to death."

"Neat," commented Kent appreciatively; "and not so bally far from the brutal truth."

"You take them yaps at Ottawa," proceeded Billy. "Do they care what happens to a homesteader? He can die an' stink for all them. They got to square a bunch of Bluenoses and Quebec Peasoups and Ontario yahoos. But the West—be damned to the West. No sir, a homesteader can't look for no help from man, an' God ain't got this far yet. But I tell you the Devil's mighty busy. I'm a Westerner an' I got no use for nothin' an' nobody what comes from the East, nor I don't know a Westerner what has."

There was a lot of work to be done before they could take the freight trail. Stove wood had to be cut and piled for the women, hay hauled and stacked beside the barns, and freight racks built.

There were no presents exchanged that Christmas, for there was no money to buy them. The shadow of approaching separation, danger, and unknown hardship hung over both families, and the first heavy snowstorm of the winter was raging without.

The two men pulled out for Riverton two days after Christmas and had to break trail all the way to the settlement after the storm.

"Want loads, eh?" said the Hudson's Bay Company's factor. "Well, I can't give you any for Beaver Island, but if you like to go on to Moose Lake there'll be two dollars a hundred more in it for you."

"We'll take it," said Billy recklessly.

The factor's eye brightened. It was hard to get men willing to freight to Moose Lake. It had already gained the name of Dead Horse trail.

Kent decided to take three thousand pounds of freight, and Billy, with his smaller team, loaded twenty-five hundred. They might reckon on close to another thousand pounds of food for men and horses, blankets, etc.

On their way home they halted at Bustard's stopping place, and encountered a gang of freighters from the old settlement, going into Riverton for fresh loads.

"Goin' to Beaver Island?" inquired one.

" No, Moose Lake," answered Billy.

The man stared, and gave a loud whoop. " Did you hear that, boys ? These fellers is hittin' the Dead Horse trail. Goin' to Moose Lake."

" Sufferin' Peter ! Where's your fur nosebags ? " queried a short man with a cocked eyebrow and a beard full of scraps of chewing tobacco. " It took old John Crawford nineteen days to make the last trip up there. They tell me he went up with two teams an' come down with one horse an' two sleighs, an' him pullin' alongside the horse, an' havin' to prop him up nights with a stick of wood to keep him from fallin' down."

A callow youth took up the tale in a twanging drawl. " Yes, the horse was that gaunt old John slid him through a crack in the ice on Swan Lake an' never seen him again. There's been seventeen or eighteen horses died on that trail since John opened her up the season before last. An' you green. You pull back to Riverton an' tell Mc-Crumbie you won't take your loads no further'n Beaver Island. He was just puttin' one over on you—he does that with green men every time."

" Well, we hired for tough guts an' we. got to fill the bill," said Billy with a laugh. " Beaver Island is too easy for us."

" Well, we'll say good-bye to you now," said the man who had first spoken. " It ain't likely we'll ever see you again."

" They seem to think we've rather put our foot in it," said Kent in a low voice.

" Tall talk," said Billy out of the corner of his mouth. " Tryin' to scare us off so they can get more freight for themselves. Leave me talk to 'em."

" You won't say anything to Mrs. Clovelly ? " said
Kent anxiously. " My wife will be anxious, you know,
while I'm away."

" Huh, it's likely I'd give Maggie a show to make
any more racket than she's makin' now."

" Mum 's the word, then."

They rested the horses at home for twenty-four hours,
and pulled out two hours before dawn, under a clear
sky, the wind light and the temperature at ten below.

Everything had been done for the women that could
be done, and Pierre Normandin had promised to look in
at both houses frequently.

The heavy loads pulled hard through the gritty snow
at first, but when the temperature rose with the rising
sun the going was easier, and in a few miles they struck
a broken trail heading in a general northerly direction,
and followed it.

The depression of parting soon wore off and their
spirits rose. The sense of freedom and relief a man
naturally feels at escaping from his wife for a season,
with the prospect of new things to see and adventures
to encounter, soon put them in a more cheerful mood
than either had known for weeks.

The country they passed through was very sparsely
settled and similar to their own. Twilight brought
them, on the trail they were following, to a lonely farm
perched on a low ridge.

As they drove into the yard a swarm of yelping
mongrels of all sizes swarmed about them from all points
of the compass.

" What the hell's this ? " said Billy. " A dog ranch ?
Must be Indians. We'll go up an' see."

With the dogs following them in a baying half-moon, they went up and knocked at the door. A very dirty small boy flung it open and stood aside with staring eyes to let them pass in.

Within, the place was a long, low room with a dirt floor, upon which sprawled and fought a number of half-naked children.

The atmosphere was stifling, for at one end stood a big sheet-iron heater, the pipe red-hot halfway to the roof, and at the other a slatternly half-grown girl fried pork and onions on a cookstove, also red-hot. The pungent smoke of burning grease filled the dwelling and furnished the prevailing perfume, but that was reinforced by many more smells, all of more power than fragrance. A stable lantern hanging from the roof shed over all its doubtful light.

The lady of the house, a large and bulbous female, with a peculiarly filthy baby hanging negligently over one arm, wandered casually about. Occasionally she trod with her naked feet upon one of the " ash cats " on the floor, who promptly set up a hair-raising howl.

" Can we put up here for the night ? " asked Billy of the woman, before the horrified Kent had time to pull him by the sleeve.

The lady spat thoughtfully in the dirt and rubbed it in with a broad bare toe.

" Suah," she replied in a soft drawl, " suah youel can stay yah. Ef youel waitahminit, Vinahel fix youel some grub." Her words slid one into another in an indescribably liquid murmur.

" No, no, no," said Billy hastily. " Thank you very much, but we got our own grub with us."

" Jussas youah please," returned the woman placidly. " We aintuh got mauch, but youel is welcome to it."

They thanked her warmly, but steadfastly declined
food, sitting down in a corner to eat what they had brought
with them after the horses had been put up. They
could not, however, avoid some coffee, served in tin
cups of more than doubtful cleanliness and having a
peculiar flavour of its own, due, as Billy surmised, to
its being made of burnt wheat.

All the time they were eating, the ash cats stood round
in an unwashed half-circle and stared with unwinking
eyes.

The opening of the door admitted a tall and lath-like
man, with hollow, melancholy eyes, and a scrubby beard
thick with tobacco-stained icicles.

He gave them a long-drawn and mournful " Good
evenahin', genelmen," and was greeted himself by the
assembled ash cats with shrill cries of " Pappy, yere's
pappy ! "

The whole family now sat down to eat, the junior
members wrangling over their food on the floor like so
many puppies. Between huge mouthfuls of pork and
onions and gurgling gulps of burnt-wheat coffee, the
man talked to his guests in the same soft drawl as his
wife.

He had a gentle courtesy of manner and speech most
oddly in contrast with his filthy appearance and surroundings. He asked no impertinent questions, and
volunteered no information except when questioned
himself. They were his guests, he seemed to say, and
his part was to make them as comfortable as his own
poor means would allow.

They learned from him that the Beaver Island trail
ran a mile north of his farm, and that they had come
somewhat out of their way. As to conditions on the
trail he could tell them nothing, never having made a
trip himself. He understood, he said, that it was a
hard trail. He accepted a pipeful of Kent's tobacco
with grave courtesy.

" I'm reahul sohy we cain't offah youel a baid, but
weah kinuh craouwded yah aouhselves," he apologized,
the younger members of the family giving strong indi-
cations that it was their time for retiring.

They hastened to assure him that they would be
perfectly comfortable in the stable with the horses
and he sighed softly and thanked them. They escaped
joyfully into the, by contrast, clean and luxurious
barn.

That was foul enough, with sundry hens roosting
on the rafters and the floor deep in half-frozen manure.
But pure, if cold, air did find its way in considerable
quantity through holes in the log walls, and a few arm-
fuls of straw made a clean soft bed.

" Jove," said Kent, drawing a deep breath, " I never
saw such a bally hurrah's nest in my life. What sort
of people are these, Clovelly ? "

" Damned if I know, Tom. Never heard nobody
talk just the way they do. It was pretty rich in there,
but they're a kind-hearted outfit—you got to give 'em
credit for that."

" I'll give 'em credit for anything on earth but cleanliness. But, for God's sake, Clovelly, let's get out of here
in the morning before they're up. I couldn't stand
another meal in that place."

"Well, I guess they won't mind," said Billy.

They rose, therefore, long before dawn, and travelled as far as the Beaver Island trail before they halted for breakfast.

CHAPTER XII

THEY followed a well-beaten trail all that day through an almost unsettled country of wide willow flats, and crossed numerous reedy sloughs. The weather was misty and the temperature relatively high, so that the horses were able to make good time.

In the afternoon they began to pass through the Jumping Horse Indian Reserve, here and there a tiny fenced field, a low log shack, or a little group of smoky tepees.

About three hours after dark, a little after six o'clock, they reached a two-story house of hewn logs standing in the midst of a cluster of low buildings by the road.

" This here must be Willy Croker's place," said Billy. " If it is, it'll be the last time under cover for us until we get to Swan Lake, from what they tell me."

Indian dogs yelped and howled at them until a man came out of the house and threw sticks of stove wood at them. To the query as to whether they could stop there for the night, the man replied with a grunt, which Billy, from some acquaintance with Indians, rightly interpreted as an affirmative. They put their horses in a substantial barn, therefore, and carried their bedding and grub boxes up to the house.

Though a peculiar odour greeted their nostrils on their entry—that dry, sour smell found wherever Indians

inhabit—the place was clean. The rough boarding of
the floor had been scrubbed white and the walls were
whitewashed to the ceiling.

The furniture consisted of some benches drawn
against the walls, and the sole illumination was furnished
by a little oil lamp on a small table. Warmth was provided by a huge box stove, snoring softly at the far
end of the room. The heat was oppressive.

Willy Croker was a half-breed, married to a full-
blooded Cree, which estimable lady, with two or three
female relatives, squatted on the floor on the other side
of the stove, the benches being solely for the convenience
of white travellers.

Willy, a man of substance and some education, as
well as sub-chief of the tribe, was not at home, and so
nobody greeted the new arrivals, for the ladies on the
floor took no notice of them.

Kent was a little at a loss, but the experienced Billy
marched up to the stove without ceremony, set down
his grub-box, and proceeded to boil water for tea and
to fry beefsteak.

Supper was eaten in profound silence. The Indian
ladies conversed among themselves in a series of liquid
clucks and gurgles, with occasional outbursts of shrill
laughter; an Indian boy drifted in from without, grunted
at them, and passed into some room beyond; the stove
purred.

" Feels like a church," murmured Kent.

They had eaten and were filling their pipes when the
dogs once more lifted their chorus outside. Sleigh-
bells chimed and stopped. Then came the sharp cracking of a whip, yelps, and a loud, harsh voice using

blistering language. A few minutes later the door was flung open and a man came charging into the room.

He gave them a gruff " Good night," dropped his grub box on the floor with a crash, and jerked a bench over to the stove. All his movements were swift and violent, and he seemed to be in a furious rage.

He was broad-shouldered and heavily bearded, of medium height, and clothed in a tattered moosehide shirt, denim overalls, much patched, and Indian-made buckskin moccasins. On his head was a small, greasy cap of black velvet, which he never removed—as they later discovered—even in bed.

His table manners were of a piece with the rest of his behaviour. He wolfed huge chunks of half-cooked pork and sucked noisily at a mugful of scalding tea. Then he filled his pipe with coarse and noiseome leaf tobacco and filled the room with acrid smoke.

" I'm John Crawford," he announced suddenly in a rasping voice. " Heard of me ? "

" Yes, sir," answered Billy, " we did."

" Yes, sir, I bet you did. Everybody on this trail knows John Crawford." He flung some words in Cree to the women on the floor, and they answered him with a shrill cackle. " They know me—you're damn right they know me. Where you headed for ? "

" Moose Lake."

" The hell you say ! Dead horse trail. First trip, ain't it ? "

" Yes, sir."

" Well, you're like a young bear—all your troubles is ahead of you. I made that trail ; I was the first man took horses right through to Moose Lake post—it was all dog trains before. It's a devil of a trail. I lost three horses out of four one trip. Damn lucky I didn't lose 'em all an' get froze to death myself. Last spring, that was—near ruint me. Well, I'll take you along with me, an' maybe you'll get back alive."

"We'll be glad of your company," said Billy politely.

"You'd need to be," said Crawford without mock modesty. "McCrumbie didn't ought to send green men on that trail, but what the hell does he care. Them what's been over the trail once generally has enough to do them, an' they won't go no further than Beaver Island."

"But you've made several trips, haven't you?" said Kent.

"Me? Sure. But I got to. It's a hell of a life: live out in the woods like a wolf, lay down in the snow with the sky for a roof an' all outdoors for a shanty. But what's man to do? I got a wife an' 'leven kids. Yes, sir, 'leven kids, six of 'em twins. That's a hell of a trick to play on a man—twins. Eat! That gang'd eat a cow while you was wipin' your nose. An' so here I am, out on the freight trail, livin' like a damn coyote an' sweatin' my soul out to keep 'em in groceries."

He said much more to the same effect, all delivered in a growling, surly tone, with short outbursts of bellowing, not pausing for an instant to listen to what anyone else might have to say.

He wound up with an abrupt, "Well, we got to be out bright an' early if we want to get to Moose Lake this winter. I'm hittin' the hay."

He rolled himself quickly in a rusty cowhide on the bare boards and seemed to fall asleep in a moment.

The squaws had long ago silently withdrawn and there

was no sound in the house. Billy filled the box stove with wood and choked the draught, and Kent made their bed by the wall.

Crawford's roaring waked them, and they pulled out as usual long before dawn, in weather like that of the preceding days.

Crawford's team were a ragged-hipped grey mare and a hammer-headed sullen black gelding, both lean and rough-coated. They walked with long slow paces, their feet almost dragging in the snow, but maintained a steady four miles an hour.

Their master jogged along behind, walking with a hitch of the shoulders and a swing of the head. His moosehide shirt seemed to be equally his wear for any temperature, as were the paper-thin buckskin moccasins on his feet. On his hands he wore unlined leather gloves.

Kent and Billy were clothed in heavy sheepskin coats, fur caps, and thick woollen trousers. They wore three pairs of socks each, and high moosehide moccasins with ankle rubbers over them. On their hands were woollen mittens and pullovers of mulehide. They found, before their return, that they were rather under- than over-clothed.

Crawford was evidently in a better temper in the morning, and with every northward mile he became more genial. By noon he was almost cordial, and when they camped for their first night in the open he surprised them by smiling.

"Looks like it's goin' to be a good trip," he said. "You couldn't beat this weather. I bet it ain't even zero."

They soon left the last of the open country behind them, and for two days pulled on through heavy spruce and jack-pine forests, or across small lakes, in fair weather and a moderate temperature.

Crawford became progressively more cheerful and companionable, willing to give others at least some share in the conversation, though generally utilizing any remark as a peg to hang his own philosophy of life upon.

" Say, why is it grub tastes so much better on the trail than it does to home ? " asked Billy idly over the fire.

" Huh, that's easy," said Crawford quickly. " Who does most of the cookin' ? Women, ain't it ? You can't learn a woman to cook—you can't do it. They got leather mouths : can't tell hog swill from chicken fixings by the taste. Well, can you learn a deef man how to fiddle ? See, understand what I mean ? "

" Oh, I don't know," said Billy doubtfully, with a glance at Kent.

Kent nodded at Crawford. " It's true enough," he said.

" Sure it's true. Nobody never learnt a woman to cook anything fit for a dog to eat. Generally they won't even try : they're satisfied. They don't know what a man's talkin' about. Tastes all right to them. Givin' good grub to a woman is just spoilin' it."

" You don't seem to have much use for women," commented Billy.

" Why, sure I have," said Crawford in surprise. " What makes you think that ? They're more nuisance than they're worth, maybe, but a man ain't happy without a woman around. He's all at a loose end. I never did

get this woman business right in my mind, nor I never
met a feller what did, neither."

He brooded on the matter for some moments and made
an impatient gesture. "Aw, forget about 'em," he said
irritably. " Can't a man never have no fun ? We don't
have to bother what hellery they'll be into next till we
get back home."

They came at sunset to the shores of Swan Lake, where
stood a small building of rotting logs. This was a
habitation built by man, and its tendency was to make
Crawford morose and gloomy and inclined to dwell on
the hardships he was forced to endure to feed his
family.

The others were glad enough to get under shelter again,
slight though it was. When they got themselves and
their horses packed inside, and the rusty old stove glowing redly at one end, the place felt like a second home,
even though the wind whistled through the gaping walls
and they could see a patch of starlit sky through a hole
in the roof.

But the halt was brief. The weather was a matter of
more than usual concern, for Swan Lake is fifty miles
wide and the freight trail runs right across it. Only
those who have tried to cross it in the face of a high
wind are entitled to speak with authority of human
misery.

Crawford was uneasy about the wind, which was
driving before it broken masses of cloud from the north-
east, and ordered a start at three in the morning.

" It ain't very likely to blow up a blizzard at this
time of year," he said. " Won't anyway unless it gets
warmer. But I'd just as lief be on my way. I wouldn't

want to be snow-bound for maybe three days in this damn shack."

Only two narrow parallel ridges marked the trail they had to follow. But Crawford's experienced team kept unerringly to these, and behind them came Kent's team and Billy's, in the order named. The men dropped to the rear and walked along in amicable converse.

The lake seemed level enough at first sight, but it was actually seamed with pressure ridges several feet high in places, formed during the original freeze-up. There was also some danger of encountering open leads, cracks several feet in width and miles long. But Crawford's horses could safely be trusted to halt at the first sign of water in the snow.

Crawford became positively genial. Now and again he laughed heartily at some whimsical remark of Kent's, one of those observations which always left Billy wondering uneasily whether the solemn-faced Englishman were really witty or merely foolish.

The weather grew thicker, and the sun rose with a wide pale halo about it. The temperature rose with alarming rapidity, and a uniform grey haze crept down until it blotted out the sun.

"Looks like one of them cursed March blizzards comin' up two months ahead of time," fretted Crawford as they halted at noon. "Just give the horses a feed of oats and hustle on. No time to light a fire."

Kent and Billy nibbled at frozen bannock during the short halt, but Crawford cut a hunk of raw fat pork from the carcass of a pig on his rack and chewed it with relish.

"Pork's the stuff for the freight trail," he said.

"Nothin' like it to keep the cold out. To the devil with beef an' bannock—they sit cold on a man's stummick. Have some."

They declined with thanks.

"You'll come to it yet," he assured them.

They were soon on their way again. The wind was strengthening and big flakes of damp snow came drifting down. Fortunately, the high temperature made the snow slippery, and the horses were able to draw their loads at a good pace.

"I want to raise that there north shore," explained Crawford. "Then if we do get snowed under an' have to camp, we'll have something to steer by when she clears."

At present nothing was to be seen but the pale level expanse stretching to the horizon on every side, and a uniform dirty grey vault of cloud overhead.

Thicker and ever thicker fell the snow and higher and ever higher rose the wind. They moved in a grey twilight that rapidly deepened to dusk and then to a blurred darkness, full of whirling particles of fine snow that bewildered straining eyes and made them feel dizzy.

Crawford took his place on the roller behind the horses, keeping the wind on his right cheek, and urging the tired and unwilling beasts on. The others climbed upon their own sleighs, each man keeping the noses of his own team glued to the rear of the rack in front.

CHAPTER XIII

CRAWFORD'S team halted. The others necessarily did the same. He came groping back to Kent.

"No use!" he shouted hoarsely. "We run into one of them ridges. Best camp—like go through the ice anyway if we kep' on."

They drew the sleighs up to form a windbreak, unharnessed the horses, brushed them off and blanketed them, and tied them in the lee of the loads. They lit a small fire and boiled tea, but the temperature was so high that the faggots soon sank into a pool of water of their own making and went out.

Crawford took a blanket and draped it over his head and shoulders, the others following his example.

"Fine night," he chuckled as they huddled in the lee of Billy's load. "Who the hell wouldn't go freightin'?"

The snow fell unceasingly, or, lifted by sudden violent gusts, drove in grey-black walls across the lake.

"Well, let's have a little singin' to keep our tails up," said Crawford, and lifted his voice in a high falsetto wail with peculiar quavers in it.

He sang old shanty-boy ballads of the Maine woods, where he had been born. Billy listened with approval, having heard many of the songs before, and Kent with curiosity and amusement.

Later they dozed uneasily for short periods, having to rise frequently to shake the accumulated snow from their blankets and stamp their numb feet.

Inky darkness turned to a grey that was neither day nor night. The wind howled like a mad beast. The temperature had fallen, and the dry snow hissed like a myriad snakes as it drove before the blast.

"Gettin' colder," said Crawford. "Likely let up after a while. Let's have breakfast."

They made another fire, which burnt without quenching itself. But the fuel they had brought with them from shore soon gave out. It was useless to think of pulling on until the sky cleared, for they had no compass and nothing to steer by. But they employed part of their time by cutting a gap in the pressure ridge.

It was late in the day before the sky cleared and they caught fleeting glimpses of the setting sun. One last mad whirling flurry in which they were almost smothered in snow finer than sand, which filled their eyes and nostrils and forced its way up their sleeves and down their necks, and the sky was swept bare of cloud.

Mighty Orion, Sirius and Procyon at his heels, took up his unending chase of the flying Bull across the southern horizon, watched by Auriga and hunted in his turn by the Lion.

"Now we'll know where we're goin'," said Crawford, wagging his head at the stars. "Them's been good friends to me many a time. There's the old Dipper. We're away."

Axe in hand, he led the way, his team following like dogs. He trod heavily, tapping the ice now and again with his axe, and gave a sudden shout of "Whoa!"

" Bad ice ! " he cried. " Watch out ! "

A thin skin of ice had formed on the surface of an open lead, and the new snow had obliterated all trace of the death trap.

" That's what we'd have run into if we'd kep' goin' last night," said Crawford. " Now, how far does this damn thing run ? You try up the other way, Billy. Holler to Tom if you find her pinch in, an' he'll give me a hoot."

The pair followed the lead in opposite directions, breaking the ice at short intervals, until Crawford stopped and cupped his hands.

" A-a-all right," he bawled. " We can get over here."

The crack had narrowed to a little over a foot in width. Crawford cut away the surface skin, so that the horses could see how far to step. His own team hopped across, but Kent's greys snorted and drew back at the sight of the black water.

" Blindfold 'em," advised Crawford. " Now, lead 'em easy. Hup, there." He struck them on the rump with his hand. The jump they gave took them across safely.

Billy's horses took the crack in a wild bound.

They hacked gaps in several pressure ridges and passed through, negotiated another hidden lead, and at last lifted the high ridge of the northern shore, lying like a dark belt of cloud on the horizon.

" Now we do have to go catty," said Crawford. " There's springs comes out under the ice along here. Never know when you're goin' through."

He moved on, sounding the ice incessantly, until the shore loomed only a rifle shot distant.

Then he gave a yell and came racing back, a big discoloured patch rapidly widening on the snow behind him.

"Near as hell stepped into it that time," he panted. "All the ice is rotten around here. You fellers keep spaced out, for the love of Mike. No sense in drownin' the whole works. We'll try along the shore till we get some place where this blank-blank ice will hold us. Think we're too far east, anyway—the hills is lower where the trail goes through."

"Ha there, you grey rat!" he shouted to his team. "Get up in the collar, Baldy, you dirty-faced son of a swill-barrel."

They tried along the shore for miles before they found a safe landfall. It grew very cold, and the coats of the horses, covered with rime, turned them all the same colour. Long icicles formed on the moustaches of the men.

"Well, we did find the trail finally," said Crawford, pointing to some little round lumps lying like beads on a string between one wind ridge and the next.

These little bits of frozen crust rounded by the wind indicated to the experienced horses a road as plainly as a line fence would have done. There was no more need to lead the way, and soon they had plunged through a deep shore drift and climbed to a heavily wooded flat, where the trail showed as a narrow and tortuous lane among the trees.

They pulled into Beaver Island post on the following day, rested for twenty-four hours, and began the final stage of the journey.

"No more good roads now," said Crawford with a grim smile. "They tell me there's been only a couple of pony teams an' a few dog trains over it this season, an' none since the blizzard. We'll have her all to ourselves. Ain't that nice?"

The weather was what the Northwest calls chilly, the temperature moving between a few degrees above zero and twenty or thirty degrees below. Billy and Kent still found their clothing adequate ; and as for John Crawford, cold seemed to have no effect upon him at all. The only concession he made to it was to draw a blanket about his shoulders when they camped.

The trail was very rough and very crooked, and each team took its turn in the lead. The road followed in general the channel of the Moose River, crossing and recrossing it frequently, for the stream encountered so many rapids that the ice upon it was never safe.

"Well, we ain't had much to kick about so far," said Crawford one evening. "We ought to strike the post in three more days if the luck holds."

"You say this is an easy trip?" said Kent incredulously.

"Best I ever made except for that little hold-up on the lake," was the answer. "We ain't bust a rack yet, nor killed a horse, nor gone through the ice. Dandy weather near all the way. What the hell more do you want?"

The time had come to keep to the bed of the Moose, for the hills on either hand had become rocky and broken. Crawford warned his companions to keep their teams well spaced out.

He took the lead himself. The morning was still young when the ice gave way without warning. The sleighs sank to the bunks only, but the horses were in deeper water and unable to keep their footing. Ahead of them the whole ice bridge collapsed, revealing a wide stretch of ridged and racing water.

Crawford stooped and jerked out the drawbolt, freeing the team. Had he not done so the sleighs must have been dragged into deep water and the precious freight, consisting mostly of flour, ruined beyond salvage.

The horses were borne rapidly downstream, to bring up at the edge of the firm ice below. But they were in too deep water to climb out unaided. Crawford plunged through the snow along the shore and reached them just in time. He flung himself on his stomach and caught them by the bridles as they were about to be sucked under.

"Easy, May," he coughed. "Ho, Baldy, nothin' to be scared of, you old fool. Damn, ain't them other bloody fools never comin'?"

But Billy had jerked out his own drawbolt and was lashing his team along the bank as fast as the drifts would let them move. Kent came plunging in his wake.

"Give me a hand," gasped Crawford, "or I'm gone too."

Kent got a grip on the grey mare's head and hung on, while Crawford devoted his efforts to keeping Baldy afloat.

"Hold on, I'm comin'," shouted Billy encouragingly, rapidly removing the stout halter shanks from his own team and Kent's.

With these he made two lines, attaching one end of each to his doubletrees and finishing the other with a running noose. He brought his team as close as he dared, and the nooses were with some difficulty passed over the heads of the drowning horses.

Billy shouted to his team and the nooses drew tight. The half-strangled beasts in the water swelled up like bladders, floating easily on the surface. A hard, steady pull, and they slid up over the edge of the ice, Kent and Crawford pulling on their forelegs.

Freed, they presently struggled to their feet, wheezing loudly but otherwise little the worse. Their harness was taken off and they were rubbed down briskly before their coats became stiff with ice.

Warmly blanketed and tied between two roaring fires, they soon ceased to shiver violently.

" Better get your load out before she freezes in," said Billy. " I'll leave you two tend the horses."

He climbed upon the back of the rack and worked forward to where the pole lay under water, pointing downstream. Standing on the end of the rack, slippery with new ice, he bent to get a loop of rope under the roller.

Crawford heard his startled cry, followed by a heavy plunge, and jumped up to see him come to the surface, beating the water wildly with his hands.

Crawford wheeled and dashed for the lower end of the lead to catch him. But Kent saw he would be too late. Billy sank, and came up, struggling feebly.

Kent flung off coat and cap and dived. He came up beside the drowning man and got a grip on his collar, turning him over on his back. He could do no more, for the icy water was rapidly paralyzing him, but it was sufficient. In another instant Crawford's muscular paw

closed on Billy and dragged him to safety. Kent followed
at once.

And now tough John Crawford was in his glory. He
snatched up eagerly the challenge of the wild. He lifted
the inert Billy in his arms and bore him to the fire.

" Off with them clothes," he ordered Kent, " every
damn stitch. Hustle or they'll freeze on you."

While Kent obeyed with numb and fumbling fingers,
he stripped Billy to the skin and rolled him in blankets.
He flung Kent a blanket and a cowhide and told him to
wrap himself up tightly.

Shouting and singing snatches of scandalous song, but
doing everything swiftly and surely, he put the billy on
to boil, stuck up branches in the snow and hung the
dripping clothes upon them, and then proceeded to rub
the half-conscious Billy with a piece of sacking as rough
as a file.

" This is a tough proposition," he chanted. " But
I'm tough too. The tougher they come the better I
like 'em. I'm that tough, when you scratch me the
sparks fly. I'm that tough they use my hide for sand-
paper. I'm that tough the Devil dassent look at me
cross-eyed. Smile, damn you."

Billy stirred uneasily and opened languid eyes under
the merciless scrubbing.

" Let up on that gunny bag," murmured Billy. " You
have the hide all chafed off of me."

" Fine," exulted Crawford. " Guess you'll do now.
I'll have some hell-fire tea to pour in you in a minute."

He sprang up and began to chop wood like a maniac.
The billy boiled and he flung in a handful of tea, stirring
it with a stick, and took it off.

" Drink her down," he ordered. " Hot ! Course it's hot. Drink her down an' hang your tongues out to cool."

He cut some more wood and piled the fire high.

" Listen : I'm goin' to sing you a song, an' you both chip in on the chorus. Nothin' in the world like singin' to warm a man up an' put heart in him—beats whisky. Come on, this is the way she goes. Let her went."

He threw back his head and roared :—

" Oh, bury me deep in a hole in the ground, a ground hog's hole is best ;
  Oh, bury me deep in a ground hog's hole an' leave me there to rest."

" Get it ? All together, now." He swung into the chorus again. " Hell, that's no good—sounds like a cat yowlin' for milk. Put some guts in her. Come on."

They did better this time.

" That's something like. Now I'll start in at the beginnin', and when I say ' Chorus,' get into it with both feet."

JOHN CRAWFORD'S SONG

Oh, the muskeeters is awful bad, they give me such a pain ;
They fill my hide so full of holes it won't keep out the rain.

Oh, bury me deep in a hole in the ground, a ground hog's hole is best ;
Oh, bury me deep in a ground hog's hole an' leave me there to rest.

The black flies chews my whiskers off : I never need to shave :
Oh, let them have my whiskers, but put me in my grave.

Oh, bury me, etc.

My horse has got blind staggers, my old roan cow is dry,
My hogs has got the cholery, an' my kids has got pinkeye.

Oh, bury me, etc.

I've stood the frost for forty years, but I am gettin' old ;
If hell was only closer I wouldn't feel so cold.

Oh, bury me, etc.

He finished by making them sing the chorus three times over. " Well, don't that warm you up ? " he inquired, very red in the face himself from his efforts.

They acknowledged that it had.

The open lead rapidly skimmed over, and Crawford's sleighs were soon fast in the ice. Kent's clothes were not dry, but Mrs. Kent had thoughtfully provided him with a change of underwear. He felt none the worse for his short immersion. Leaving Billy by the fire, he and Crawford unloaded the rack and drew it out backwards with the team after working it loose with axes and levers.

They made less than ten miles in all that day, for Billy's legs would bend under him and it was too cold to ride for long at a stretch. Crawford's team, too, had been weakened, and the grey mare developed a slight limp.

CHAPTER XIV

THREE days later they crept into Moose Lake post—a store, a few squalid log shacks, and some dirty tepees.

They were a trail-worn outfit. The ribs of Kent's fine greys showed through their staring coats. They hung their heads and dragged their feet, woefully unlike the well-fed, clean-stepping pair who had pulled out from the homestead.

Billy's horses, light-limbed, tough bronchos, were thin but looked stronger. Crawford's May was limping from a cut on the knee, sustained in breaking through the ice; but hammer-headed Baldy was unchanged. Day after day he had slugged along from camp to camp at the same unvarying gait, had methodically cleaned up his oats at every feed, and taken the up and down of the trail with a sort of resigned gloom.

All the men were drawn and hollow-eyed from lack of sleep. All were more or less frostbitten. It is impossible to sleep for long in the open when the temperature is much below zero, and for five days now they had done nothing but pull and camp. Three hours on the trail, two in camp, from dawn till noon, from noon till dark, from dark till midnight, and round again to dawn.

It was dark when they drew up before the store, so they left their loads where they stood, knowing that no one would dream of touching them. In a stumbling, uncertain manner they got their horses into the stable, unharnessed, watered, and fed—for a freighter must look to his horse before he thinks of himself.

They carried their bedding and grub boxes into a dark and filthy little bunkhouse. They lit one of their lanterns and the stove, and brought in some hay and laid it on the floor for a mattress. They put on the billy and the frying pan, and lay down to rest until the meal should be ready.

Kent awoke and found himself chilled to the marrow. The lantern had burnt down and was beginning to smoke, the stove was cold and empty, the billy dry, and the frying pan contained some small pieces of charcoal.

Moving like a man in a dream, he relit the stove, made a feeble attempt to cut some more meat, and fell into a doze. He roused a moment later, stared around with blank and unseeing eyes, dropped upon his blankets and pulled them over his head with a grunt. Neither Billy nor Crawford had stirred, nor had Kent any after remembrance of having relit the stove.

It was Crawford's roar that finally woke them. He was sitting up with a lighted match in his hand.

" 'Tain't mornin' yet," grumbled Billy.

" You're damn right it ain't," said Crawford. " I bet it's night again. If we ain't slep' the clock around I'm a Dutchman. I know my belly thinks my throat's cut."

They roused out and found another lantern, went out and fed the horses, and dragged some wood into the bunkhouse. Then they indulged in a gorge royal, and lay down for another sleep.

In the morning they sought the factor to check off their loads.

He was a morose and surly old Scotsman, full of the idea, not uncommon among the older employees of the Hudson's Bay Company, that he was satrap to an all-powerful empire.

John Crawford, with his inherited American distaste for all empires, was inevitably at feud with him.

" Don't let him put anything over on you," he warned Kent loudly. " That feller'd skin a louse for his hide."

The factor pointedly ignored him. " Yer first trup ? " he said to Kent. " Ye're in dom bad company. Yon lad ocht to be in preeson. He's no honest an' a leear forbye."

" Speak English, Scotty," jeered Crawford. " Them boys don't savvy Cree."

" Shut yer heid," rasped the Scot. " Whut d'ye ken o' English, ye uneducated, illeeterate, haverin', heathen fule ? "

Amid such amenities the loads were checked over and a receipt given. The factor retired into his store in a very ruffled frame of mind, with a curt injunction to them not to hang around the post, for he would have no thieving loafers on the Company's premises.

Crawford roared after him to come and chase them away. The factor slammed the door. Crawford marched up and down outside, daring him to come out and fight, until dragged away by the others.

The few Indians left at the post, the majority being away on their hunting grounds, listened to the dispute with awe and admiration, but took good care to keep out of sight.

First honours lay with the American, but the dour old Scot had the last word. Food was running low. The trip had taken longer than they expected, and Kent and Billy had gravely under-estimated the gargantuan appetites the trail bestows on its followers. Their beef was all gone and they had only two bannocks left. Crawford's pig was being rapidly reduced to a mere skeleton. All they had in sufficiency was tea and tobacco.

" I've nae instructions to sell ye ony grub," said the factor with grim malice, when Kent appealed to him. " Ye're supposed to bring yer ain."

It is a pity that Crawford's comments on the subject will not bear repetition.

" Have to see if I can dig up a Nitchie an' trade white-fish for tobacco or something," he concluded.

He finally discovered an elderly Indian, who, though in deadly fear of the factor, agreed to let them have some fish if they would meet him a couple of miles down the trail.

In exchange for some of Crawford's poisonous leaf tobacco, a hunting knife of Kent's, and a pound of tea, he gave them some three hundred pounds of frozen whitefish. Then he made off into the bush as fast as his dogs could pelt.

It was forty below that day, but Crawford looked up at the steely sky and shook his head.

" Sixty below by mornin'," he predicted.

" Well, we're goin' home," said Billy cheerfully. " Lucky it didn't hit us when us an' the horses was all tuckered out, an' the loads to pull."

They made only short camps that night, for the horses

began to stamp and shiver after standing still for an hour or so.

It was in the two savage hours before the dawn that John Crawford made his first concession to the weather. He put on a pair of woollen mittens in place of his leather gloves and drew a blanket about his shoulders.

Cold and fatigue woke a grinding ache in all their bones, and they drew the stinging air into their lungs sobbingly. Their faces were covered with frost and ice and every exposed inch of skin felt like a blister. Kent scooped handfuls of snow from the ground as they walked along and rubbed it upon his swollen and aching nose.

The grey mare rose into the air with a sudden squeal. The ice had closed her nostrils. Crawford sprang to her head, whipped off his blanket and flung it over her ears. He hung on like a bulldog, muffling her head in its folds, while she struck out madly with her forefeet. The warmth of the blanket presently thawed her nostrils and she became quiet, panting heavily.

They pulled on again. Large drops of blood began to drip one by one from the nose of Billy's Sam. Nothing could be done to stop it, for its warmth kept the poor brute's nostrils from freezing like the mare's.

The sun rose in a sky of steel. In the motionless air it was impossible to estimate distances ; every outline, far and near, was equally sharp and distinct. The snow was like powdered glass. The smoke of a fire ascended vertically in a slender column, mush-roomed out, and dissolved into nothingness.

All that can be done in such weather, if no shelter is available, is to keep moving : every halt numbs the blood. They went on all that day, making brief halts.

There seemed to be no heat in the fires they built. Even when they approached the flames so closely that their clothes began to scorch, the cold stabbed them in the back. When they turned, their faces froze.

"Raw pork," said Crawford hoarsely. "Chew on it, boys; it'll help you."

Without repugnance they gnawed the last scraps that remained of his pig.

"Never thought I'd come down to eatin' raw hog," mumbled Billy. "But this fat tastes like grub pile in Heaven to me."

"Archangel food," corrected Kent.

There was nothing left now to eat but whitefish, and by Crawford's advice they ate that raw too. White fish has a certain amount of oil in it, which is lost in boiling, and the great craving in intensely cold weather is for fat of any kind.

Except when they camped, even the solace of tobacco was denied them, for their pipes quickly froze up and refused to draw.

Day passed into night, and night waned. The horses plodded on with nodding heads; their sleigh-bells chimed flat and thin; and behind them their drivers stumbled along in a little knot, too weary, cold, and miserable to exchange a word.

Billy's team was in the lead, and halted. All the horses had taken to doing that of late.

"Hey there, Sam, Jimmy, get up," coughed Billy. But the team did not move.

"What in hell's holdin' 'em?" he mumbled, and waded forward through the deep snow beside the trail.

His sudden sharp yell brought the others up on a shambling run. A small Indian pony lay in the midst of the trail before them. It was hitched to a rough home-made jumper, and in the jumper sat a motionless figure, leaning back in the seat in an easy attitude.

"Froze stiff," said Crawford sombrely. He bent and scrutinized the rigid features. "It's poor old Jean Perrault. Well, I guess the old lad's made his last trip."

"What'll we do?" asked Billy.

Crawford shrugged. "Ain't much we can do."

"Yes, but hadn't we best take him down with us?"

"No. Why would we? He don't belong down there. He hangs out at Moose Lake, an' his folks wouldn't thank us for buttin' in an' haulin' him off south. No, best leave him right where he is. This is the main travelled road and somebody'll happen along any day. We can't turn back now with him. Come on, come on, or we'll be froze as stiff as what he is."

Feeling depressed and uneasy, they drove their sidling snorting teams around the grim obstacle. Crawford lingered a second to give the body a friendly pat on the shoulder.

"So long, old-timer," he said. "You was a good old scout, an' I'll keep you in mind, if that's any consolation to you."

The incident cast a deeper gloom upon their depressed spirits. At their next camp, Billy was moved to say :—

"I give anybody leave to kick me as finds me on the freight trail again. Once is enough for this chicken."

Kent concurred with a grunt.

Crawford became suddenly bitter again. "This is

what twins does to a man," he grumbled. " I'll travel this trail again—I'll have to travel it—an' one of these here days I'll be found dead on it like poor old Jean Perrault. An' that'll be if I'm lucky. I'm more liable, with my luck, to go through the ice on Swan Lake or get drownded in the Moose, an' nothin' ever seen of me any more. Eleven kids, and six of 'em twins. Leave it to a woman to put it over on a man."

The temperature moderated by imperceptible degrees, and they arrived at Beaver Island post in the midst of a half-blizzard.

Here they had shelter and a twenty-four-hours rest. But they still had only whitefish to eat.

" I'm growin' fins," grumbled Billy. " If I ever take another trip up this cursed trail I'll bring a couple of dead steers with me."

" Huh, we're lucky we got whitefish to eat," said Crawford. " I seen a whole band of Indians die of starvation because they couldn't find the fish one year. Oh, this is a sweet country. Don't know why in hell I ever left the States."

When they came to Swan Lake, snow was no longer falling, but a furious north wind was sweeping drift down the lake in great clouds.

" Well, a man does have a little luck once in a while," said Crawford grudgingly. " Anybody comin' up the lake to-day is goin' to be happy, but we're goin' to have it soft goin' down."

He showed them how to rig blanket sails on their racks, and they sat snugly in front of these while the wind drove them along so fast that the horses had sometimes to trot to keep the sleighs from running them down.

But by now Crawford's good humour had definitely departed. The fate of Jean Perrault and the incidence of twins formed the twin subjects of an eternal monologue.

"Three pairs of twins," he repeated. "One's bad enough, an' two's playin' it about as low down on a feller as you can go, but three . . ." And again : " I don't know but what Jean was lucky, at that. The very same thing'll happen to me one of these here days, an' I don't care how soon she comes, neither."

When he turned off the trail to go to his own home, he shook hands with them gloomily.

"You're good lads, both of you," he said. "Don't you waste your lives on this here freight trail. I got to ; I'm down where I can't help myself ; an' it'll get me in the end. But you stay off of it if you have to eat your horses."

The two wayfarers received a cordial welcome on their return.

"Well, what's the news ? " demanded Billy eagerly.

"Lucy's cut another tooth," said Maggie.

"She was cuttin' that when I went up," said Billy. "Gosh, I feel like I been away a year."

"You didn't seem so long," said Maggie. "The time went pretty fast. It was awful cold an' I had to keep big fires, an' me an' Mrs. Kent visited back an' forth fine days, and Pierre Normandin looked in every day or two. I was a little lonesome nights. The new cow's awful cranky : she come pretty near hookin' me. An' Lucy run right out in the snow one day, the little monkey. I don't know how she got the door open.

I was out in the barn an' I seen her, an' dropped the hayfork . . ."

The placid wifely monologue droned on and on, while before Billy's eyes passed a panorama of lonely lakes and frozen rivers, of snow-clad hills and fires twinkling in the frostbitten nights. It was a hard life, but there was uncertainty and adventure in it. This was pleasant enough, but dull. He began to feel he ought to take another trip. The one just completed would not keep them long.

" Tom, you mustn't make any more trips," said Mrs. Kent in her emphatic manner. " I absolutely forbid it. You look perfectly ghastly with all the skin peeling off your face, and your nose is a sight. And you're so thin, down to skin and bone. I never saw you with a beard before, and I can't say it improves your appearance. Do hurry up and shave it off. Really, Tom, I do hope you're not going to be silly enough to go again."

" Well, my dear, we'll see," murmured Kent with a twinkling eye. " Can't say I'm infatuated with the freight trail, but we must have money."

When the men met they looked at each other shyly and hastened to talk of indifferent matters. One day they went into the bush together for a load of logs. A silence fell between them.

" Well, old-timer, how about it ? " asked Billy at last with a grin.

" Pining for John Crawford's company ? " chuckled Kent.

" Something like that," admitted Billy. " You know, things is pretty slow around here, an' I need more money before spring opens."

"We'll have to pay another visit to our friend Mc-Crumbie," said Kent.

Maggie acquiesced: life was hard and it was useless to repine. Mrs. Kent voiced a strenuous objection, but relented after Kent had harnessed his horses, and kissed him good-bye.

"Want another load for Moose Lake?" grinned McCrumbie.

"Just that," said Billy. "The long haul pays us best."

"I wish I had a few more good sports like you," said McCrumbie. "The new settlers seem a soft lot."

The February weather was raw and chilly, but they were fortunate in having a southerly wind on Swan Lake. Beyond Beaver Island they fell in with John Crawford, in company with a half-breed who drove a team of rat-like ponies.

The spirits of the American were evidently on the downgrade again, for he was on his way home. He jerked a scornful thumb at his companion.

"That's all the company I can get on this damn trail," he grumbled. "I got to put up with it or travel alone. Why the devil didn't you tell me you was takin' another trip?"

"We didn't think we would when we left you," said Kent.

"Huh, you'd ought to have more sense than to do it again. Well, I got to be pullin' on home: the damn twins'll be bawlin' for grub."

The factor at Moose Lake, seeing them unaccompanied by the hated Crawford, was almost civil, and gave them a load of whitefish each to haul to Riverton. They were thus able to make the trip pay both ways. Altogether the journey was safe, profitable, pleasant, and—uninteresting.

The only incidents of importance were Billy's remarkable use of his trail sense and a stupendous display of northern lights at about two in the morning on Swan Lake.

By the first he discovered a short cut through a notch between two hills that eliminated seven miles of the crooked and treacherous Moose River. It was known thereafter as Clovelly's Cut-off.

The performance of the aurora began abruptly with a broad band of green light sweeping from east to west across the whole vault of the sky. Changing flames of purple and blue and amethyst flickered like the spears of the army of Valhalla all along its northern edge. In the south a mysterious crimson glow lay like the reflection of some great fire afar off on a bank of clouds. But there were no clouds, and the glow came and went in mid-air. The stars were dimmed, and formless shadows fled and dashed in pursuit and battled and merged and broke up again upon the green-tinted snow of the lake, and there was a slow, rustling beat in the air like the wings of passing angels.

Emboldened by success, they made a third and last trip, and nemesis swooped upon them.

They broke Kent's rack against a stump and lost a day building another one. They were storm-bound on Swan Lake for two days, while a raging March blizzard made it impossible to see five feet ahead on the open ice. Later they broke through the ice on Moose River, and lamed one of Kent's horses for a month.

They lost the can containing their tea somewhere on the road, and had to drink melted snow water, a dismal beverage. On this trip, too, they subsisted very largely on raw and boiled whitefish, because their meat was consumed in the various delays.

The one bright spot on the whole wretched journey was their meeting with John Crawford a few miles north of Swan Lake. With characteristic hardiness he was making the dangerous trip alone, but as his back was turned on home he was in the best of spirits, and greeted them like long-lost brothers.

He was good enough to sing them his ground-hog song again, and they joined in the chorus.

They lost themselves in a blizzard on Swan Lake, and by the time they got ashore and found the trail again all the hay had been eaten, and from there to Willy Croker's the hungry horses had nothing to eat but a little oats.

Worn to skin and bone and half dead with fatigue, they limped home, swearing mighty oaths that the freight trail should see them nevermore.

CHAPTER XV

THE annual miracle was performed. A frost-bound, snow-covered, inhospitable waste was turned in the space of a few weeks into a warm and fruitful garden.

For Billy it meant only the drudgery of ploughing and harrowing and seeding. The freight trail grew fair in receding memory, and the mosquitoes stinging at his sweaty neck woke in him a sudden longing for snow and an absence of insect pests.

For the Kents it was an initiation into real farming. Henceforth they would have to live on the land and by the land. Mrs. Kent had been given to talking about " going home to England," and treating their homesteading experience as an interlude in their real life.

She spoke no more about that in public, and gave herself seriously to the care of her garden, her cows, her calves, her poultry, and the schooling of her sons.

Kent, in a mask of sweat and dust, wrestled with the stubborn earth. He had to farm, and he proposed to do it well. He worked his land before seeding with a care and thoroughness that aroused Billy's amusement. His own lumpy field, full of roots and grass clumps, contrasted strongly with Kent's smoothly harrowed acres.

On a bright June morning a slender young man with a flowing tie and a black slouch hat drove up to the Clovelly homestead in a handsome new one-horse rig.

"I'm representin' the Wolfe-Butcher Implement Company," he announced. "We're prepared to sell farm implements to sound farmers on easy terms. You been recommended to us as a progressive leader in the community."

Billy was impressed with the young man's discernment. He did his best to look sound and progressive.

"Well, you see," he apologized, "my neighbour has an outfit an' we work back an' forth with them. I ain't got a big enough crop to need a whole outfit of my own. Besides, I ain't got the price."

The young man waved his hand. "Don't think about the price. We'll take care of that. But listen to this. Whose hay is cut first, eh? Yours or your neighbour's? Ain't it his land that is seeded first? Who has first call on the binder at harvest time? Who gets the fine weather to cut his crop in? What you get is leavin's—ain't it, now? An' suppose you fall out with your neighbour—mind, I ain't sayin' you will—but just suppose you do, eh? What then?"

"That's so," agreed Billy doubtfully. "I do have to kind of wait on him. But how am I goin' to pay for all these things? I got no money, nor I ain't likely to have by the way things look."

"That's right—not the way things are," said the salesman. "But if you have your own outfit an' can go right ahead without waitin' on anybody. Why, I knew a man pay off all his debts with just one good crop."

He did not mention that the man had settled within two miles of a railway, while Billy would have to haul his grain twenty-five times as far over bad roads.

"Well, come on up to the house," said Billy, glad enough of an excuse to knock off work for the morning.

Maggie came to the door with Lucy in her arms.

"Well, now, if that ain't a fine new settler," burbled the salesman. "Born right here on the homestead, eh? Well, you won't find many finer children than that anywhere. I guess not, I guess not."

Maggie beamed. She and Billy listened in a happy daze while with lightning strokes the implement man converted the ragged bush homestead into a little agricultural paradise. All this magic would be performed almost without effort by the Wolfe-Butcher farm implements.

"But where am I to find the money?" protested Billy feebly.

"Tell you what," said the salesman with a keen glance about for possible eavesdroppers and an impressive lowering of his voice. "This is in confidence, mind. We don't want everybody to know. My company ain't puttin' this proposition up to everybody. We're just pickin' the ones we know'll make good. We're willin' to carry 'em an' treat 'em right. If we know a man's the right kind, suppose he does have a streak of bad luck an' gets a little behind—why, we won't press him. We know we'll get our money in the end."

" But you ain't in business for your health," said Billy with a feeble gleam of sanity.

The salesman laughed heartily and wagged his head in admiration.

" No, sir, you're right, we ain't. But, listen here —we figure to sell that man a lot more implements. That man's goin' to be an asset to us. We treat him right an' he's a man we can count on to buy from us. It ain't likely, is it, that we're goin' to do anything to lose us his business ? I put it to you, as a reasonable man, as a man who knows his way around—is it likely ? "

This was a far-sighted view that appealed to Billy. The salesman produced swiftly a fountain pen and a little book. " Yes, sir, all we need now is just your name. A mower an' rake, binder an' seeder. That'll come to . . ." He named the price. " We'll say six, twelve, an' eighteen months to pay, eh ? "

He wrote swiftly and handed the pen to Billy. " Sign these, please. Right there."

Billy shied like an unbroken horse. " What's them things ? Notes ? "

" That's all," said the salesman with elaborate carelessness. " Just a formality. You can always renew, you know. Pay what you can, an' let the balance run."

But here Maggie intervened. " I wouldn't like to run into debt, Billy. We kep' out of it this long, an' I guess we can go on like we been doin'."

The unabashed salesman turned upon her his most

beaming smile. " That's right, Mrs. Clovelly, don't let your man run into debt until he knows what he's doin'. But he can't go wrong here. He's not the kind that'll be in debt long. When a man's got a good wife an' a good quarter, an' is the right kind himself—why, he won't be long gettin' on his feet. All he needs is a start, an' that's what I'm here to give him."

The argument was protracted. The bemused Billy would by now have signed anything put before him, even though he knew that the signing of promissory notes is one of the widest avenues to ruin of the pioneer. It is so easy to sign them—and so difficult to meet them when they fall due.

The inexperienced Maggie was left to battle alone. She yielded point after point, but against the seeder she set her face like a flint. The agent gracefully left her in possession of that stronghold, praising her clear-sightedness and thrift in glowing terms.

Thereby the signing of the remaining notes became in the nature of a generous act on his part. Even Maggie was anxious to have them signed. He took a cordial farewell of them both, and departed merrily on his piratical way. They never saw him again. The next agent of the Wolfe-Butcher Implement Company to call upon them was of a very different stamp.

" I'm kind of sorry you signed them notes," said Maggie remorsefully that evening.

" Aw, shoot, we'll be all right," replied Billy. " What's the use of worrying ? "

The steady trickle of immigration into the country continued. Quarter-sections were taken up here and there. The effects were not immediately apparent : the trails were still open and there were hayland and grazing enough for all.

They had to put up more hay that season, for Billy had now two cows and two calves, and Kent's little herd was growing fast.

Then came harvest and proved the wisdom of Kent's more careful methods. The season had been rather dry, and Billy's wheat-field was patchy and the straw very short. Kent's yield was much higher and the grain of higher grade. He also had a better yield of oats.

Pierre, taking another line, had seeded his first little field of barley, and had invested in two brood sows in the spring.

" I cannot eat de barley," he explained. " But peeg eat him—I eat de peeg. It is too far for haul grain to Riverton, too many treep. I keel my peeg, put him in mine vagon—one treep, an' better price, hahn ? "

But the population of the settlement was not increased solely by outside immigration : a few took a more direct route. Thus arrived William Clovelly, Junior, in the small hours of an October morning, and already the little shack began to be crowded for room.

Lucy had grown from a creature prone to shrill clamour at unseasonable hours, who sent her mother nearly insane with anxiety over mysterious ailments, and Billy flying over to Mrs. Kent for advice at all hours, into a small and fascinating imp of mischief, who pestered her adoring father.

There were also strange doings at the Darke homestead.

On a day in July Billy met the formidable man on the trail and, after the leisurely fashion of the pioneer, stopped his horses for an exchange of news and views.

The ex-sergeant was driving a newly purchased bay team, and their points had to be discussed, and the weather, and the crops, and the new settlers.

Darke seemed to be labouring under some pleasurable excitement ; his stern face was wreathed in smiles, and he spoke of the country with glowing enthusiasm.

" Wonderful climate, Mr. Clovelly—wonderful climate you 'ave 'ere. The effect it 'as 'ad on Mrs. Darke, you wouldn't believe. She's a changed woman." He bent forward confidentially. " For the first time, Mr. Clovelly —for the first time she 'as given me 'ope—real 'ope, I mean. You're a family man yourself, Mr. Clovelly. You know 'ow I've always 'ankered for children."

" Oh," said Billy, a light breaking. " An' you think it's goin' to be all right this trip ? "

" We do," said the sergeant reverently. " We 'ave prayed, Mr. Clovelly, an' it looks as if our prayer is at last about to be answered. If only—oh, if honly it's a boy, Mr. Clovelly, I'll 'ave nothin' else to wish for."

Billy checked his inclination to smile. Reverence was no part of his nature, though courtesy was.

" Well, sir, I wish you all the luck in the world," he said cordially.

This being part of the budget of news a pioneer was expected to bring home to family and friends every time he went abroad, Billy mentioned the matter to Mrs. Kent.

" I must see if there's anything I can do for the poor woman," she said at once.

On a fine Sunday afternoon she rode over on her black pony.

The sergeant's experiment in house building had been highly successful. He had constructed a neat, warm, two-room shack, and added a small kitchen at the back. A stable and a byre on the same principle stood at mathematically exact distances, *en échelon*, and a well house represented, as it were, the advance guard. The hole was enclosed in a picket fence. There was also a well-tended garden, and beyond it a thirty-acre field of grain.

Darke, a thrifty man, had saved money during his army service, and his small pension kept him supplied with ready money—something extremely rare in the Northwest of the day. He could give his whole time and attention to the cultivation of his farm, and keep clear of debt.

He was not at home, but Mrs. Darke came to the door as her visitor rode up. Recognition was mutual and swift. Mrs. Kent dismounted with agility and held out her hand.

" Why, how d'you do, Phillips ? I never expected to meet you out here."

" My lady ! " exclaimed Mrs. Darke, wide-eyed.

" No, Phillips, not ' my lady ' ; just your neighbour, Mrs. Kent, come to pay you a friendly visit."

" But, but . . ."

" Not a word, Phillips. I'm Mrs. Kent, and you'll

do me a favour by keeping anything else you know about me to yourself."

" Very well, my—Mrs. Kent. But we can talk about The Family when we're by ourselves, can't we ? Mr. Darke is not at 'ome. 'Ow's Lady Mabel ? "

" Quite well. You know, of course, she's married —twin boys and a little girl. Aren't you going to invite me in ? "

" Certainly, certainly, my lady—I mean Mrs. Kent. I'm afraid the place is in an awful state—I didn't expect you."

" Don't be silly, Phillips. Of course you didn't expect me. My own house isn't nearly as nice as this."

They had a long talk, and it was arranged that Mrs. Darke would send for Mrs. Kent when her time came. Mrs. Darke also faithfully promised to keep the secret of her rank, and actually did so for years.

Mrs. Kent left before the sergeant returned, for supper had to be got ready and milking cows do not observe Sunday.

On a blowy November evening, a week after the birth of Maggie's second baby, there came a messenger in hot haste with a fast horse and buggy, and carried Mrs. Kent to the home of the formidable man.

On account of her age, the labour was long and painful, but Mrs. Kent battled grimly.

" Now, Phillips, pull yourself together."

" Yes, my lady," whimpered the frightened woman. " But it do 'urt so. I'm going to die—I know I'm going to die."

" Nothing of the kind. I'm going to be very angry with you in a minute. How dare you drag me all this

way through a beast of a snowstorm and then behave
like this ? "

The poor woman yielded herself to her pangs. Hours
later she brought into the world a son—a very small
son, and one in whom the light of life flickered like a
candle in a draft. Mrs. Kent shook her head privately
over him, but hoped for the best.

The mighty and terrible sergeant had gone all to
pieces and sat in a corner sobbing like a child. The
winter wind howled around the shack, and Mrs. Darke
looked as if death had already claimed her.

At daylight there arrived a woman engaged by Darke,
who had been brought up by the same man who had
brought Mrs. Kent. She was elderly, but clean and of
long experience.

She looked at Mrs. Darke. " More scared than hurt,"
she whispered to Mrs. Kent. " Them old ones. I'll
bring her around. Let's see the kid."

She examined the baby with interest. " He'll live
too, likely. I must say you done a good job. You look
to me like you need more doctorin' than what she does.
Best get along home. I'm goin' to have enough to look
after without you, an' I'm goin' to chase that big fool
bawlin' in the corner. Men make me tired."

Kent drove up soon after for his wife, and Mrs. Kent
left the house confidently in the hands of the masterful
midwife. The sergeant tried to express his gratitude
to her and broke down again.

" You didn't behave like this in the presence of the
enemy, Mr. Darke," she reminded him gently.

He snapped to attention, and her last view was of
him standing stiffly at the salute.

She arrived home to faint, and Madame Normandin had to be brought over to nurse her.

Mrs. Darke rallied, the ex-sergeant regained his courage and drove the midwife from his home after an engagement of great fury, and Master Kent Darke, after a period of uncertainty, began to thrive.

CHAPTER XVI

THEY took the freight trail again that winter as a matter of course. Their crops, when hauled fifty miles to Riverton, and bought by the usual rascally elevator man, hardly sufficed for winter groceries.

They left home with their first loads the day after Christmas, and had the luck to run into John Crawford just as he turned in off his own private trail upon the main road.

He wore his old moosehide shirt, his buckskin moccasins, and his little black cap. Being still close to the settlement, he was full of gloom, but it was now the need of feeding twelve children that he lamented, for another had arrived during the summer.

He had with him a slender, saddle-coloured youth of eighteen, with the almond eyes that bespeak Indian blood, who drove a team of piebald shaganappies the size of mastiffs, pulling a thousand-pound load. He was Crawford's eldest son and making his first trip. His father roared at him ferociously.

" Old man scares hell out of you, don't he ? " said Billy with a grin to the lad during the noon halt, Crawford chopping wood at a little distance.

" He thinks he does," said the boy with a smile and an affectionate glance in his father's direction. " He makes considerable noise, but he ain't never laid a hand on none of us kids in his life."

This was a new light on the terrible John, and caused Billy to note that though he used blistering language to his horses he never touched them with whip or line.

"Think the old man's just a windbag?" he inquired privately of Kent.

"The Right Honourable John? Well, no; he's just ashamed of being too kind-hearted. He's one of the most lovable old fools I ever met."

"I guess you're right. Wonder what he'd do if he really had to fight."

"He'd fight, my son."

They had excellent weather and encountered a party of freighters on Swan Lake, returning empty from Beaver Island.

"Watch out for Dan Cooley," said one of them with a grin as they passed. "He's got a mad on."

John Crawford's ragged whiskers bristled. "That's one man I got no use for," he snorted. "No man what uses horses the way he does has got a right to have horses. One of these here fine days I'm goin' to have to take a poke at that guy—I just won't be able to lay off of him."

Farther on they spied a black spot on the ice, which gradually resolved itself into a team of tired sorrels, one of which limped painfully and was being savagely whipped by a very tall man in a black dogskin coat.

Crawford, who had been growling to himself ever since they had passed the freighters, broke out angrily.

" Just look at him now, look at the . . . By the livin',
pink-eyed . . . I can't stand to see that."

As they drew abreast, Cooley, without ceasing to
belabour his wretched horse, favoured them with an
ugly scowl.   The fact that he was cross-eyed and
had a crooked mouth detracted nothing from its
hideousness.

Crawford spoke in his loudest and harshest voice :
" Any man what uses a lame horse that way ought to
have his damn worthless neck twisted."

" Come an' do it," roared Cooley in answer.

" I wasn't meanin' you," said Crawford, with
every hair on his face bristling, his eyes gleaming, and his yellow dog teeth bared. " I was meanin'
a long, limber, cross-eyed shyster, with a crookit
mouth, what's a liar an' a bum an' a yaller dog. His
name is Dan Cooley—anybody seen the dirty bastard
around ? "

Cooley lashed out with his loaded blacksnake. He
was quick, but not quite quick enough.   Crawford
ducked in under the lash and closed with him.   The
fight which began was not conducted according to any
set rules :   it was primitive in the extreme, but it was
a great fight.

All apparent odds were on Cooley's side. He was
over six feet in height, raw-boned and muscular, and
outweighed his opponent by many pounds. But he was
wearing a great deal of hampering clothing and was
further handicapped by his long fur coat. Crawford
wore little but his moosehide shirt and his overalls.
Moreover, he was very compactly built, and sinewy
and agile as a wild cat.

An overhand smash set the blood spurting from Cooley's nose. Cooley retaliated with heavy thumps between the shoulder blades, for the American kept his head down out of harm's way.

They waltzed grotesquely on the snow, clasped in each other's arms and striking occasional wild blows. Cooley jerked away and tore off his fur coat, received a stinging clout on the jaw, and grappled again.

Both men began to breathe hard ; both were smeared with blood from Cooley's dripping nose. Once Crawford was lifted off his feet, but contrived to get a thumb in his opponent's eye. Once he tripped the tall man so that he stumbled, but he recovered himself.

They parted and stood watching each other warily, while each panted for breath. Crawford was the first to rush in, and the battle raged again. He fought with a set grin, Cooley with a fixed scowl.

A hammerlike blow on the temple sent the American to his knees, but he flung himself to one side, rolled clear, and was up again before the slow-moving Cooley could follow up his advantage.

But Crawford's little black cap was knocked off, and for the first time in living memory his totally bald pate was bared to public view. It seemed to bewilder him. He clapped a hand to his skull with a dismayed expression, and was knocked off his feet by a terrific swing.

With tears streaming down his face, young Crawford was for rushing to his father's assistance, but they held him back.

" Leave 'em be," said Billy, " leave 'em be. Your old man's got lots of fight in him yet an' he wouldn't thank you for buttin' in."

Cooley sprang upon his fallen foe, but, either by accident or design, Crawford caught him full on the bridge of his sore nose with an elbow.

The tall man reeled back, tears of agony in his eyes, giving the American time to rise and grip him again. In the ensuing scuffle Crawford's right ear came within reach of Cooley's mouth, who promptly fixed his teeth in it.

Crawford made his first outcry, a weird and un-earthly bellow. He strove to jerk his head away, but Cooley hung on with locked jaws. He reached up a fumbling hand and got a grip on the long hair at the base of his enemy's skull. Then came a test of endurance.

Cooley made a muffled, wild-beast noise, but did not let go. For a long moment they stood thus, swaying back and forth on motionless feet.

Cooley's mouth slowly opened, back and back went his head. Crawford heeled him smartly and down he crashed. Crawford leaped upon him, but there was still lots of fight left in the big man. He brought up his knees and tossed his enemy away like a kitten.

Both of them scrambled up, and they stood facing each other again. Crawford suddenly put down his head and charged. His hard skull, driven with the force of a battering-ram, took Cooley in the midriff. He doubled up like a carpenter's rule, and lay writhing and gasping on the trampled snow. Crawford stared at him dizzily, rocking on his feet and fingering his bald head aimlessly.

Billy took him gently by the arm. " He's beat, old-timer. You give the dirty skunk his needin's."

Crawford nodded. He thrust his head forward and glared at his prostrate enemy. " Hey, you," he rasped. " Had enough, or shall I kick the daylights out of you ? "

Cooley, still unable to speak, groaned and nodded.

" Well, then, I'm takin' your whip along with me, see ? An' if I ever meet you on the trail again with a whip, or poundin' a lame horse or any horse, I'll maul you so there won't be but a grease spot left."

They had been joined during the fight by a half-breed driving a team of ponies in a jumper, who had stopped to witness the argument, grinning with delight.

As Cooley got slowly upon his feet and staggered over to his rack, the half-breed whipped up his shaga-nappies and whirled away down the lake.

" Get up," mumbled Cooley to his team. Slowly they limped away, dwindled to a speck, and faded out.

They tied up the American's mangled ear and cocked the little black cap atop. He was so sore and stiff that they had to roll him in blankets and lay him upon his rack. But he was full of pride and joy, and sang his ground-hog song at intervals all the way across the lake.

The half-breed witness spread the tale of the great battle all up and down the freight trail, and the dis-honoured Cooley forsook the country.

They made three round trips that winter again, were
hungry and frozen, encountered manifold perils and
misfortunes, and secretly enjoyed themselves, though
never ceasing to lament the hard fate that forced them
to take the trail.

CHAPTER XVII

THE notes fell due. Billy found mail waiting for him on his return from each trip. He could well have dispensed with it, for it consisted entirely of duns.

He paid the interest, and tried to explain matters to the company in rambling, misspelled letters. The company had received many such letters, and coldly reiterated its demand for money.

Anxiety pervaded the Clovelly household. Not that Billy worried very much—it was not his nature. His constitutional melancholy was careless of material things. When spoken to on the subject, he merely damned the company heartily, and talked about other things.

It was Maggie who visioned their being turned out into the snow, ruined and penniless. She drove Billy at length to seek assistance from a Riverton bank. The bank manager inquired blandly what security he had to offer for a loan. Billy was thereby furnished with two institutions to curse.

He went dismally about his spring work. It was a cold, backward season, and his horses were thin from their winter on the freight trail.

Kent, having no interest to pay to anyone, bought himself a third horse, and got through his work more easily. His herd had increased to twelve, while Billy had only five.

"Oh well, he had the start an' I didn't," said Billy.

His three years were up, he had completed his homestead duties and won his bet with the government, and that summer he received his patent.

It was what the implement company had been waiting for, the law not permitting them to acquire a homesteader's land until he had secured title to it.

A little before harvest there appeared one day a burly, red-faced man, with cold, fishy eyes and a pursed-up mouth. He represented the implement company, he said, and would like to see Mr. Clovelly.

Maggie invited him in and gave him a chair to await Billy's arrival for dinner. Anxiously she studied the stranger for signs of amiability, but found none. Little Lucy came and prattled to him, but shrank away from his hostile glance.

Billy came in and invited the stranger to the meal as a matter of course. Maggie vaguely hoped that food would soften his heart. But the company did not choose its collectors for amiability, and this one was an old hand at his dismal calling.

She pressed upon him such small delicacies as their poor table afforded, but he waded through his food like a surly pig in a trough. Billy was sullen and refused to open his mouth, and no effort at sociability on the part of the anxious Maggie could lighten the cloud of gloom.

At last the stranger pushed back his chair. "Now, let's talk business, Mr. Clovelly," he said brusquely.

"Uh," grunted Billy.

"You know them notes of yours is long past due,"

pursued the collector remorselessly. " You ain't even paid all the interest on them."

" Uh," agreed Billy.

" The company has to have its money ; it can't do business that way, Mr. Clovelly. What are you goin' to do about it ? "

" Well," mumbled Billy, " I been havin' kind of hard luck, what with one thing and another, but when I get my crop off I figure to be able to pay something."

" Hm, I seen your crop as I come by," said the collector. " Not more than twenty-five acres, an' not lookin' very good."

" Well, what can I do ? " cried Billy wildly. " It's all I got. I can't make money, can I ? I'm havin' hard scratchin' just to live the way things been goin'. The man what sold me them implements said the company wouldn't push me if I got a little behind. He said them very words, settin' right where you are now. My woman heard him. I wouldn't have bought 'em only for that. I didn't really need 'em."

The collector shook his head and let his heavy lids droop over his fishy eyes.

" It ain't what he said that counts, Mr. Clovelly. He's out to get the business, of course. The company ain't responsible for how he gets it. All the company says to him is, ' Turn in your orders an' you get your commission.' That's business. If he likes to stretch a point, why, it's up to him. The company don't look to that at all : it looks to what's wrote down in black an' white. You signed them notes, didn't you ? "

" Uh-huh."

" Very well, that's what the company goes by. It

says on them notes in black an' white, with your name
to it, it says that you promise to pay so much at such
and such a time, with interest. Now, when that time
comes, the company expects to get its money. That's
business."

"I wisht I'd never bought the damn things," said
Billy sulkily.

"But you did buy 'em, Mr. Clovelly. You wanted
'em. The company let you have 'em; let you have
'em on time, too. They trusted you."

Billy gave a short derisive laugh.

But the other went coldly on. "They trusted you;
they didn't think you was the kind of man to buy a thing
an' turn around an' try to wiggle out of paying for it."

"But I ain't," protested Billy. "I'm goin' to pay
just as quick as ever I can."

"Well, then, let's have the money an' no more said."

"But I ain't got it, I tell you. Ain't I just been tellin'
you I can't pay till I get my crop off?"

Again the collector shook his head. "We need something better than that, Mr. Clovelly; we need something better than that."

"Well, what in hell do you want, then?"

The collector became more cordial at once. "Well,
we don't want to push you too hard, Mr. Clovelly, but
we need a little security. That's business."

"Yes, but what do you want?" asked Billy, still in
the dark.

"Now, how would it be," insinuated the collector,
almost purring, "if you gave us something against your
land? It's just a formality, of course—that's all it is.
But you see how it is: we need the security."

"Is it a mortgage?" inquired Billy, with acute suspicion.

"Well, it is a kind of a one. It's not just the same thing exactly."

"No sir, no sir, I'll sign no damn mortgage," said Billy loudly, shaking his head. "I know all about mortgages. You can't put a thing like that over on me."

There followed half an hour of wrangling. Billy was defiant and suppliant, sulky and noisily rebellious, by turns; the collector grimly insistent. He wound up by invoking the dread name of the law.

The word "law" was even more grimly terrible to Billy than the word "mortgage." Brought up on the edge of the raw wilderness, far from courts and lawyers, the law had only appeared in the guise of an oppressor. The law meant to him men beggared, broken, and imprisoned. He looked upon even the Royal Northwest Mounted Police with suspicion, for bailiffs frequently had to appeal to them for protection, and they had haled more than one defiant farmer of his acquaintance off to jail.

He was of law-abiding, Anglo-Saxon stock. He had no criminal traits, but, with Anglo-Saxon independence, he felt himself amply capable of protecting himself and his from violence and wrong.

Here, however, was a power he could not fight, against which all his courage and resolution would be powerless. He sat silent.

With a grin meant to be conciliatory, but bearing a much greater resemblance to a cat gloating over a mouse in its paws, the collector produced a paper.

"Just a formality, Mr. Clovelly," he purred. "No

call to get so excited over it. The company wants to do what's right by you. Just sign here."

Maggie had listened in silence, but now she suddenly got up.

" You ain't goin' to sign that thing, Billy," she said. " You signed too much already. If you hadn't signed them notes we wouldn't be in this jack pot now. An' if you sign that there mortgage we'll be in worse trouble before we're through. Things is plenty bad enough right now—no sense in makin' 'em any worse."

The collector made the mistake of affecting to ignore her. " Sign here," he said brusquely.

Billy meekly took the pen.

But the paper was jerked from his hand, the stove lid clanged, and Maggie was standing defiantly in front of it.

The collector sprang up with a snarl. " Give me that paper."

" I won't. I put it in the fire an' there it's goin' to stay," she flung back.

He pointed a minatory finger at her. " Do you know what you're doin' ? Do you know I can turn you out of this place, put you right out on the road with nothin' but the clothes you stand up in ? "

She hardly doubted him : for her, too, the law was the mysterious and terrible oppressor of poor folk. But she was fighting for her home and her children.

" Go ahead an' do it " she retorted. " Turn us out if you can. But my man ain't signin' no more papers. Now you go on about your business. We'll pay for them implements when we can, or you can take 'em away if you like, but my man ain't goin' to sign no more papers."

The collector went away, muttering threats.

Billy regarded his wife gloomily. "Now you done it, kid. We're liable to see a mountie up here next thing we know, an' me behind the bars lookin' out."

"If a mountie comes around here lookin' for you I'll scratch his eyes out," she cried. "I don't care nothin' for their old law, so I don't. We ain't done nothin' wrong, an' I won't have you put in jail. I'll go there myself an' take the kids along. They can't let the kids starve."

"Well, you're hot stuff, anyway," said Billy with a rueful smile. "Gosh, I thought you was goin' to have that feller's ear off."

"I would, too—I would if he was a dozen men," she screamed, and suddenly flung herself face downward on the bed and burst into a passion of tears.

For some days they felt like felons in the condemned cell. The sight of a man on horseback caused Maggie to turn pale. When a buggy rattled up to the shack late one evening, Billy reached desperately for his shotgun, but it was only a land-seeker who had lost his way.

But the wheat was ripe in the fields and the rush of harvest drove their terrors into the background. Billy had a fair crop that year, a far better yield than the appearance of his field warranted. He hauled it down to Riverton and turned the proceeds in on his debt.

He thus, through no virtue of his own, escaped the fate of so many settlers, who passed into a state of virtual servitude to the implement companies, working without hope, seeing all the fruits of their labours swallowed up in interest payments. Some of them gave up the fight and became homeless wanderers, and only a very few regained their independence by dint of terrible toils and privations.

But as he had no money he turned naturally to the freight trail again. Kent did not go that winter. His crop had been a good one, and he was kept busy hauling it to town until it was too late to take the freight trail.

Billy paired off with a new settler called Berry, and met John Crawford and his son and fell into their arms. He was caught on Swan Lake in another blizzard, and went through the ice on the north shore and was nearly drowned with all his outfit. He wrangled with the domineering old Scot at Moose Lake, with whom he had by now a healthy feud of his own. He smashed a rack on Moose River when his load went over the bank. He acquired the usual extensive collection of frostbites, and looked starvation in the face once more.

So that winter passed, and plough, harrow, and seeder had to be brought once more into requisition. Maggie became once more a mother that year and bore him twins a boy and a girl.

" I got the curse of John Crawford on me," said Billy.

There was no room in the shanty for the six of them, and he built a wing of logs, converting the old shack into the kitchen and living-room. He also put up a new barn.

The little farmstead retained its pioneer appearance, though across the slough Kent was enlarging his house and adding a frame loft to his biggest barn.

The increasing settlement was beginning to have

its effect. Haying resolved itself for the first time into a bitter struggle with needy neighbours. All the uplands were dotted with scrub cattle, and men kept watch over particular sloughs so that others should not get in first and cut the initial swath.

Billy sat up all one night with a shotgun on guard over the slough below Kent's. At four o'clock Martin Oslen, a Swede from Minnesota, drove up with his mower.

" I'm here first," said Billy, the gun in the crook of his arm.

They glared at each other. " You take dis side and I take de udder," said Olsen. " I got to haf some hay."

" All right," said Billy reluctantly.

They sat and watched each other while the sun rose. Hay cut with the dew on it is worthless. But the Swede was in motion while tiny drops of moisture still glittered on the long grass. Billy had to follow suit. It developed into a race as to who should cover the largest area in the shortest time.

The slough was full of lumps, anthills a foot or more high, and old buffalo skulls. There were also old muskrat channels, deep narrow ditches.

Billy had the lighter mower and the faster team and started off at a trot, the knives of his mower clattering like mad. His reckless career ended suddenly in a muskrat channel, into which one wheel sank over the hub. He found he had bent a brace, and had to straighten it before the knife would run freely in its channel.

The Swede turned in his seat to wave a derisive hand, and Billy ground his teeth.

The Swede stopped with a violent jerk. His blade
had run full tilt into an ant hill. Now it was his turn
to descend and make hurried repairs while Billy drove
jubilantly by. Next, Billy picked up a rotting buffalo
horn and broke off a blade with it.

The Swede got himself bogged in a maze of muskrat
channels, and Billy charged an old dead log and nearly
wrecked the mower.

Both teams were by now soaked in sweat and panting.
Both mowers showed signs of being ready to fly to pieces
at the next collision with anything. Smoke was rising
from Billy's bearings.

The drivers began to show a little more discretion.
The race was not to the swift, but to the most skilful
in avoiding obstacles. They swung round the lower
end of the slough and came face to face. Each man
drove doggedly on until the opposing teams touched
noses. Then they had to turn and drive side by
side, each jockeying to get a little ahead and edge
over.

The horses halted knee-deep in the slough. The
drivers glared at each other until a slow smile wrinkled
Billy's face.

" Hah," grinned Olsen. " Ve haf a hall of a time,
me 'n' you. Yumpin' Yesus, I tank my mower ged
drownt ant my team back dere. But you didn't put
vun ofer on me, eh ? "

" No, we come out pretty even, Martin. Now I'll
beat you up to the other end, or somebody else'll be
cuttin' in on us."

The race was resumed. Billy had a little the best
of the return journey, Olsen getting badly bogged in

the same place as before. They had, however, ringed an approximately equal area on either side of the long slough. Both teams, splashed with black mud to the withers, were very tired.

There was a law written or unwritten—I never learned which—that gave to a man all the hay he could enclose in a swath. No other mower could drive across cut hay. But the law was not always observed, and fights developed all through the district.

Two men started in the same slough àt the same time, one inside the other. The argument was settled by the more hasty of the pair with a small rifle, one of the men going to hospital and the other to jail. As many as four different outfits would begin to cut hay simultaneously in the same large slough, the resulting confusion not infrequently culminating in a free-for-all.

Kent and Billy each got just enough for his own needs, but the shadow of what was to come already lay heavy across the land.

Then harvest, with an early frost to decrease the yield and lower the grade. What had looked like a thirty-bushel stand of fine clean wheat threshed out eleven bushels to the acre, tough, a grade below milling quality and only fit for pig feed.

So Kent had to take the freight trail again that winter, and collectors harried Billy for money until he was nearly insane.

His implements were wearing out already, though they were not yet paid for.

The Canadian Government was touting the West far and wide, while allowing every kind of commercial pirate to batten at will upon the unfortunates who flocked into the country.

This year and the ones which immediately followed were dark years for the pioneers. Starvation and ruin grinned at them from harvest to harvest.

CHAPTER XVIII

YEAR by year the trickle of immigration swelled to a stream and from a stream to a flood. For three years it was at a standstill in the district, and then came the deluge.

During those three years, though every even-numbered section fit for habitation had been filed on, the odd-numbered sections were withheld. The settlers, therefore, still had a little elbow-room.

In the beginning a homesteader had been able to trap and hunt in winter, raise small crops for food, put up big stacks of hay, and, for the rest, allow his scrub cattle to wander at large over the whole face of the land.

Trapping came to an end first. Then began the quarrelling over hay and grazing lands. More land was broken up, and that made the situation worse, for the haul of fifty-odd miles to Riverton was prohibitive of grain raising, and the hungry cattle were crowded into yet narrower areas. Fat cattle came to be almost unknown, and the buyers would not pay high prices for lean and stunted stock.

Hardly a settler but was in debt up to his ears.

The collector swept through the land like a scourge. The population of the West was not large enough to have political weight at Ottawa, where the two political parties, engaged in the ancient struggle for the fruits of power, had no time to waste on anything but votes.

Communication, strangely enough, became worse instead of better. The old trails, such as Billy had made, had followed the high land and the open levels that were easiest to plough. When the land was taken up such places were the first ploughed, and the trails were driven down into the woods and marshes.

That led to road disputes and fence cutting, assaults and law-suits. Lawyers added themselves to the parasites preying on the settlers.

Travel, especially in the spring, became almost impossible, and even in summer the roads were a dreary succession of stumps and mudholes. In winter the trails took naturally to the level sloughs, and people could get about freely.

Flimsy bridges were thrown across some of the utterly impassable bogs, but there was no one responsible for their upkeep and no system followed in their erection.

Matters got to such a pass that many families found themselves almost as much cut off from the world in summer as if they dwelt on so many islands.

It was gradually ceasing to be a man's country; the frank, easy comradeship of the frontier was passing. With closer settlement the women got about more and inevitably set up social feuds and intrigues into which they dragged their husbands. The settlers split up into small cliques—" clicks " in Western parlance—mutually exclusive and hostile. There was as yet no community feeling and no co-operation for common ends.

The Clovellys, the Kents, the Normandins, with the Darkes as a sort of outpost, formed one such clique, and a feud grew up between them and some families to the westward.

The westerners harried the Kent-Clovelly-Normandin cattle, and Billy and Kent retaliated by fencing off the westerners' most direct route to town, compelling them to make a wide circle round a large swamp. That led to a worse harrying of the wretched cattle.

" It's no use, old man," said Kent one day. " We're not a tribe of bally—ah—aborigines, hunting each other's scalps. I'm goin' to hold out the olive branch to the Groats and Collinses."

" Huh, I'd liefer hold out a club to 'em," said Billy. " Well, go on. If you don't get back I'll come after an' gather up the pieces."

Kent drove over to Silas Groat's place. Old Man Groat came out and shook a fist at him.

" You get to hell off of my land," he bawled. " I'll have you pinched."

Kent went on to his son's place. Young Si was sulky. " I stand by the old man. You got no right to close that trail."

" Stop chasing my cattle and I'll open the trail," offered Kent.

Young Si shook his head stubbornly. " Your cattle got no license on them sand-hills."

But the Collins brothers, bachelor homesteaders, were more reasonable.

" Let us put a gate in our line fence an' drive along the edge of your field," they offered, " an' we'll cut back our fence where it runs into the slough an' let your cattle by that way."

It made a longer way round for the herd, but it opened

to them a stretch of vacant land hitherto barred to them.

The Groats, outmanoeuvred and deserted by their allies, sent over a peace offering in the shape of a turkey each to Billy and Kent.

" To hell with them," growled Billy. " I'd just as lief be on fightin' terms with them as not."

" Wrong spirit, old man," dissented Kent. " A compromise is always better than a scrap to a finish. Old Groat is a hasty old owl, but he's not really a bad fellow. I'm not asking you to kiss him on the whiskers . . ."

" No, nor I ain't goin' to kiss nobody's whiskers : I ain't a Peasoup."

" Metaphorically speaking, my son—purely a figure of speech."

" Huh. Well, if you're goin' to let him go through, all right. But if he ever dogs my cattle again, I'm goin' to nail his hide to a door."

So that feud was healed.

There cropped up another matter of the first importance—that of education. In a sound and vigorous community of people, most of whom were under forty, the birth rate was naturally high. The children were in danger of growing up illiterate little savages.

Mainly by Kent's efforts, the Cloam School District was formed. He was also created a justice of the peace about this time.

A small log schoolhouse was put up and a young woman engaged as teacher. One Theodore Battle, from Nebraska, opened a store near the school and was made a postmaster. It was no longer necessary to travel eighteen miles to the old settlement for mail or to buy a plug of tobacco. The mail came out from Riverton by team twice a week, and newspapers became common in the settlement.

A road gang made its appearance, and there was talk of a government road going through about a mile north of Billy's place.

About the same time a Dominion election was announced. Work went on vigorously on the road until after election, and then stopped. There would be no more government road work in that section until the next election.

A stout, cordial, perspiring individual toured the country as Government candidate. He visited individual farmers and held meetings in schoolhouses. He said he was proud of being a Grit, a real dyed-in-the-wool Grit; he would be proud to represent so progressive and intelligent a community; he was proud to know he had so many fine supporters in the district.

He pointed out that if they elected him they would have a member who was on the right side, one who was right close to the Government, who could keep his district right in the foreground and get his share of anything good that was going.

He abused the Opposition with great heartiness. But as to the real issues of the election, it was plain to the discerning that he knew nothing. As the great majority of those whom he addressed were as ignorant as he, it did not matter much.

His opponent was a gentleman who habitually chewed tobacco and used filthy language. He appealed to the electorate on the ground of being a plain man, a man without any frills, a man who knew what the people

needed and was out to get it for them. If they wanted
a feller to make them dirty grafters in Ottawa set up
an' take notice, he was their man. They couldn't put
anything over on him, no sir. He couldn't get up an' make
fine speeches, but he knew what he wanted an' what
the people wanted, an' there wasn't nobody could make
him back water once he got started. His collection of
dirty stories for private circulation was unsurpassed.

He had himself been acquitted on a charge of horse
stealing, but his opponent was suspected of being a
fraudulent bankrupt. Both were, therefore, equally
fitted for Parliament.

Both candidates called on Kent. He was of opinion
that they were both most awful cads, but that possibly
the Grit was the less putrid of the two.

Billy refused to be interested, not even troubling
to vote.

" They're all grafters together," he said, " the whole
damn works. It don't make no difference which a man
votes for, it won't do him nor the country no good. The
country's all right—it's a damn good country—only
it's run by crooks. An' the main, chief, principal trouble
around here is too damn many neighbours."

The campaign was a spirited one. The settlers liked
their politics hot and an election was a break in the
monotony of existence. Charges and counter-charges
of corruption were freely bandied about, and were not
at all difficult of substantiation.

Election cigars made their appearance. These required a technique of their own to smoke. A knitting
needle passed from one end to the other was necessary
to create a draught, and it was best to smoke them in the

open air. Even hardened smokers were overcome when several of them were going at once within doors.

Just before polling, whisky made a mysterious appearance. Cases were found cached in the bush, though the candidates themselves were sublimely unaware of their existence.

The whisky was on a par with the cigars. Some of the settlement's best drinkers dropped dead, to all appearance, at about the third drink. The survivors howled and fought about the poll for hours. As women did not vote in those days, absolutely nothing marred the festivities.

It was generally conceded to have been a very good election.

The Grit won, but it appeared later that men many years dead had risen from their graves to vote, and suspicious people brought the charge that the ballot boxes had been stuffed. Still, it was a very good election.

Preachers of various denominations made their appearance in the settlement. The women welcomed them, but the general attitude of the men was one of tolerant contempt. Services were held quite regularly in the schoolhouses.

Men drove their wives over, but stayed outside themselves to talk or pitch horseshoes.

The Kents attended service when an Anglican curate happened to pass that way. Neither of them was very religious, but the Church of England is the church of the upper classes and it is the correct thing to countenance it.

Billy refused to attend church. " When preachers commence to snoop around, that means the country's

all shot," he said. " I knowed this district was goin'
on the bum, but this proves it. It's gettin' around time
for me to move on."

" Why, Billy, I didn't know you was such a heathen,"
said Maggie. " You used to come to church back in
Wenderton with me."

" Uh-huh, I used to go with you," grinned Billy.
" Back in them days I'd go any place with you. But
I seen a lot of you since then, an' I ain't so anxious."

They had one of their differences of opinion, an
affair of hot words, shouts, tears, a swift reconciliation
and kisses. But Billy continued not to go to church.

A young and earnest minister came to interview him,
counting on Maggie's moral support.

" You get my woman," gibed Billy. " Don't want
me around too, do you ?"

The missioner looked shocked.

" Now, Billy, you talk nice to Mr. Burt," chided
Maggie.

" What did I say now ? " inquired Billy with inno-
cently raised eyebrows.

" I can't do a thing with him, Mr. Burt," said Maggie.
" You talk to him." She went into the house.

Billy's face became resigned. He looked at the square,
humourless, zealot face before him, and rubbed his
nose.

The missioner spoke with great earnestness for ten
minutes.

" I heard all that before," admitted Billy. " Lots
of times. My ma had them ideas, an' my old dad got
that way towards the end, when he was breakin' up.
He got pretty hard to live with before he died ; it took

all the fun out of him. I ain't old enough yet to go to worryin' about my soul."

" Don't you believe in God, Mr. Clovelly ? " said Burt sternly.

" I don't know what I believe. I guess there is a God : you got to blame this here world on somebody. But I never noticed Him watching over me. When any hard luck come my way I most always had to dig my way out from under by myself."

" It's a sin to say that."

" Your sayin' so don't make it so."

" You ought to pray to God to help you."

Billy turned on the man with a tightening of the jaw and a spark in his blue eyes.

" I ask help from nobody, mister. I take my luck as she comes an' tough her through. I been give some sour medicine in my day, too."

Burt was distressed. He was an honest and sincere young man, and his greatest desire was to save souls. But his training no less than his nature made it impossible for him to understand the aloof and solitary soul of the born pioneer.

He turned the conversation into other channels, hoping to find an opening in Billy's armour.

It was not long before Billy reiterated the remark now so often on his lips, that the trouble with the country was too many neighbours.

" But we are commanded to love our neighbour as ourself," was the reproof that rose irrepressibly to the preacher's lips.

" As how ? " said Billy. " That's the kind of fool talk what always gets my goat. Preachers is full of it,

I tell you, my family's got first call on me. Until my kids is fed, my neighbours can starve for all me. I'm a lone wolf an' them's my cubs. I don't ask no help of my neighbours. I'm civil to them if they're civil to me ; I want them to keep their nose out of my business an' I'll keep my nose out of theirs. I like a good neighbour about five or ten mile off, where there's room for both of us to turn around. It's gettin' so around here there's somebody breathin' in your neck all the time. A feller ain't got room to spit."

The missioner went away after assuring Billy that he would pray for him.

" Pray for yourself," retorted Billy. " I ain't payin' you nothin'."

CHAPTER XIX

THE odd-numbered sections, hitherto closed, were thrown open for homestead entry, and now indeed came the deluge. Some hundreds of Swedes, direct from the same district in Sweden, chose that particular district to settle in.

They came like a flight of locusts and devoured all the land. No homestead was too poor for them to take up ; some perched on barren sand-hills fit only for grazing, others upon islands in swamps where only muskrats would thrive. A few of them had money, but the wealthiest had not much. Many were almost destitute to begin with.

The spruce bluffs, already considerably thinned, were wiped out to provide building timber. The slough lands whereon the settlers had cut their hay were ploughed up by men the rest of whose land was under water. Fences sprang up everywhere and trails almost disappeared. There were, of course, the road allowances, but these had been laid out geometrically in straight lines that took no account of hills and swamps. Traffic was in danger of coming to a complete standstill.

For the first time men had to guard against thieves. Locks and bars had been unknown ; owners left their houses on the latch while they were away, lest any needy wayfarer should lack shelter ; private property stood by the roadside until its owner had need of it.

But now everything began to be stolen. Farm implements left out in the fields were taken apart in the night and carried away piecemeal. Billy lost his hay-rake that way and never saw it again.

One unfortunate bachelor left his shack to put in the winter in the logging camps. He returned in the spring to find only the walls and roof standing ; even the flooring, the door, and the windows had been stolen. He discovered some of his property in the possession of a Swede, and the man went to jail.

By no means all the stealing was done by the Swedes, though they got all the blame for it. They were aliens to begin with, and their coming had made an already hard struggle almost desperate.

Many of the wretched Swedes were literally starving. After they had trapped every remaining muskrat in the country, and all but exterminated the rabbits and other wild game, there was nothing left for them to eat.

They were an independent people, who would sooner starve than beg, but sooner steal than see their children starve. Who can blame them ? Their condition was made harder by their ignorance of the ways of the country and of its language.

In the face of this menace all the old settlers drew together, forgetting their private feuds. The influence of the cliques was greatly weakened, but the cleavage between the newcomers and the old-timers was wide and deep. They would even pass each other on the trail without speaking, hitherto a thing unheard of.

The Swedes did not all arrive in the same year, and among the last to come was one Ole Petersen, who filed on the quarter-section lying immediately south of Billy's. Over a hundred acres of it was under from three to twelve feet of water, the rest hay meadow.

Having cut hay there every year, Billy had come to consider the slough almost as his own property. He hated Ole Petersen as a man who had robbed him. He departed so far from the traditions of his upbringing as to refuse to speak to the man.

"No Sowegians in mine," he declared. "Bunch of damn thieves. If I had my way I'd shoot the whole works or run 'em out of the country. What the hell do they want to bring a bunch of lousy foreigners in here for ? There's five times too damn many people in here now. I don't have no truck with no Sowegian if he was dyin'."

He had already cut the hay on Petersen's place, and made haste to haul it away before the man could claim it.

He saw the house the Swede had built from a distance and sneered at it savagely. The poor devil had run up a wretched little shack of crooked poplar logs on a narrow peninsula, with water on three sides of it. Though it rose not ten feet above the level of the slough, it was the highest piece of land in the whole quarter-section.

The freeze-up came early that year, but a Chinook delayed Billy's departure for the freight trail. All the farm stock were out enjoying the warmth, and he was loafing in the house.

A loud cackling among the hens, some of whom had strayed over toward the poplar bluff behind the corral, made him jump up and take down his gun. He was always willing to exert himself mightily for a shot at a prowling coyote.

He raced out bareheaded, tore round the corral, and halted dead, for the tracks that led into the bluff were not those of a wolf but of a man.

"One of them damn Sowegians," he snarled. "Chicken stealin', eh? I'll fill his lousy hide so full of holes it won't hold water."

He swiftly mounted the tall hill behind the house. A man was going at a curious staggering run in a southerly direction. Over one shoulder he bore a sack which jerked grotesquely.

Billy dropped on one knee and got the broad of the man's back between the sights. Then he sighed and dropped the weapon.

"I'd ought to shoot him," he said. "But I'll get him yet. I'll put him behind the bars."

"What's the matter?" asked Maggie, as he burst into the house.

"Got that Petersen swine dead to rights," he exulted. "Just seen him run off with one of my chickens in a bag."

He struggled into his jacket, and caught up the gun again.

"You can't take that gun along," said Maggie, laying hold on it. "You might get mad an' shoot the feller. Leave it here an' go along."

"Well, he'd ought to be shot. But I won't shoot him; I'm just takin' it along to scare him."

"You leave it right here. If you can't handle that man with your two hands, you best leave him be an' call the police."

"Well, hell, have it your own way. Can't stand an' argy with you all day."

He left the weapon in her hands and ran out. He headed directly for the Petersen place, cutting across the frozen slough and approaching the shack under cover of the willows that lined the shore. He had gained a vantage point within a hundred yards of the shack by the time that Petersen, who had made a wide detour, came in sight in the opposite direction.

Keeping the shack between himself and his quarry Billy stooped and ran forward to confront the thief almost at his own door. The Swede stopped dead, an expression of utter despair in his staring blue eyes. He panted and his knees knocked together.

"You damned thief," roared Billy, and gripped him by the throat.

The man collapsed under his hand in a heap on the ground.

"Get up," growled Billy, and stooped to jerk him to his feet.

Petersen came up with scarcely an effort. He was literally skin and bone, and hung in Billy's muscular grasp like a rag. The bones of his face were clearly outlined under the stretched yellow skin, and his hollow eyes were dark-rimmed.

"Well?" demanded Billy, shaken out of his rage by the wretch's emaciation.

Petersen's lips moved, but the sounds he made were

so faint and broken that Billy could not catch their drift even when repeated.

"'Keets hunkry.' What in hell does that mean?" he demanded.

Petersen pointed mutely to the door of the shack. Picking up the sack, in which a surprised and indignant hen still kicked and squawked, Billy pushed his captive thitherward.

The place within was so low that Billy could not stand upright. One end was taken up with a bunk of poles and hay, overlaid with some tattered rags of bedding. At the other end stood a tiny sheet-iron stove and beside it a large packing box. A single pane of glass admitted a faint ray of light.

"Keets hunkry," repeated Petersen, pointing with a skinny finger at three emaciated children, barefoot and in rags, huddled on the dirt floor about the stove.

"Voman hunkry," said Petersen, and Billy saw a woman crouching in a dark corner. With a face as pale as death she offered a milkless breast to a wizened baby, who turned away from the dry nipple with a feeble wail.

Petersen comprehended the whole in a gesture and threw himself face downward on the bunk, his shoulders heaving with dry sobs.

Billy stood appalled. Never in his life had he seen such utter misery. Meaningless profanity bubbled from his lips. He fled from the shanty.

He burst into his own house, raving in a way that made Maggie fear for his sanity.

"Starvin' to death! Oh, God damn it, starvin' to death! Christ, right at our door—little kids—little

babies starvin' to death! Get me some grub—get
milk, for the love of Christ. Hustle—come on now—
bread, blast you. Don't stand gappin'. Damn you,
get a move on—can't you hear me?—they're starvin'
to death."

He began to upset everything in the shack in a mad
hunt for food.

When she understood what he was talking about,
she was not less eager than he. In a few minutes he
was running back with a can of milk in one hand and
a loaf of bread and some butter under his arm.

He found the family as he had left it, the man still
lying on the bunk and the rest huddled apathetically
about the stove. They had not even closed the door
he had left open in his flight, and the hen still kicked
in her sack.

They stared vacantly at him when he entered, but
said nothing.

He set his burden on the packing box and looked
about him. There was a battered kettle on the stove
and an empty pot on the floor by the children. There
were no other utensils. On a shelf were a few tin plates,
some spoons, and a tin mug. Of food the hovel held
no trace.

He caught up the mug while the family continued
to stare at him in ghastly silence, filled it half full of
milk, poured in some hot water from the kettle, and
offered it to the woman.

She tried to put it from her with a hand so thin it
was almost transparent.

"Come on, drink it," he said roughly. "Don't
keep the kids waitin'."

She drank meekly. He refilled the mug and held it to the lips of the youngest child on the floor.

The parents had evidently denied themselves for their children, for though piteously thin they had not the deathly pallor of their elders.

The child sipped the mixture doubtfully, then seized the mug with both hands and drank with such eagerness that the liquid trickled from the corners of its mouth. The other two set up a shrill clamour and held out their hands beseechingly.

As fast as he could fill the mug he gave it to them to drink. In a moment the milk can was empty, and still they clamoured for more.

" Got a knife ? " asked Billy, unwrapping the bread and making gestures.

No one answering him, he tore the bread to pieces, took out his knife, gave the tobacco-stained blade a thoughtful polish on his trousers, and proceeded to spread the hunks with butter. The starving children snatched them from his hand and retired behind the stove, gnawing at them like little wild animals.

Billy looked up to see slow tears stealing down the woman's cheeks.

" Oh, for God's sake, don't cry," he begged. " It's all right, everything's all right now. Here, take this."

He thrust a piece of bread and butter into her hand, and gave another to the man. They began to eat languidly, as if they had lost all desire for food. The man choked at the second mouthful, and fell back in a faint. After a few bites the woman let hers fall, and continued to weep silently.

At this moment, with Billy almost out of his wits with

pity and horror, there came the quick beat of a galloping
horse. Mrs. Kent hurried in. Maggie had run over
to tell her the news, and she had lost no time in hastening to the rescue.

Billy retired into the background with relief.

" You fix 'em up," he said. " I'm goin' all around
among the neighbours an' tell 'em what's doin'. This
is too big a job for one outfit to handle."

By the time the short winter day had ended, Mrs.
Petersen and her baby were in bed at the Kents' ; Billy
took Petersen, too weak to walk, home in his wagon,
and the three children were carried off by Martin
Olsen.

Consternation reigned in the district. They had
almost permitted a whole family to die of starvation
in their midst. The old settlement would jeer at them.
It was the first waking of the community spirit.

The Swedes indignantly denied that Petersen had
ever told them of his situation. Had not his stubborn
independence broken down at the sight of his children's
suffering, impelling him to wander forth in desperation
and steal the first edible thing that came to hand, all of
them would have perished before anyone was aware
of their fate.

Offers of assistance poured in from all sides. The
Swedes strove to prove the sincerity of their regret
by being among the foremost. Even the poorest of
them had something to offer.

A monster bee ran up a new shack beside the old
one, and stocked it with potatoes, meat, and groceries,
all voluntary gifts. A dozen teams hauled a huge pile
of firewood. The old shack was converted into a barn,

and one of Mrs. Kent's milk cows and a heifer given by Darke were stabled there.

Under Mrs. Kent's care, Mrs. Petersen and her baby both recovered, and the Clovellys fed Petersen back to a semblance of his former self. The children, as they had suffered least, made the quickest recovery.

About the time of Billy's return from his first trip of the season, the Petersens were inducted into their new home. It was in the nature of a public ceremony in which the whole countryside participated.

Kent made a short speech :—

" Good neighbours : We all feel, I think, that we have brought disgrace upon ourselves by allowing such a thing to happen among us. We have done what we could to repair that disgrace, and we feel that instead of Mr. Petersen being in our debt we are grateful for being allowed to show our—ah—sincere repentance for our past negligence. Life is not always easy for any of us in a new country. We need the neighbourly spirit, and I'm afraid that we have not always shown it of late. I think, I believe, that you will all agree with me in this. A thing like this ought to bring us all closer together, and make us sink our small personal differences for the good of the community in which we live, and make us neighbours not only in name but in fact. Let us henceforward be good neighbours. Am I right ? "

" You bet ! Hurray for Cloam district ! " bawled a man called Rush. The crowd echoed him.

Petersen tried to express his thanks and could not. Then he begged for the names of his individual benefactors in order that he might repay the debt, but this was refused him.

The crowd cheered the Petersens and also themselves. They shook hands with the family all round, and went home in an excellent temper. It was the beginning of a better understanding between the Swedes and their English-speaking neighbours.

CHAPTER XX

THAT was Billy's black year. Hitherto he had been lucky, as luck goes on the freight trail. He had never lost a horse. But on the forty-below-zero day, half-way between Beaver Island and Moose River, poor gallant Sam succumbed to some mysterious horse ailment and the Dead Horse trail had claimed another victim.

The tears froze on Billy's cheeks as he took the harness off his faithful servant and left his body to the coyotes. He had been on the return trip with a small load of fish, and he managed to struggle somehow into Beaver Island with Jimmy drawing the whole load by himself.

He had to go into debt to buy another horse, a sway-backed roan with a sulky disposition and a confirmed tendency to shy. He finished the winter poorer than he began it.

Spring came with a rush, though belated, and sent a river of polluted water running from the manure pile down the slope into the well. It had happened before, but it had happened once too often this time.

Billy cleaned the well out and thought no more of it. But the twins fell sick. They were the weakest of the six young Clovellys that now crowded the little house. After they had lain in a high fever for two days, Mrs. Kent heard of it from the worried Maggie.

She came at once and took in the situation at a glance.

"Typhoid," she said. "I knew it was going to happen sooner or later with that beastly well of yours. Clovelly, my man, go for the doctor at once—at once. Why wasn't I told of this sooner? Don't stand there staring, man—hurry."

Typhoid, "the fever," already a dreaded and epidemic scourge in that healthy land. In a country pre-eminently of pure water and pure air, five out of six of those who died were stricken down by consumption or by typhoid; polluted wells and overheated, unventilated houses the cause.

Billy had to drive all the way to Riverton to find a doctor, who demanded thirty dollars in advance before he would make the trip. Billy borrowed the money at the bank.

There was little the doctor could do when he arrived, nor could he stay to watch the patients. He left medicines and directions, the one of no more value than the other. Maggie nursed her children with the utmost devotion. Billy dug a new well beside the house and cleared away the huge manure pile.

Dot, the girl, recovered. Danny died.

Maggie wept unreservedly, but Billy was dry-eyed.

They buried the little wooden box in the cemetery beyond the schoolhouse, already beginning to fill with like victims. Burt conducted the funeral service, and tried to say a word of consolation to Billy afterwards.

"You ain't told me anything new," said Billy in a flat voice. "I can't do nothin' for the little feller no more : where he's gone he don't need me. I done my best for him while I had him, but now he's gone. Words don't mean anything to me. Talk to my woman—maybe she'll get some good of that stuff."

He never spoke of the lost Danny again, nor would he let Maggie speak of him. " Quit talkin'," he said. " If a woman could only learn to shut her damn mouth sometimes. Do you think I'll forget him as long as I live ? "

It was a bad spring ; too wet in the beginning and too dry afterwards. The grain germinated late and came up to be shrivelled by a blazing sun. Cutworms were also bad that year. The fields were a sight to make a farmer weep.

There was no grazing. The cattle, having starved all winter on straw piles, searched their cramped pastures hungrily for scant mouthfuls of grass. Even in mid-summer they were racks of bones.

There was no price for anything. Dressed beef brought three cents a pound, dressed pork five, butter and eggs were difficult to dispose of at any price. Wheat, oats, and potatoes had to be hauled forty, fifty, sixty miles to town and sold for what they would fetch. Only hay was high in price, but there was no hay.

The grain companies and the cattle buyers cheated the settlers systematically. The implement companies, the mortgage companies, the banks, reduced them to slavery and wrung out the last cent of interest, like drops of blood. The Government at Ottawa, engaged in the fascinating game of pitting Quebec against Ontario, and rewarding its heelers with jobs, sent out ringing appeals for more immigrants.

Kent and Billy discussed the situation : it was the one topic of discussion throughout the settlement in those black years.

" The only thing to do is to pull out," said Billy. " Go where there ain't so many people. All that's wrong is too many neighbours."

" You may be right, old man, but I'm going to stick on. What I'm going to do is cut down my herd. I haven't grazing enough for them in summer or hay enough for them in winter. The only thing I see for it is to keep fewer and better beasts and grow my own hay. I'm going to sell mine at once, before they cease to have any value at all."

" You'll go broke over it," opined Billy. " No money in pure-bred stock. They can't tough the climate."

" I don't intend them to tough it : I'll take good care of them."

" Then you'll go broke all the quicker."

" Well, I might as well go broke in a good cause. It seems I'm on the path to bankruptcy in any case."

" Huh, you ain't had to take the freight trail the last three seasons," said Billy enviously. " An' you ain't loaded down with debt an' kids like what I am."

" No, I've been luckier than you," said Kent generously. " But if my wheat doesn't pick up pretty soon I'll be with you again this coming season."

But the crop was not an utter failure. The yield was light, but the grade high. Kent stayed at home, but Billy took the trail with Jimmy and the sway-backed roan.

CHAPTER XXI

LIFE in the settlement, even in the black years, was by no means all hardship and misery. There were times when the people gathered and forgot hard times, hard work, and low prices ; when they ceased for some hours to worry about drought and early frosts and hungry weeds, about interest payments and taxes overdue.

An occasional summer picnic, and more numerous dances and concerts during the winter months, brought people from as far as twenty miles away, driving often through heavy blizzards or bitter cold.

A concert and dance was held at Cloam schoolhouse in late October. It was the first of its kind to be held in the immediate vicinity, and the Kents decided that in order not to seem snobbish they should go.

Maggie, an enthusiastic dancer before her marriage, hungered for a little relief from the unending round of milking, churning, baking, washing, mending, and feeding children, calves, pigs, and chickens. What to do with the children was a problem, but Ted Battle announced that he would throw open his store for the night to all women with children under ten.

Everybody came to the dance. Battle's store was filled with children of all ages whom their mothers were trying to get to sleep. Some of the older ones, utterly refusing to be left, had to be taken into the schoolhouse, where they fell asleep in uncomfortable positions and were occasionally trodden upon.

Everybody had come determined to have a good time, and therefore they had a very good time. Job Winkle was there with his fiddle and Pat Grogan with his—indefatigable men both. And old Dad Croup, silver-haired and silver-voiced, the best caller-off in the country, was floor manager.

The concert came first. Ted Battle obligingly lent his piano. It was a trifle out of tune, but it would still make a gratifyingly loud noise if hammered vigorously.

A young Englishman sang a London music-hall song, and was encored. Everything was encored, until there appeared the danger that the concert would last all night, and the people had come there chiefly to dance.

Ex-sergeant Darke obliged with " Rocked in the Cradle of the Deep."

" He's got a great bull roar on him, ain't he ? " was the delighted *sotto voce* comment in various parts of the hall.

Pierre Normandin, on being pressed for a French song, struck an attitude, threw out his chest, and delivered the Marseillaise like a challenge to the universe. Mrs. Kent played all the accompaniments, and gave them " Coming through the Rye."

It was decided to postpone further vocal music until supper. The fiddlers struck up for a square dance, and twelve couples took the floor, Billy and Maggie among them.

Dad Croup threw back his head, stood on one leg, and let an estatic quiver run down the other. " Balance all in the corners all," he chanted. " Join your hands and away to the West."

" Whoop ! " yelled the men. " Whee ? " And made their boot-heels rattle on the floor.

The figure proceeded, everyone dancing with tremendous vigour. Dad Croup was in his way a genius. He did not tie himself down to any set sequence, but allowed his imagination free play. As most of those present had danced frequently under his direction the result was in general very pleasing and harmonious.

" Allamen left. Shake them feet. Swing that gal. Ladies bow an' gents bow-wo. Ladies chain."

The men whooped like Indians and the women let out high squeals of delight.

" Hoe her down," yelled Billy, grinning like a wolf, in the very heart of things.

Dust rose in clouds ; the schoolhouse rocked to the thunder of heavy feet.

The essence of the square dance is movement : there was here no dreary wriggling and shuffling by close-locked couples in an area of a few square inches. These people covered ground. The men leaped into the air and clapped their heels together ; the women spun on their toes and went whirling down the line from partner to partner.

Mrs. Kent became restless in her chair ; her eyes began to shine and her feet to tap.

" These people are enjoying themselves," she said to her husband, sitting stolidly by her side, though with the usual solemnity of his expression giving way to amused wrinkles. "Tom, I'm going to try it. I'm going to ask Billy Clovelly to dance with me."

"Go ahead, old girl."

"But you've got to dance too—and shout. I'd love to hear you shout. You're such a solemn old duffer. Go and ask Mrs. Clovelly."

"Sure, Mrs. Kent, tickled to death," said Bill.

And Maggie dimpled as if she were nineteen again when Kent bowed and requested the pleasure of the next dance.

Mrs. Kent, still slender and light-footed, acquitted herself to admiration, responding swiftly to Dad's mellifluous accents.

Kent had rather to be hustled through. Dad adjured him to shake them feet, and reminded him that he was not nailed to the floor.

"You're doin' fine, Mr. Kent," said Maggie kindly.

"Shout, Tom," commanded his wife as she flitted by him on Billy's arm.

Kent let out a single deep whoop.

"Go to it, old-timer," yelped Billy, pirouetting on one leg. "Whoop her up. Whee!"

Flushed and out of breath, but bubbling with glee, Mrs. Kent returned to her seat. "Haven't enjoyed myself so much for years, Mr. Clovelly," she declared.

"By Jove, I'm having the time of my life too, Mrs. Clovelly," chuckled Kent. "I wonder if I can get a dance with that pretty girl in blue."

"Tom, I thought I'd cured you of flirting," flashed his wife.

"No, just lack of opportunity, my dear."

"That's Olga Gunderson," said Billy. "I'll give you a knock down to her, Tom."

Kent led up the Swedish beauty for the next set, and Mrs. Kent found a partner in the younger of the Collins brothers. Billy and Maggie had also secured partners.

The fun was now fully under way ; five sets, all the schoolhouse would accommodate, were in action at once. The noise was terrific.

But perhaps no one there enjoyed himself more than Pierre Normandin. He bounded about the room like a rubber ball, never understanding more than half of Dad's commands, and continually getting in somebody's way. He apologized right and left with sweeping bows and flashing eyes and smile.

Madame Normandin did not dance, but sat looking on with an occasional smile on her pale and immobile face. To her Pierre returned after every set with a bow ; and bowed, too, each time he left her to take part in another.

"Ah, zis is grrand," he beamed. "But me, I am ze bool calf in ze glass case, hahn ? Pouf, I brreak somesing effery time I turrn. *Mais allons, mes braves* ! Hoopla ! "

Dad Croup, to rest his voice, permitted a few waltzes and schottisches, though these were not very popular. Mrs. Kent waltzed better than any woman in the room, and found an excellent partner in young George Rathlau, a handsome Dane.

Though there was much noise, there was no rowdyism. Dad Croup was a strict disciplinarian and the spirit of the crowd was against it. The forms and conversation were not the forms and conversation of high society, but the spirit of courtesy and good breeding prevailed.

" Are you sweatin' much, Mamie ? " inquired the gallant Joe White of his fair partner, after a particularly strenuous set.

" Well, I should smile, Joe. Ain't a dry rag on me."

CHAPTER XXII

MIDNIGHT arrived. The baskets the women had brought with them were unpacked and supper eaten, the women seated on benches, the men on the floor. There was more singing and then the dancing began again.

Things began to drag a little. The older people grew sleepy, took short naps sitting up, and woke cramped and fretful. Mothers stole away to visit their offspring in the store and did not return. Only the young and vigorous kept the fun going.

Winkle and Grogan spelled each other off, their fiddles growing thin and squeaky. Dad's voice temporarily gave out and Billy relieved him with one set.

The formidable man, Sergeant Darke, was in the cloak-room with a few friends, smoking and indulging in grave conversation. He had brought his wife to the dance, but she sat rather forlornly in a corner, talking to Mrs. Kent in a low voice when that sprightly lady was not on the floor.

The sergeant eschewed the square dances as undignified, but moved stiffly through the waltzes with the air of a man worthily performing a painful duty. He was sitting nearest the outside door when there came a heavy bang upon it, and three late-comers entered.

He recognized two of them as bachelor neighbours,

Steve Daws and Joe Hayworth ; the third he did not
see clearly.

Steve thrust a bottle of whiskey under his nose.
" Just got back from town, old scout, an' hustled over
to get in the fun. Won't you smile a little ? "

" You'd better take that filthy stuff away," said Darke
severely. " We don't want any 'ooligans 'ere."

" ' Ark at the old perisher," cut in the third man.
" Callin' oil of paradise filthy stuff. Somebody ought
to sit on 'is 'ead."

The voice seemed to waken a train of memory in
Darke's mind. He rose and stared at the stranger,
a big slouching fellow with a dissipated face.

"Ah, I thought I knew that voice," he said. " I
'ad you under me on the square, didn't I ? In the
orkard squad, you was. You was a dirty insubordinate,
inefficient, drunken rookie, an' you made a dirty, inefficient, insubordinate, drunken soldier. Many a
time I crimed you, but at that I didn't crime you 'alf
as often as you deserved. An I can see you 'aven't
himproved, Sam 'Obbs—not as it was to be expected,
seein' what you was."

" Gor strike me blind ! " gibed Hobbs, staggering
back in simulated amazement and striking his forehead
after the traditional manner of the melodrama stage.
" It's 'im—it's old Tripey, me old friend, swag-bellied
Tripey, dear old Tripey Nigger Darke."

The formidable man flushed a red that verged on
purple.

" Look 'ere, me lad," he said in a restrained but
terrible tone, " we ain't in the Harmy now, an' I'm a
man of peace. But I won't be miscalled by any man

livin'. If you can't keep a civil tongue in your 'ead you'd better 'op it an' 'op it blinkin' quick."

" Don't you come none o' that on me, Tripey," snarled Hobbs, with drunken truculence. " You're bloody right we ain't in the Harmy. Don't yer try an' come the 'igh an' mighty wiv me, Tripey. I howes yer a bit—ah, above a bit—for all the times you crimed me. For a bleedin' 'a'penny I'd bash yer ugly face in."

" 'Op it," growled the sergeant, moving upon him. " 'Op it."

But Hobbs did not hop it; instead, he smote the formidable man a mighty wallop on the jaw. It was very poor policy. In the open, by superior agility, he might have done the slow-moving Hercules a great deal of harm, but in the narrow cloak-room he had little chance.

The music stopped dead within and the women gathered in a knot, listening to the wrangling and the drunken yells of Daws and Hayworth egging Hobbs on. The men were all jammed in the narrow doorway, anxious to get a glimpse of the fight.

Darke waded doggedly in under a shower of heavy blows until he had Hobbs pinned in a corner. Then he doubled his man up with a single push of his ponderous fist, and smashed him on the jaw with the other hand. Hobbs fell upon his face and lay quiet.

Without a word the sergeant turned. He gripped Hayworth by the collar, and tucked little Daws under one arm. The intruders had left the door open behind them.

He shook Hayworth dizzy, while maintaining a firm

hold upon the struggling, kicking, blaspheming Daws, and cast them both forth into the night. Then he dragged the limp Hobbs upright, pushed him to the door, and kicked him down the steps. He closed the door and put his back against it, panting a little from his exertions.

" I'm a peaceable man," he said, mopping his forehead vigorously with a large silk handkerchief. " But I can't stand 'oolligans—never could."

" Open the blank-blank door, you blank-blank-blank," from Daws without, accompanied by heavy kicks upon the panels.

" I've 'eard 'em carry on like that in the guard-'ouse," said the sergeant placidly. " Don't take no notice of 'im an' e'll soon stop."

He proved to be right. The kicks were not repeated and the belligerent voice died away. The men, feeling pleasantly excited, went in to reassure the women, Grogan struck up a jig, and the dance recommenced.

It came into the sergeant's head to go and visit his son, asleep in Battle's store. His whole being revolved about the child, and he could not be happy with the boy out of his sight.

With a word of excuse to the others he went out. A few minutes later a woman coming from the store stumbled over his unconscious body, and her screams brought the dancers tumbling out of the schoolhouse in a body.

They bore Darke in and laid him on a hastily gathered pile of coats on the floor. He was breathing stertorously and bleeding profusely from a wound at the back of his head. Search revealed a blood-stained stick of firewood with which he had evidently been treacherously struck down from behind.

Mrs. Darke flung herself upon his body with a despairing cry. Some of the women began to sob and others ran about aimlessly.

Mrs. Kent's clear high voice was heard giving directions.

" Somebody get me some water in a basin. Will you go over to the store, Mr. Clovelly, and get me some white sheeting, or anything suitable for a bandage ? Tell Mr. Battle to charge it to me. And somebody go for the new doctor in Mussel Creek. Harry," to her eldest son, " you'd better take your pony and go. And don't come back without him."

Mrs. Darke was removed to a chair. Assisted by the inscrutable Madame Normandin, whose calm no circumstance seemed able to disturb, Mrs. Kent set about rendering first aid to the injured man.

The men went off in search of the would-be murderer.

Steve Daws was discovered in the stable, lying under the feet of the horses, an empty bottle clasped lovingly to his heart. It took two pails of icy water and some punching to make him open his eyes. But he merely smiled vaguely, made some inarticulate remark, and fell asleep again.

Of Hayworth and Hobbs there was no sign. Horses were brought out and the men leaped upon their bare backs. Dawn was breaking and the dry grass underfoot was crisp with hoarfrost. As they rode forward in a long line in the direction of Hayworth's shack, a figure was sighted progressing in a series of staggering runs, punctuated by falls.

It was Hayworth, too drunk to know what he was doing, but proceeding homeward by a sort of instinct. Ridden down and surrounded, he rolled stupid eyes at them, made threatening gestures, and told them in a thick voice to leave him alone. They asked him where Hobbs was.

" He's drunk," said Hayworth solemnly. " I left him. He's drunk. Leave me go 'ome."

" We'll get nothing out of him in this state," said Kent. " Even if he knows, he probably won't tell. Scatter and look for Hobbs. He's most likely the man who did it. Collins and Haley, will you please take this man back to the schoolhouse and keep him under guard ? "

The score or so of riders spread out like a fan and moved on. Billy, on the extreme right of the line, saw a figure moving at a run from one thicket to another, and gave chase.

His shout brought the rest pounding after him. The fugitive gained a willow thicket and plunged into it. Billy dashed round to the other side and met him emerging, armed with a bludgeon.

" Keep off," shouted Hobbs, brandishing his weapon.

Billy's answer was to jerk hard on the rein, making his horse swerve violently. It was neatly done. Before Hobbs could swing his club, Billy had leapt from his horse upon his shoulders, and borne him heavily to the ground.

Hobbs fought with desperation. He was a powerful man, but his recent debauch had sapped his strength. They rolled over and over on the grass, but by the time the rest of the posse rode up Billy sat astride his captive, pinning his wrists to the ground.

Upon being allowed to rise, Hobb's first words were :
" 'Ave I killed the old blighter ? "

" He'll probably die," said Kent sternly.

Hobbs laughed recklessly. " 'Ope so, anyway," he
said with bravado.   " Serve 'im bloody well right."

After that he was stubbornly silent.

He was led back to the schoolhouse, where a crowd
of worried and fretful women, with no means of getting
home, since their husbands had gone off with the horses,
were trying to get breakfast for their hungry children.

Darke, still unconscious, lay in the darkened school-
room, under the care of Mrs. Kent and Madame Normandin, with his grief-stricken wife sitting in stony
despair beside him, clasping her weeping and terrified
boy in her arms.

Kent, in his capacity of justice of the peace, held
a little court and committed Hobbs and Hayworth
into custody.   Daws was still in a drunken stupor,
guarded by a couple of settlers.

The married men gradually harnessed up their horses
and went home, leaving the bachelors to guard the
prisoners.

Harry Kent, having spread the news through the
old settlement, whence word was dispatched to the
mounted-police post in Riverton, returned about noon
with the doctor.

The medico was hopeful. Concussion of the brain,
but a very good chance of recovery, he said. The
bachelors, who had deserted their prisoners to hear the
verdict, set up a cheer, and Mrs. Darke came out of her
dumb misery to weep.

Hobbs, who had somehow contrived to loosen his

bonds, chose this moment to make a dash for freedom. He caught a saddle pony and went away at a gallop. One of those badger holes that make riding on a prairie a doubtful pleasure was his nemesis. The pony went to its knees, and Hobbs landed on one shoulder and broke his collar bone. He was soon caught after that.

Darke was carried out and laid on some blankets in a wagon box, Madame Normandin and the doctor in attendance, and driven home. In twenty-four hours he regained consciousness, but his mind was a blank from the time he left the schoolhouse until he awoke in his own bed at home, considerably astonished to find himself there.

Hobbs came up for trial at the spring assizes in Riverton.

Billy was one of the star witnesses for the prosecution, and was consequently very severely handled by counsel for the defence. He was so badgered and bullied that he lost his temper and asked the pleader to step outside. Thereupon he was browbeaten by the judge, and in general confirmed in his belief that courts and lawyers were direct inventions of the Devil.

Hobbs received a two-year sentence; Hayworth was acquitted; Daws had not been held.

As the prisoner was led out of the dock, he pointed his finger at Billy. " I won't forget you, you bastard," he said.

CHAPTER XXIII

THE spring fever smote Billy that year with especial virulence. The vision of the Desirable Land was before him night and day. He babbled of far fields and lonely trails. The idea filled Maggie with terror. She had struck deep root; she was anchored to the homestead by a thousand associations, not least by the little green mound in Cloam cemetery.

It is not in women that the pioneer spirit stirs; the horizon does not beckon them; hills and rivers are to them a barrier, not an invitation to explore. It was men only who pressed on across the great plains; the women had little more to say in the matter than the horses who drew the wagons in which they sat. Where women had the deciding word no move was made.

It was not until the man had encountered an impassable barrier, or his vision of the Desirable Land had grown dim, that the woman descended from the wagon and proceeded to fulfil her destiny by turning a wilderness camp into a home.

Maggie had made her move when she was young, when marriage had made change inevitable, and she was willing to follow her man to the ends of the earth. But now she was prepared to fight to the last ditch to retain what with so much patient toil she had built up.

She and Billy had the first real difference of their married lives. She sat tight-lipped and frowning while he raved at her, cursing the country and all in it, and commanding her to rise up and follow him into an unpolluted land.

" Billy, you're crazy. I ain't goin', I ain't goin'. We wouldn't be no better off there. We'd have to start all over again among strangers. I had it hard enough here. Why, we're just beginnin' to get a start. You got the biggest crop in you ever had, an' the railroad commencin' to come out from Riverton."

She would not be turned.

The wrangle lasted until he turned and dashed out of the house into the night. But poetry had vanished out of the landscape. No loon spoke the magic word to him, for the loon does not love crowds. Billy found himself hemmed in by barbed-wire fences upon which he tore his clothes. The fences enclosed muddy ploughland that stuck to his feet, or pastures rutted deep with cattle paths. There were roads everywhere, deep in foul mire.

He returned home tired and savage, and did not speak to Maggie for three days. By that time the worst of the fever fit had passed, and she knew that he would be safe for another year. But she looked forward to the coming spring with dread. How long would she be able to hold him ?

Yet brighter days were already dawning for the settlement. The long-awaited railroad was at last pushing out from Riverton. The survey line ran just south of Cloam schoolhouse, not three miles from Kent's.

And Billy's complaint of too many neighbours was on the way to being remedied to some extent. Many who had homesteaded on utterly worthless land had given up the fight : sold up for taxes, dispossessed by mortgages, or simply disgusted. It had been proven that a man had to farm half a section or more to survive.

Kent was one of those who enlarged their holdings. He had long had the idea in mind of draining the collection of sloughs to the south of him. There was a whole section of land there, most of it under water, owned by four Swedes, of whom Ole Petersen was one.

Petersen had made a gallant fight, but he was glad to sell his title for five hundred dollars, as were each of his three neighbours.

In former days all the country round had been a paradise for beaver. Uncounted generations of them had dammed every tiniest trickle of water at intervals of a few hundred yards, until the whole territory had become a checkerboard of beaver ponds. The beaver were gone, but their work lived after them.

The first settlers had plenty of dry land, and were too busy to spend time draining swamps. Later a start was made here and there, and often only a short channel through some old dam was required to drain areas of many acres.

Kent went into debt for the first time, borrowing heavily from the bank at the iniquitous rate of eight per cent. With a gang of men and teams he cut a deep, wide channel through three big dams into Kent's creek.

By autumn wide stretches of swamp were mud, and he ran a fire through the forest of tall dry reeds left bare by the falling water. The spring snows melted and flowed along the drain instead of filling the swamp to the brim.

He had his recompense in the following season, which was wet.

A great deal of hay was drowned, and the soft ground would not hold up teams and mowers. Hay was scarce and high in price throughout the settlement.

Kent cut five hundred tons of hay on his reclaimed land and cleaned up his indebtedness to the bank at a stroke.

There was great activity in the infant village of Cloam. An elevator was going up, together with a creamery and several store buildings.

Road building was also taken seriously in hand ; hills were graded, bogs filled, and bridges erected. Now that the settlers would have a near-by market for their produce, a feeling of great optimism prevailed. Even Billy caught the infection, and began to entertain golden visions of being out of debt.

As he harnessed his team to the mower one sultry August afternoon and drove past his wheatfield toward the slough, where he intended to cut hay, he was in high spirits. The grain stood waist-high, a fine even stand with long heavy heads already touched with the red-gold of harvest. It was the finest crop he had ever had.

He busied himself doing complicated sums in mental arithmetic while the mower knife whirred through the tall grass. If he got so many bushels of wheat and

got so much for it, how much would that come to ?
Since both yield and price were uncertain, the problem
could be infinitely varied.

He looked up to notice a heavy black cloud rising
swiftly in the north-west. The thick, close atmosphere
stirred and a chilly wind swept by in moaning gusts.
Only a thunderstorm—or hail ? The chill in the wind
was ominous. Whatever it was, it was coming fast,
as swiftly as a galloping horse. He must make for shelter
if he did not desire a drenching.

He lifted the mower knife and turned homeward.
The black cloud covered half the sky. A moment, and
the face of the sun was veiled. A furious gust bent
the standing grain almost to the ground. A few big
raindrops splashed down. He urged the horses into
a trot.

There came a lull, but the storm was only gathering
its forces. The great question was whether he was
directly in its path, for these storms commonly only
sweep a narrow area.

He was still half a mile from home when the blast
struck him. The wind rushed out of the dark sky like
a charge of cavalry. He was struck a sharp blow on
the head. Little white balls hopped along the ground
and bounced off the back of the horses, who plunged
and snorted. It was hail, then.

The gust passed. Billy swiftly unhooked the traces.
The horses set off for the stable at a fast trot, and he
tore along behind them with the reins wrapped about
his wrists.

The hail came down again in earnest. His head and
back smarted and stung. The team broke into a gallop,

and he followed in great bounds.   The air filled with
a deep drumming : the hailstones were playing a quick-
step on the sun-baked earth.

A dazzling, blue-white streak of flame smote the
ground before them.   Up went the horses on their
hind legs. A paralyzing thunderclap brought them
down again. They bolted. Billy was jerked off his
feet and flung on his face. He was dragged twenty feet
before the reins unwound from his wrists.

The merciless flagellation of the hail drove him to
his feet, and he staggered the few remaining yards to
his door, which the anxious Maggie flung open for
him.

His face had been cut in his fall and the blood from
the wound mingled with the mud with which his face
was plastered. His back felt as if he had been beaten
with rods.

" I'm near killed," he groaned.   " What happened
the horses ? "

" I seen 'em run in the barn, Daddy," piped Billy,
Junior.

" Well, the crop's all shot to hell," said Billy grimly,
watching from the window the hail knock the grain
flat, and with insensate malice break the straw into
fragments a few inches in length, an utterly irreclaim-
able ruin.

The storm was over in half an hour, but it would
not have mattered had it continued all night. The only
thing to be done with the wheatfield was to plough it
under at once, lest the cattle get into it and kill themselves with overeating.

The sun came out again ; everything was fresh and

cool and fragrant, though the ground was littered with broken branches and the grass wore a trampled look.

When he had assured himself that his own case was past help, Billy walked over to see how Kent had fared. His neighbour was soberly surveying his own ruined fields.

" Well, ain't it hell ? " burst out Billy. " What do you know about a country like this ? Ain't a man a fool to stay here a minute longer 'n he can help ? "

Kent cocked a quizzical eyebrow at him. " Well, old man," he murmured, " we won't need to pay a thresh-ing bill this year, anyhow."

" Oh, you be damned, Tom ; you ain't goin' to make me laugh this trip. I'm sore all the way through. Why, I won't even have seed for next spring."

Kent winced, for his own carefully tended plot of ground, in which he had been trying experiments with different varieties of wheat, had been more completely wiped out than any other portion of his crop.

By one of those exasperating tricks fate plays, they had been the heaviest sufferers by the storm. It had worked its worst havoc along a path less than a mile in width and only a few miles in length. Outside that area there had been very heavy rain only.

The farmer is the world's most hopeless gambler.

Kent had suffered a heavy loss in the destruction of his crop, but he had forty head of good fat steers to dispose of and some pedigreed heifers. His experi-ment in cattle breeding had proven profitable.

It was far otherwise with Billy. Since he had

obtained title to his homestead he had been able
to borrow money at the bank, and, like most of his
neighbours, he lived merely from one crop to the
next. The bank skimmed all the cream of his efforts.
But this fall he could not even meet the interest on
his loan.

Once more he made up his mind to sell out and leave
the country. His temper was so savage that even Maggie
was daunted. Her hope was that he would talk himself
out, while she opposed to his proposals the force of
inertia.

He found many places to choose from. There was,
for instance, British Columbia, where a man could make
a magnificent living off a few acres of fruit-trees. Or
Washington or Oregon. Or there was California with
its orange groves, where it never got cold and a man
could make a fat and easy living almost without working.
He even got hold of some vague information about far-
away New Zealand, a pleasant land and a fertile, where
a man might make a fortune out of sheep ranching in
few years.

" You don't have to work your damned head off in
them places," he explained to Maggie. " You get something for what you do. Not like here."

" If there was any place in the world where people
could live without workin'," she replied shrewdly,
" everybody'd be there. I don't believe you can live
any place without workin' just about as hard as what
we do here."

" That's because you never seen nothin'," he retorted.

She sniffed.

"That's just like you," he shouted. "I can't get a notion but what you turn your nose up at it. I certainly crabbed myself right when I got married. I ain't knowed a happy moment from that day to this. A man'd a heap better be in jail than the way I am. I can't say a word about here, you're that cranky. Jump right on to me the moment I open my mouth. But I'm gettin' to blazes out of here, I warn you that, one of these here days. Maybe when you least expect it. Huh, well I guess."

Maggie was alarmed, but maintained a wise silence. She had no doubt that she could defeat him in a pitched battle, but she feared that after one or two such defeats he would one day leave her in pursuit of his mirage.

She was determined to keep him and to keep him at home.

She made private inquiries and learned that he could not legally sell the farm without her permission. This was a weapon in her hand. The cattle had always been recognized as hers, as the horses were his. The status of the pigs was undefined, but the chickens were hers by prescriptive right.

Her position was impregnable enough in one respect, but she knew enough of Billy not to clank his chains. She kept her information to herself, for production only in case of extreme need.

Billy was absent-minded. He had just heard of the Peace River district in Northern Alberta. Here was a land where a man might pasture his cattle over ten thousand acres and neighbours were not. The land was so far out on the edges of civilization that it must be many years before railways could ruin it.

He did not speak to Maggie about it. He was beginning to feel that she was his enemy, his jailor, and he looked upon her with a suspicious eye.

The pair manoeuvred all through that autumn in one of those matrimonial campaigns that have to be fought out to the bitter end in most cases, and in which the woman is always the loser, even when she wins.

CHAPTER XXIV

KENT brought over a letter one October day. The envelope bore the name and address of a law firm in Manitoba.

" Wonder what the deuce this is," said Billy. " Don't owe nobody down there no money."

After he and Maggie had stared at it and felt it and held it up to the light to see what was inside, an inspiration came to them and they opened it.

" Here, you read it, Lucy," said Billy, handing the letter to his daughter.

There were words in it that even the educated Lucy could only vaguely comprehend, but amid much excited talk they arrived at a fairly clear idea of its contents.

" Well, I be hogtied," said Billy. " Why, that's my old uncle Billy, him I was named after. Derned if I didn't near forget I ever had a uncle. An' the poor old lad's dead, an' died—what did you say he was, Lucy ? "

" Intetsate—no, it's intestate, Daddy."

" Well, whatever that is. Guess it means he left all his property to be equally divided among his relations. Tosh, them lawyers sometimes says a lot in a few words —but mostly they seems to use a lot of words an' say nothin' at all. Anyway, that's what it seems to amount to, eh, Lucy ? "

" I guess so, Daddy. It says he left no will."

" That's so, too. Well, then, how the devil could he be insestate ? You never can tell what them lawyer crooks is talkin' about. It don't matter much anyway, just so long as there's a chunk of property comin' to us. Wonder how much it'll be. It don't say, does it Lucy ? "

" No, it says the estate will have to be wound up first."

" Wound up, yes. I guess when them law sharks gets through winding it up it'll be wound so tight nobody'll get nothin' out of it. I guess we're stung, all right. I got as much use for a lawyer as I have for a preacher, an' both of 'em'd steal the feedin' bottle from a blind baby. Well, I'll take the letter over to Tom Kent an' see what he says, but I don't guess we'll get much out of it."

He returned from Kent's in a much more cheerful temper.

" Well, Tom thinks we will get something. Anyway, he's goin' to fix it up for me. I can trust him, an' I guess he's pretty wise to lawyers. Maybe we will get some money after all."

Now came the fascinating game of deciding how the money was to be spent when it came. As to how much it would be, Billy had only the vaguest notion. His uncle had been reputed a highly prosperous farmer, and his only relatives, so far as Billy knew, were the children of his only brother, Billy's deceased father. Billy thought he had seven or eight brothers

and sister living, for his mother had recently died
and severed the only link that bound the scattered
family together.

However, this left all the more to the imagination,
and added zest to the game. The legacy might be anything from a few hundreds to a few thousands. Billy
declared for the thousands, Maggie, more cautious,
for the hundreds. Her pessimism so infuriated Billy
that she kept her opinion to herself.

In fancy, he rebuilt the house from the ground up
with great magnificence ; he purchased vast domains
and stocked them with herds of pure-bred cattle. He
would maintain a regiment of fine horses, an army of
hired men, and a threshing machine of his own. Maggie
and the girls would have fur coats and new dresses,
and he would start each of the boys out on a fine farm
of his own.

Every evening he had a fresh inspiration and modi-
fied the original plan.

Automobiles were beginning to make their appearance on the newly graded roads, frightening sober horses
into convulsions, and causing their drivers to threaten
dark deeds with shotguns.

Billy, having denounced the things with furious
bitterness, suddenly changed his mind and announced
that one of his first purchases would be a big car.

Maggie sat silent through these glowing anticipa-
tions. She was content if even a part of them came
true : Billy no longer pined for fresh fields. But Lucy
was a true child of her father, and outran him in
imaginativeness. Whenever his fancy flagged, she was
ready with a brilliant new suggestion.

They had plenty of time to decide what they would do. The law moved with its usual deliberation. All old William Clovelly's surviving relatives, scattered through the length and breadth of the prairie provinces, had to be found and their relationship verified. There were reams of correspondence, and acres of documents to be signed and attested.

Meanwhile there was no money. Creditors had to be staved off somehow, and the family had to live. The bank manager did not view with enthusiasm Billy's application for a large loan in view of his expectations. With chilly insistence he asked for repayment of the loan already overdue.

There was nothing for it but the freight trail. Billy did manage to go in debt for another horse and, with Berry, made up three teams between them. He consorted once more with John Crawford, who had two sons with him that season. He renewed his acquaintance with the genial Willy Croker, who still kept a stopping place. He had more long-drawn-out wrangles with the Scotch factor at Moose Lake, whose temper had not improved with age.

He had the most successful season of his career, for the rate had been raised, the road considerably improved, and the winter was a mild one.

It was not until he returned home from his final trip that he found the money had arrived and was waiting in the bank.

Nine hundred and forty-three dollars and thirty-nine cents. It was more than Maggie had anticipated, but far less than he had confidently expected. Uncle

Billy, like rich relations in general, proved a disappointment.

But there was, after all, nine hundred and forty-three, thirty-nine, and the question of its expenditure had yet to be decided.

Maggie said inflexibly that it was to be used to pay their debts. Billy turned from the idea with a shudder of horror. Lucy sided with him. The smaller children did not actively participate in the great battle, though their sympathies were with Billy. He was not a good father, but he fascinated all his children.

Maggie, though she knew the odds against her to a nicety, was not in the least daunted. She had no doubt that she would win, however hard the battle might be.

Billy, with the uneasy consciousness that she usually had her own way in the end, opened hostilities aggressively. They were all sitting round the stove that evening, while dying March flung defiant snowflakes in the face of approaching spring.

" Well, anyway, I'm goin' to get a new team of horses out of this. Old Oscar Swenkison has a dandy team of greys, go fifteen hundred apiece, just goin' on five. He's willin' to sell 'em for five hundred cash. You couldn't get a better team in the country at the price."

Maggie, sitting with folded arms, pursed up her lips and shook her head.

" Well, why not ? " demanded Billy noisily. " Ain't it my money ? Didn't it come from my Uncle Billy ? He ain't your uncle. You can't lay no claim to this money. I guess not. It's my money, an' I guess I can do what I like with it."

Maggie scratched her bare elbows and said nothing. It was always a good plan to let Billy exhaust himself before she launched her counter-attack.

" That's just it," said Billy, raising his voice and working himself into a fine appreciation of the many injuries he had suffered at her hands. " That's just it. You want it all—I don't get nothin', not a smell. I can go out an' work myself to death. I can get hailed out an' nobody cares. I can get froze to death on the freight trail an' nobody cares.

" Long as I hand over every cent I make it's all right; that's what I'm for, I guess. I got no rights around here. No, but when I want something for myself— any little thing at all—then there's all hell to pay. It ain't that I look for very much—just a little consideration for my feelin's once in a while. But do I get it, eh ? Ever anybody seen me get it ? Huh, I guess not, I guess not. All I get is the dirty end of the stick. Every time."

He paused, out of breath. Lucy shot a reproachful glance at her mother and squeezed his arm. Maggie continued to scratch her elbows and say nothing.

" Well, don't set there like a lump of mud on a hoe," cried Billy. " Say what you want. Don't mind me ; I don't count around here. It ain't what I say goes. All the use I am around here is to keep this gang. An' then I can go to the devil for all anybody cares."

" I was thinkin'," said Maggie in calm tones. " The way it looks to me, it would be best to pay off

our debts an' start square again. We been in debt
so long I'm fed up. All we make goes in interest and
taxes. Now, if you was to pay off Ted Battle the two
hundred dollars we owe him, an' hand the rest to the
bank, we wouldn't only owe about a hundred dollars."

"Yes, that's just like you—that's just about what
I thought you'd say," retorted Billy furiously. "We're
not going to get no good out of this money—just the
bank. The bank never done nothin' for us, damn 'em,
but you're quite willin' they should get it all. If
I thought I could get any sense in your head with
a axe . . ."

"Well, but they got to be paid sometime, ain't they?"
she countered.

"Aw, you make me sick. Course they got to be paid
sometime, but we don't need to hand 'em over every
cent of our money the minute we get it. Why, don't
you understand that money's my capital? That's what's
been the matter with us right along—we ain't had no
capital. Now we got some capital we want to hang on
to it, not hand it over right away an' be in just the same
fix as we was before."

But Maggie was not concerned to refute economic
fallacies.

"What of it?" she rejoined with spirit. "I'd sooner
be out of debt, even if I didn't have no capital, than have
capital an' be the way we are now. What I say is, let's
get the debts paid. If I can't have capital without
paying my debts, well then, I don't want capital, that's
all."

Billy threw up his hands. "What's the use of tryin'
to argue with a woman? Can't I make you see nothin'

at all ? All you can talk about is them debts—you give
me a pain. Here am I tryin' to explain to you about
capital, an' all you can do is blat about them old debts,
like a sick calf."

" I don't need to know nothin' about capital," she
answered doggedly. " All I know is we're in debt,
an' we always been in debt, an' I'm fed up with it."

" Well, but, for the love of Pete, can't you see if we
blow in all our capital just when we got it we're goin' to
be back just where we was ? If a man can't keep his
capital, how can he ever get ahead ? "

This argument seemed to have a peculiar effect on
Maggie.

" Well, suppose you're right," she said, almost meekly,
" what do you figure to do with the money ? "

It was not often Billy had won so easy a victory.
She had yielded to his superior intellect and he felt that
he could afford to be magnanimous.

" Well, is there anything you'd partic'ly want ? " he
inquired graciously.

" Well, there sure is," she replied with animation.
" For instance, ain't we been livin' in this here old
shack about long enough ? You don't suppose it's any
fun for me with nothin' handy. You don't remember
how many years it was since you promised you'd build
me a good house. No, but I do. Another thing, d'you
know how long it is since I had any clothes fit to wear ?
An' look at them kids, all rags. An' all their shoes near
wore out. An' Lucy ain't got a decent dress to her name.
Do you think maybe I couldn't do with a sewing machine,
an' a new churn—the old dasher'd kill a horse,—an' a
washin' machine, an' some new furniture,—not old

packin' boxes an' such,—an' some blankets, an' maybe a carpet on the floor, an'——"

"Here, here, here, stop. Let up. Have you went crazy?" bawled Billy.

"No, why? You asked me if there was anything I wanted, an' I started in to commence to tell you. An' I no more'n get started, neither, when you commence hollerin'."

"No more'n get started, eh? See here, woman, don't you know it'd take about a million dollars to get all the things you said? An' what about our debts? You figurin' on blowin' in all that money, an' not leavin' a nickel to pay on what we owe—is that it?"

"Never mind them old debts," she retorted recklessly. "We always been in debt, ain't we? Well, then, it won't hurt to let 'em run a little longer. Let's have a little fun out of life, anyway."

"You're talkin' like a fool," said Billy severely. "Nice fix we'd be in if we didn't pay our debts. We always have paid our debts, an' we're goin' to keep on that way as long as I have anything to say around here."

"Don't care if I am a fool," said the shameless Maggie. "All I want now is just to get spendin' some of that money, an' havin' a few things I need."

"Well, that's all right, we got to get some things; but we can't blow all the money that way. It just shows how unreasonable you are : first you want to hand it all over to the bank, an' now you want to run crazy an' shoot it all in. Here's me been tryin' an' tryin' to explain to you about capital, but it don't seem I can make you savvy a single thing."

"What's the use of havin' money if you don't have no good of it?" she queried. "You answer me that, Billy Clovelly."

They wrangled fiercely for an hour. As the argument proceeded, Billy found himself confronted by only two choices: either he must pay his debts, or hand the whole sum over to Maggie, to be spent, as she frankly avowed, in luxuries.

Her shameless and growing rapacity forced him finally to refuse all further argument.

"No sir," he said firmly. "I've listened to you all I'm goin' to. It's my money, an' I'm goin' to have the say how it'll be spent. That money's goin' to pay our debts an' put us square. It'll give us a new start. I'm goin' down in the mornin' an' pay Ted up, an' then right over to the bank an' give 'em the rest. See. I got something to say around here even if you don't think so."

"Well, but ain't I goin' to have something out of it?" she persisted. "I got some rights, too, ain't I? I guess I do a little bit of work around here as well as you."

"Well, I tell you, I'll give you fifty dollars, just to shut your mouth."

"It ain't enough. Why do you need to pay them old debts? An' besides, I want——"

"That's enough, that's enough," interrupted Billy with finality. "Fifty dollars or nothin', I said. What'll it be?"

"Oh, well, I guess I'll take the fifty dollars."

"All right, that's settled. Lucky there's somebody around this joint with a little common-sense. But for me you'd had all that money blowed in an' nothin' to show for it. Now, let's get to bed; it's late an' I'm sleepy. It takes a devil of a time to make you see reason some days."

Not until Billy was snoring peacefully by her side did Maggie permit herself a quiet smile.

CHAPTER XXV

People began to realize that their children were growing up. The children of the original settlers were all about of an age, and they all burst into flower, as it were, simultaneously.

Lucy Clovelly had been merely a schoolgirl, long, thin, and awkward, full of small chatter about her teacher and her playmates. She was a useful help to her hard-worked mother, but she was still a child in Billy's eyes until the evening of a certain dance in Cloam, where a dance-hall had just been erected.

It was held in June, during the short lull between seeding and haying. All the young people of the settlement were to be there, and it was to be Lucy's first dance—her coming out, as it were.

Mrs. Kent had designed an inexpensive frock for her, and round her slender throat she wore a thin gold chain and locket. The skirt was at least two inches longer than anything she had hitherto worn, and the bodice at least an inch lower. Also her wavy brown hair was piled high on her small head.

Billy stared at her on her appearance in the kitchen. He was not certain whether he ought to be pleased or annoyed. But she was his favourite : she had to go very far amiss to do wrong in his eyes.

" Figure you're a old woman, don't you ? " he taunted.

She tossed her head at him. " No, I'm not old ;
but don't you think I look pretty nice now, Daddy—
don't you ? "

" All dolled up like a clown at a circus."

She pouted, and he made haste to recant.

" Why sure, kid, you look dandy. Bet there won't
be a girl at the dance to touch you."

They drove to the dance together. Maggie said she
was getting too old for dances.

" Huh, I ain't," he said. " I can step it with any
of 'em."

But when he got there he was less sure of himself.
It was a dance in the new fashion. The change had
been going on gradually, but as he had attended few
dances he had not noticed it.

The tango was new in those days and had not reached
so far. Jazz as yet was not, and the fox-trot was to
come. But their immediate predecessors were in full
bloom. There was only one solitary old-fashioned
quadrille danced that night ; the rest were waltzes,
schottisches, and the passé but still popular polka.
Billy could not dance a step of any of them, and sulked
most of the evening in a corner.

But Lucy—she had been taking private dancing
lessons from Mrs. Kent—Lucy was on the floor the
whole time. Billy watched her with surprise, in a joy
tinged with sadness. This bright-eyed, laughing girl
in a pretty frock was graceful, she had charm, she had
soft immature curves where she had been all angles.

Other people also noticed her for the first time.

The elder Kents were not present, but Harry and
Ted Kent had come. Harry looked very like his father

—heavy, slow-moving, quiet, but inexorable. He had
been his father's right-hand man for five years now,
and had been admitted a partner in the Cloam Stock
Farms on his twenty-first birthday.

Ted was also to be admitted to partnership on his
majority, but he showed no enthusiasm for the idea.
His mind was of a mechanical bent, and he was happiest
driving a car or tinkering with the Kent dynamo, recently installed. All the machinery on the place was
under his charge. He took after his mother in appearance—slender and active.

He had always been excellent friends with Lucy:
he had patronized and showed off before her. It came
to him as something of a shock that she was pretty.
She inspired him with a new emotion, a peculiar and
strained feeling in the throat, and a vague sensation
of flushed temples. He could not have defined his state
of mind except as a general uneasiness, an indefinite
foreboding. He approached.

She was cruel. She rejoiced in her new importance.
She realized for the first time that she was precious
and desirable. There was a new look in the eyes men
turned upon her, a look that gave her a thrill of dreadful
joy.

And she knew at once whom she could hurt most.
This knowledge was part of her very being: no one
had taught her. She could feel Ted's soul quiver under
her soft finger-tips: she swung her hips and smiled
at him—and turned her back to talk to someone else.

She refused him the dance he begged—and brought
him out of a fit of furious sulks in a corner by asking
him to eat supper with her. She told him how much

she admired Billy Faulkner, who was his very antithesis, but refused Billy's request for a dance on Ted's plea.

She enjoyed herself. She attracted wantonly young Walter Brownell, and played him off against Ted Kent. Finally, she drove home with her father, resisting the pressing invitations of both her admirers, flushed with triumph and bubbling over with delight.

But Billy was filled with a gloom that endured for days. He was not yet forty, but he had been distinctly of the older generation. The youngsters held the floor and led the revels. They seemed to speak almost a different language and had different views. They enjoyed themselves, but not with the unrestraint of older days : there was a complicated etiquette to be followed which he found unfathomable.

And yet there was no doubt that he was nearly forty. He had been sitting still all these years. He was no nearer the Desirable Land. Life was passing and his task was unfulfilled, almost unattempted. He had halted too early on his westward march.

He was in better financial condition than he had ever been. He was not prosperous, but there were few indeed in the settlement as free of debt. But he was not content. He began dimly to realize that he would never be content, that not even the wastes of space beyond the Pleiades would glut his desire for the unknown and far-off.

Into this deep unrest of spirit came the war, almost casually. To the native-born farmer of the Canadian West it was a happening like the Russo-Japanese War, or the more recent Balkan wars.

" None of our business," said Billy. " Them fellers over there is always fightin'. Don't seem to have nothin' else to do. Don't know why the Old Country wants to get into it for. 'Tain't like the Boer War ; that was in British territory. I come dern near goin' to that myself. This is in Europe—them Peasoups an' Dutchmen an' such woolin' each other around."

" The Kent boys is goin'," said Maggie. " An' Jack Martin an' Phil Openshaw—all the young Old Countrymen."

" Oh, they're fed up with bachin', that's all," said Billy. " All they want is a free trip home to see their folks. The war'll be over long before they get there. If I was young an' single, don't know but what I'd sign up myself. Just for the fun of the thing."

Ted Kent met Lucy Clovelly driving the cows home one evening. It was with design on his part. They stood facing each other on that warm August evening, with only a few lazy-eyed cows to watch them.

" I'm goin'," said Ted.

" Where to ? " she inquired, with widely innocent eyes.

" Why, to enlist," he answered, the harmless pomp stricken out of him suddenly.

" Oh, well, you won't be away long," she said cheerfully. " You won't see any fightin'. Daddy says the war'll be over before you get there."

" Oh, yes, I suppose so," he said glumly. " But still —well—will you write to me ? "

The idea was attractive, but a request too easily granted falls flat.

" If you write to me first, I might," she conceded.

" Oh, well, all right."

He desired to be sentimental, but she was too cool.
He had intended to ask her for a kiss, to have an affecting
farewell. An unwonted bashfulness tied his tongue.

" I'll write to you," he said. " And mind you write
back."

" All right. I guess I got to get home now; it's
past milkin' time."

" Well, good-bye, Lucy."

" So long, Ted."

He halted on the ridge. Presently she looked back
and waved a careless hand. His flung up in answer.

He and his brother left Cloam on the morning train.
Mrs. Kent saw them off with a strained smile : her
tears were for the privacy of her home. Kent was restless,
but he was now fifty, and someone had to stay and look
after the farm.

Pierre Normandin came to see them a few days later.
" I am conscrip'," he said. " To-morrow I go. You
will see Madame sometime, no ? "

" I will do anything I can for her, Mr. Normandin,"
said Mrs. Kent warmly. " It's too bad you must go."

" It is for France," he answered simply.

Madame remained on the farm to tend the pigs, out-
wardly calm as usual.

The formidable man snuffed the battle from afar
like an old war-horse, but he returned from Riverton
bowed with the weight of shame and sudden years.

" They wouldn't 'ave me," he said, with tears in his
eyes. " They wouldn't 'ave me. The M.O. said I
was too old—said I 'ad flat feet, me that can march
as well as ever I did—ah, a sight better than lots of
young chaps. I'm fifty-five, but put me in front of one

of them low, dirty, sausage-eatin' Germans with a bay'nit an' see. An' the M.O. said I was near blind of an eye. I know my sight ain't what it was, but I don't sight with my left eye, do I ? An' I can see to use a bay'nit with the best."

News came at intervals in carefully censored letters, from Valcartier, from Salisbury Plain, and, after a long period of silence, from " Somewhere in France."

The craving for news was universal. Life came to revolve about the telegraph office and the newspapers. A letter from the front was to be treasured. Lucy treasured Ted's and wrote long replies.

Ted had been wounded at First Ypres—shrapnel, a mere scratch, but it would give him the coveted wound stripe on his sleeve.

An official letter for Madame Normandin. Mrs. Kent, dreading its contents, took it to her in person. Madame was feeding her pigs. She wiped her hands on her apron and took the envelope with fingers that scarcely trembled.

A long silence. The letter slipped from Madame's fingers and fluttered to the ground. Madame stood quite still with a face like stone.

With a steady step she entered her house, and cast herself on her knees before her crucifix. Mrs. Kent lingered, but Madame made her a slight gesture. She would be alone with her grief and her God. In grave doubt, Mrs. Kent left her.

The Frenchwoman was early to see her on the following morning. No face could be paler than hers habitually was, but Mrs. Kent trembled at her eyes. She spoke to her one friend in the land of her exile in the language of her own country, that country for which she had never ceased to long.

"Pierre is gone," she said. "There was no one like him. I am alone. I am only sorry I cannot die too, but that does not appear the will of the good God. I shall sell my farm and return to France."

She went. It was undoubtedly the best thing for her. She sold her pigs for a good price, for all food prices were rising steadily. Kent bought her land.

She maintained her inscrutability to the last moment. It was not until the time came to say good-bye that she embraced Mrs. Kent, kissed her on both cheeks, and wept. Mrs. Kent wept too, though she was not a woman addicted to tears. They were never to meet again, for Madame died during the influenza epidemic of 1918.

The war laid hands on Billy. He passed from indifference to interest, from scepticism to credulity. He came to believe implicitly every piece of propaganda that came his way. It seemed to him the blood of the whole German race would not atone for all its crimes.

But that was not until his own youngest brother had been killed overseas.

In the last year of the war, Maggie only kept him from enlisting with the greatest difficulty.

But the war brought him greater prosperity than he had ever known. Kent, deprived of his sons, had to have assistance. Hired men worth anything were scarce and grew scarcer, but the call for foodstuffs was incessant and anxious.

Both men worked very hard during those years. Billy was able to clear himself of all debt and to improve his house and barns, all by now falling into decay.

Mrs. Kent's only brother was killed on the Somme. One of Kent's died of wounds in Mesopotamia.

The winters brought a respite in the hideous casualty lists. But now Ted was reported missing. He had taken part in a trench raid, and had not returned.

" I won't believe he's gone until I know," said Mrs. Kent.

Kent aged visibly under the blow. Ted was his favourite, as Harry was his mother's.

Lucy became disconsolate and inclined to look upon herself as a woman whose life's happiness had been taken from her in advance. There was a certain amount of sentimentality in this, but the wound went deeper than perhaps she knew.

CHAPTER XXVI

" I HEAR that Sam Hobbs is back," said Billy.

He and Kent were repairing a fence where the big prize bull had broken through.

Kent merely grunted. He had become very silent since the news of Ted's disappearance.

" Remember Sam ? " asked Billy, determined to make him talk.

" The man who clubbed Darke ? "

" Uh-huh. He went overseas when he got out of the coop. No, he must have got out before that. Anyway, he signed up when the war started. It seems he was hit by a piece from a trench mortar bomb, an' then while they was waitin' for dark to take him out, another bomb come along an' buried him."

" Pull on that strand a little," directed Kent. " All right. What were you saying ? "

" Well, they give him his discharge an' he come back to Cloam last week. He's been hangin' around town. They say he acts like he was a little funny in the head. Bob Jones told me I better keep out of his sight, account of what he said that day at the trial, you remember ? "

He grinned at Kent. " Funny if he'd start a little war over here, an' him with the experience he's got, eh ? I'd have to hunt my hole."

Kent smiled faintly.

" He seen Darke on the street day before yesterday an' says to him, ' Hello, Tripey,' he says. I bet Art was mad."

Kent's eyes wrinkled at the thought of the dignified ex-sergeant's indignation. But his face became suddenly serious again.

" By Jove, this looks like your friend now," he said with a note of anxiety in his voice. " And he doesn't look very friendly."

Billy looked up to see Sam Hobbs staring at him from a distance of thirty yards. They had not noticed his approach. He stood in a slouching attitude, a double-barrelled shotgun over his arm, and mumbled something they could not catch.

Billy said loudly, " Why, hello, Sam, how are you to-day ? "

But the innocent remark had a totally opposite effect to the one intended. Hobbs's eyes dilated. He stepped back a pace and flung up the gun.

" 'Ow am I ? " he said in a hoarse broken voice. " Ah, you may well arsk that. 'Ow am I ? You as tried to get me 'ung. 'Ow am I ? Blarst you, can't you see 'ow I am ? Can't think, can't sleep. Bombs —crumps—whizz-bangs. Up they come—sossiges —turnin' over an' over—can't tell where they'll come down. Right on top of you. An' then— bang ! "

He shuddered from head to foot and crouched, the light of insane terror in his eyes.

Billy took a step towards him. " Now, now," he said as one speaks to a frightened horse.

Hobbs flung up his gun. "Stand back," he said sternly. "Stand back there."

His crazed mind went off on another tack "Why ain't you in uniform ? What're you doin' of 'ere, livin' on the fat of the land ? Like bloody dukes. An' us in the trenches—in blood an' muck—sossiges comin' over —bloody great sossiges—blowin' us to 'ell. I'm goin' to kill you, I am—both on you. It's my duty. Ah, an' then I'm goin' to kill Tripey—old Tripey Nigger, what crimed me, blarst 'im, day in an' day out. You pervented me killin' of 'im larst time. Never again—I caught you bendin' this time."

He grinned, menacing the pair with the shotgun. "Ah, that puts the wind up you. Which shall I kill first ? "

"Look out," shouted Kent in peremptory tones. "Here comes one now."

The lunatic crouched and whirled to look over his shoulder. Kent leaped upon his shoulders, and Billy snatched at the gun. It went off with a double roar.

Hobbs seemed to freeze. He dropped the gun. With a scream he tore himself out of their grasp and fled.

Kent raced for the house to telephone far and wide the news of a dangerous lunatic at large. But for two days Hobbs evaded all pursuers with a wild-beast cunning. When he was finally discovered in a straw stack, he fought seven men for half an hour before he was finally overpowered.

Another blow for the Kents. Harry had been danger-ously wounded in command of a mopping-up party, having won his commission in the field.

More cheerful news : his wound, though severe, was not mortal, but he would never be fit for active service again. Mrs. Kent was frankly and unashamedly glad. She said that Harry had done enough, and she had sooner he lost his leg than have gone back to the front.

Still no news of Ted.

And then Kent came whizzing back from Cloam in his car, narrowly missing the gatepost, and halting with the fender crumpled against the verandah.

"Lucy, Lucy, Ted's safe. Here's his letter. He escaped into Holland—interned for the rest of the war."

Mrs. Kent laughing and crying at once, and repeating, "I told you so, I told you so. I knew the boy was alive. I'd have known in a minute if he'd been killed."

Kent striding over the ground and Billy hastening to meet him, anticipating some such news from the Englishman's unusual excitement.

"Good boy, Tom, good boy. You know it'd hit me as bad to lose one of my own kids as Ted."

Lucy happy and wondering why Ted had not written to her also. Restored to serenity a week later by a letter of her very own.

Kent roused out of his listless taciturnity and full of plans for improvements "to show the boys when they come home."

Harry writing home of one Nellie, a V. A. D., whom he had met at his grandfather's. Mrs. Kent seriously alarmed, more even than at his wound, but reflecting that anyone received at her father's house could hardly be socially undesirable.

It appeared that Nellie had had her hand badly crushed in an automobile accident, and had been forced to leave

the service, since she could no longer drive the heavy
motor truck she had been driving at the time.

His last letter said that he and Nellie were to be
married at a registrar's, and that he was bringing her
back to Canada with him.

Mrs. Kent's maternal jealousy blazed with white
heat. She hated the pilferer of her favourite son's
affections.

Harry arrived home just before harvest, pale and
sharp-featured, limping with the aid of a cane, but
glad to be home and anxious to take up stock breeding
again.

Nellie proved to be a tall girl of sturdy build. She
had a wonderful English complexion, spoke a curious
language composed of a slang unknown outside England, and wore a glove on her maimed hand. She had
an almost offensive directness of manner, smoked more
cigarettes than was good for her, but was unmistakably
a gentlewoman.

She and Mrs. Kent met like two gladiators. They
measured each other with hostile, glittering eyes. Their
tongues were like two rapiers. But they were both
well-bred. There would never be anything stronger
than a tepid friendship between them, but they respected
each other, and each realized that their mutual antagonism
must be kept from the men.

With her father-in-law Nellie was successful from
the first. Her diplomatic interest in his beloved Short-
horns completed the conquest. Her cigarette smoking
alone made him uncomfortable, and she had the wit
to see it and to smoke very seldom in his presence.

She and Lucy met like two strange dogs ; Lucy on

the defensive, and Nellie, the elder by two years, inclined to patronize.

Nellie prided herself upon her riding, but when Lucy jumped upon a barebacked pony, only a halter shank in her hand, and put the beast over a four-rail fence, she had to own her mistress.

Girls and women worked all over the West in the harvest fields during the last two years of the war. Side by side, in overalls such as the men wore, the two girls stooked grain and pitched bundles, and became as friendly as the unfriendly sex ever become.

With Harry at home and Ted safe in Holland, the direct connection of the two families with the war came to an end. Their interest did not languish, but the poignancy was blunted.

On the raw November evening of the Armistice there was a torchlight procession in Cloam, and Billy got imperially drunk on home-brew, and was with difficulty brought home by Kent and Harry. He was quite impenitent.

"I ain't been pickled since the day I married you," he told Maggie. "An' if a feller ain't got a right to be full once in his married life, I want to know it, see."

And now Ted wrote that he expected to embark for Canada shortly. Then a long silence. Mrs. Kent began to fret more openly than she had ever permitted herself to do during the war.

"Oh, he'll turn up," said Kent irritably. "Don't worry so, Lucy."

He was standing in the corral one afternoon. He appeared to be contemplating meditatively a bunch of yearlings, but actually he saw nothing at all. He had become listless again of late. Nearly two months had gone by without news of Ted. He had been expected in March and it was now the end of May.

A car drove into the yard. He did not turn his head, expecting that Harry had returned from Cloam.

Then he heard a shout. A tall figure sprang out of the car, vaulted over the high-railed corral, and came to meet his outstretched hand. Father and son met for the first time in four years of peril and anxiety. But there were no embraces, no tears. That is the English way. They shook hands.

" Well, Dad, how's she going ? "

" Not too bad." Kent had picked up some Western expressions—a very few. " Your mother 'll be glad to see you."

They went up to the house. Mrs. Kent heard the double tramp of feet in the hall and came hurrying out of the kitchen.

" Ted."

" Mother."

She gave him a big hug and a kiss. " You bad boy, you bad boy. Why didn't you write ? We've been nearly out of our heads worrying about you."

" I did, Mother. I wrote and said that I was held up at Shorncliffe."

" We never got it."

" Not my fault, Mums. Me good boy. Anyway, when I got to Riverton I found the train didn't go till to-morrow, so I hired a car. I couldn't get here any quicker."

" Oh, well, now that you're safe home I'll forgive you. Had your tea ? "

" No, and I'm hungry as a bear."

That was all.

Harry and his bride came in, and Ted was introduced to Nellie. " Harry isn't as slow as he looks," he said gallantly. " I was looking for a girl just like you all over England, but I couldn't find her."

" Harry, I'm going to elope with your brother."

" Go on ; I won't stop you. He'll soon be sorry, though."

" Beast."

They sat down to supper, served by a Swedish maid, but after the meal Ted began to fidget. " How's Lucy ? " he inquired for the third time.

Mrs. Kent's brows drew together. " You might be willing to stay with your own mother for a little while, after being away for four years, instead of rushing off the minute you set eyes on her," she said reproachfully.

" But, Mums, I am," he answered contritely.

Mrs. Kent relented. " Oh, go along with you," she said with a forced laugh. " I mustn't be greedy."

And, indeed, according to her lights, she had some cause for disappointment. She had been brought up herself in all the pride of patrician birth, had married a man of patrician birth, and her eldest son had married a girl of unquestioned breeding. But Lucy was distinctly a pleb. Old prejudices die hard.

He understood a good deal of what was passing in her mind, and rightly took her words as an honourable surrender. He hugged her gratefully, picked up his cap, and, with a nod and a rather sheepish smile to the rest, went to look for Lucy.

He took the path across the now dried-up slough, encountering little Donald Clovelly, who stared as country folk will. Four years is a long time for a child to remember, and Ted had changed. He had gone away a boy and he returned a man. His face was harder of outline and there was a broad scar from the temple halfway down his cheek where the German shrapnel had gashed him at Ypres.

"Well, son," said Ted kindly. "Which one are you ? "

" I'm Donald," muttered the boy shyly.

" How's all the family ? "

" Fine. Pa an' Ma's in the house."

Ted went on fast, Donald, trotting curiously at his heels.

Maggie came to the door, stared, flung up her arms, and cried, " Why, if it ain't Ted ! Billy, here's Ted. Come right on in, stranger. When did you get back ? Your folks didn't know where you was."

Billy jumped up from his chair, where he had been smoking his pipe and dreaming of the good days before there were too many neighbours. " Well, hell, how are you, Ted ? Tickled to death to see you. You're lookin' fine. That where the shell hit you ? Some crack, eh ? Well, well, well."

But there was no Lucy to welcome him. The disappointed Ted sat down and answered mechanically the questions showered upon him. He learned that Lucy was over at Groat's, though expected back at any time. Good breeding forced him to be content with that, and he listened and replied for another half-hour.

"Well, guess I'll go along now and see if I can meet her," he murmured, rising at last.

"What's your hurry?" inquired Billy.

But Maggie was more tactful. "Sure," she said, "go along. She'd ought to be on her way by now."

He gave her a grateful glance and escaped. Billy Clovelly, Junior, would have accompanied him, had he not been forcibly restrained by his mother.

Twilight had begun. Ted passed by the poplar bluff and down across the old corduroy road through the runway, still used in wet springs. Vega and the Swan were again high overhead, and Antares blinked a red eye upon the horizon. Other stars came out one by one as the dusk deepened. The ever-restless poplar leaves danced and whispered in the light air, and the scent of the first wild roses was like the breath of Paradise.

Mosquitoes had grown fewer with the draining of the sloughs, and there were few abroad that night.

Ted saw Lucy before she saw him. She came quickly down the trail, lost in thought. She had grown no taller in the years since he had seen her last, but the immature curves of that day were now full and firm. He could not see her face in that dim light.

He stood still in the shadow of a tree. There was an awe upon him almost amounting to dread. He was one of those strange individuals, not so uncommon as might be supposed, a one-woman man.

Lucy had been his first love; she still remained his only love. His fate was in a very special sense in her hands. Such men never learn that the difference between one woman and another is only slight and superficial, and that nearly all lips are sweet.

Then she saw him and halted. Her hand went up to her heart, that ancient and appealing gesture.

" Lucy," he said in a thick voice.

" Ted ? " inquiringly. " Oh, Ted, how you scared me ! "

He took an uncertain step forward, laughing unsteadily. " Well, aren't you going to shake hands even ? "

She gave him her hand, but it was cold and limp, and slid quickly out of his grasp. " I—I wasn't looking for you so soon," she said.

He entered into a breathless explanation, but she seemed to be thinking of something else. He moved closer to her and inhaled the fragrance of her divine youth. His temples throbbed with the powerful beat of his heart. He desired to say words that would express his emotions, but all he could think of seemed cheap and silly.

A puff of chilly air from the rising north wind struck through her light dress. A shiver passed over her.

" Oh, you're cold," he said. " Here, let me put my jacket round you."

" No, no, no, I'm all right, Ted. Really I am. But we'd best be getting along home."

They walked a little distance in silence. He tried to speak lightly. " Well, aren't you glad to see me after all these years ? You might pretend you are, anyway."

She nodded only, quickening her pace.

" Say something, Lucy," he begged. " What have I done ? What's the matter ? Lucy, Lucy."

But she put her head down and only walked the faster. It was now quite dark under the trees and the trail was rough. In her heedless haste she stumbled over a root. He threw out his arms and caught her.

"Lucy, Lucy, sweetheart," he panted. "Tell me."

She turned her head obstinately away, pulling at his hands with shaking fingers. Something warm and wet fell upon his hand, and he realized suddenly that she was weeping. The knowledge put him beside himself.

"Don't, sweetheart, don't; I can't bear it. Don't you know I love you?"

She ceased to struggle, but her body remained stiff and unyielding.

"Why didn't you tell me that before?" she demanded. "How was I to know you weren't just making a fool of me? Isn't there any girl in the Old Country?"

"Not for me," he said exultantly. "The only girl I ever loved is right here. I don't want any other girl. If you want me to say I love you, I'll tell you that as often as you want. I love you, I love you, I love you. Now!"

She relaxed, burying her face on his shoulder. Gently he kissed the tip of her ear. Still she would not lift her head. He put his hand under her chin and brought her face round until he could kiss one eye. At the third attempt he found her lips.

"Now, say you care for me too," he begged.

She laughed. "No, of course I won't."

"Please, Lucy," he coaxed.

She put up a hand and drew a folded paper from her bosom. "Do you know what that is? That's your last letter. Now you know, and if you're only fooling with me you ought to be ashamed of yourself." She kissed the paper and put it back.

Billy and Maggie were sitting up for them. Lucy wore Ted's jacket over her shoulders.

" Well, you got here," said Billy with a grin. " Gosh, it does take some folks a long time to walk the little ways from Groat's."

CHAPTER XXVII

THERE was excitement and wonder in the Cloam post office. An official-looking letter had arrived addressed to Lord Mountalban, and nobody knew who Lord Mountalban was.

Mrs. Petworthy, the postmistress, squawked and fluttered like a demented hen. A lean, envious, spiteful creature, Mrs. Petworthy, with a long red nose, a mouthful of crooked yellow teeth, and a slanderous tongue.

" All I says is," she declared for the hundredth time, " if there is a real lord somewhere about 'ere, don't let 'im try to lord it over me. We're all equal in this country, an' I ain't the one to bow down to no lords, that I ain't. But 'oo can it be ? They must 'ave the wrong address. I never 'eard nobody call 'imself a lord anything about 'ere—not when they was sober or not jokin'—an' it stands to reason nobody that was a real lord wouldn't 'ide it."

" Maybe it's Tom Kent," suggested Billy mischievously.

Mrs. Petworthy tossed her spiteful head. " It's likely, ain't it ? 'Im an' 'is stuck-up old 'en of a wife that gives 'erself such hairs. 'Ardly speak to me, she won't. Why, if she was the wife of a lord there'd be no 'oldin' 'er. Thinks she's a lady—'er ! I know 'er kind—barmaid in some swell pub."

Mrs. Kent had recently declined too close an acquaintance, and had thereby earned the postmistress's undying hatred.

The formidable man, with his wife and son, drove up, and while the ex-sergeant went over to the garage for a new tyre Mrs. Darke entered the post office and asked for her mail.

Mrs. Petworthy, delighted to have a new listener, at once produced the mysterious letter, already much thumbed by curious hands.

" Ah, so 'e did come into the title after all," said Mrs. Darke with keen interest.

" 'Oo ? " demanded Mrs. Petworthy.

All the people in the post office craned their necks.

" Mr. Kent, of course," replied Mrs. Darke. " One of 'is elder brothers was killed at the front, an' I suppose the other, 'im as 'ad the title, 'as gone an' died. As 'e was a bachelor, Mr. Kent will natually in'erit. The other one left only daughters."

" Well, I'll be damned," ejaculated Billy. " An' me been callin' him Tom all these years."

" For 'eving's sake ! " gasped Mrs. Petworthy. " An' so 'is stuck-up old 'en of a wife is Lady Mountalban now. But just let me catch 'er puttin' on 'er hairs with me—I'll show 'er. She ain't no lady, whatever title she 'as, an' so I'll tell 'er to 'er face."

Mrs. Darke bridled. Since she had presented her husband with a son, secure in his affection, she no longer hesitated to speak her mind. She fixed upon Mrs. Petworthy an indignant eye.

"My lady was always a lady, let me tell you, Mrs. Petworthy. Before 'er marriage she was Lady Lucilla Broadacres, youngest daughter of the Duke of Cloamshire. I was lady's maid to 'er sister, Lady Mabel, before I married Darke. An' let me tell you, Mrs. Petworthy," pursued Mrs. Darke pugnaciously, "she was always a great deal too good for the likes of you. You ain't fit for 'er to wipe 'er boots on, narsty, spiteful old talebearer."

Mrs. Petworthy was quite overborne by the onslaught. The end of her long red nose turned purple, her skinny throat twitched, her clawlike fingers worked convulsively. But before she could collect herself and retaliate in kind, Mrs. Darke had picked up her mail and sailed majestically out.

"That's another woman I can't abear," said Mrs. Petworthy venomously. "I'd like to know 'oo she thinks she is. Lady's maid—'er! Scullery wench, more like. Barmaid in some low pub, sellin' 'alf-pints to drunken sailors—that's about 'er size."

"Why, here's Tom Kent comin' now," said an interested loafer near the door.

Kent halted at Darke's hail, and remained in earnest conversation with the pair for a moment, while the door and window of the post office were black with staring heads.

Then he nodded, lifted his hat to Mrs. Darke, and approached. The spectators held their breath in rapture. Mrs. Petworthy's nose paled, and flushed a belligerent crimson.

Kent entered coolly, nodded to the company, and inquired of Mrs. Petworthy, " I hear you have a letter

for me, Mrs. Petworthy, addressed to Lord Mountalban.''

"Yes, I 'ave a letter addressed to Lord Mountalban,
Mister Kent. But I don't know as you're 'im. I 'ave
to be careful 'oo I give letters to.''

There was a subdued titter. Everybody enjoyed
Mrs. Petworthy's insolence, when they themselves
were not the victims.

Kent preserved his habitual calm. "Quite right,
Mrs. Petworthy. But you will make no mistake in giving
me that letter.''

"'An' 'ow do I know that?'' she inquired malig-
nantly.

"I think,'' said Kent, with a slight tightening of the
jaw muscles, "that my standing in the community
should be sufficient warrant for my—ah—veracity.
If not, Mrs. Darke and her husband would be able
to inform you that I am telling the truth.''

"Oh, 'er! That woman'd say anything.''

"Mrs. Petworthy,'' said Kent in an ominous voice,
"am I to understand that you refuse to give me that
letter?''

The postmistress had only recently been in trouble
for withholding mail to gratify a private grudge, and
she had received a broad hint that such a thing must
not happen again. The post office was her only means
of livelihood, and she realized that she had gone as
far as she dared.

"I take all you people to witness,'' she said solemnly,
"that I honly parted with this letter under collusion,
an' if this man turns out a low, dirty swindler it won't
be my fault.''

But Kent only picked up his mail and walked out. Billy followed him.

" Give me a ride home ? " he asked.

" Jump in," said Kent laconically.

Kent, having shoved his mail into his pocket unread, drove on in a thoughtful silence that the curious Billy had not at first the courage to break.

But five minutes of it was all he could stand. " So you're a real lord now," he burst out.

Kent gave him a quizzical sidelong glance. " It seems so, Clovelly."

" What 're you goin' to do about it ? "

" Don't know. Haven't made up my mind yet."

Billy sat in puzzled silence. Then he began to chuckle.

" Well, don't it beat all ! I never thought I'd be drivin' along this here old road with a real live lord." He spoke as if an imitation dead lord would have aroused no astonishment in him at all.

" A real live lord ! Me hittin' it up the freight trail with him an' old John Crawford ! That 'd make old John's eyes stick out, eh ? I'd like to hear what he'd say. What do you know about me bein' pulled out of the Moose by a lord ! An' me learnin' you to swing a axe an' bawlin' you out for ridin' the saw ! Gad ! "

He hugged himself and rocked back and forth in his seat, gurgling with delight.

They had by now arrived at Kent's gate, and he stopped the car. " Come over and see me after supper, Clovelly," he hinted.

" Sure, you'll be wantin' to talk it over with Mrs. Kent. I get you. Well, I'll hustle along an' tell Maggie. She'll be tickled to death to know she's been livin' right next a real live lord all these years. An' never knew it. Gosh, if that ain't the limit. Well, so long."

Maggie swallowed the amazing news with avidity, though her first remark was sceptical.

" Billy, you're foolin'."

" Honest to God, I ain't. ' I'm Lord Mountalban,' he says, ' an' you cough up that letter or there'll be hell apoppin'.' You'd ought to seen old Ma Petworthy's face. An' old lady Darke. ' She's Lady Luciller Board-walk, daughter of the Dook of Boardwalk,' she says, ' an' you ain't fit to carry swill to pigs,' she says. ' You red-nosed old turkey hen ! ' she says. Oh, she give her hell. You'd died laughin'."

" Billy, you're makin' it up. I never see such a man to tell yarns."

" All right, don't believe me. Go over an' see for yourself. I ain't tellin' you no more."

" Well, I didn't say I didn't believe you. But, you know, you do say such things. Go on, Billy, tell me some more."

" I told you enough. If a feller's own wife calls him a liar it's time he shut his head."

" Billy, if you ain't enough to drive a person crazy ! You come across now, before I take the stove lifter to you."

" All right, I'll be good. Let up, now, Mag—that damn thing's hot. What do you want to know ? "

" All about it, an' cut out them yarns."

He repeated the story more soberly.

" Well, I don't know what to make of it," she said, shaking her head. " I can't believe it. He ain't never acted like a lord. I never knowed a man put on less than what he does. Mrs. Kent she can go up in the air if she thinks anybody's gettin' fresh with her. But he's that even-tempered an' good-natured . . ."

" He ain't even a drinkin' man," agreed Billy. " Take a drink now an' again, but not as if he liked it. I thought real lords was roarin' drunk all the time. An' he's a good worker, too. I don't know any man what'd do a better day's work than him. I know damn well I wouldn't work if I was a lord. Maybe I wouldn't raise hell an' put a prop under it ! "

" Not if I was around you wouldn't."

" If I was a lord I wouldn't be married to you."

" Another crack like that, old feller, an' you get the hot stove lifter in your eye."

" It's easy seein' I ain't a lord, or you wouldn't dast get gay with me."

" Cut out the foolin', Billy. What're we goin' to do about this ? "

" Well, I don't know that it's up to us. We'll just go along as we been goin'. If they want to put on dog . . . Hell, Tom's too much of a man for that. I don't know about her. Women's different. Anyway, I'm goin' over after supper, an' I'll let you know how it goes."

It was with serious misgivings that their long and intimate friendship was about to end that he took the slough path.

Kent was in the barn feeding his prize bull, and grinned at Billy's solemn face.

" I suppose you'll be pullin' out for the Old Country now ? " said Billy.

" Well, no, there's no particular reason why I should."

" No ? But you got a big house over there, an e-state,
ain't you ? There'll be a whole raft of guys, all dolled
up like a circus parade, to wait on you, eh ? "

Kent shook his head. " The old place is gone long
ago," he explained. " The poor old pater left his affairs
in a bit of a mess when he died. The estate had to be
sold."

" Oh, that's too bad. But say, I been callin' you
Tom right along. I suppose that's all off now ? "

" My name's still Tom," replied Kent, with a chuckle.

" No, is it, now ! Well, that's fine. I thought you'd
be puttin' on dog, gettin' too high-toned to know your
old friends, maybe."

A more generous thought moved him—jealousy for
his friend's honour. " But, say, that wouldn't be right :
you just got to put on some dog."

Kent laughed outright. " I don't think so, Clovelly.
A title isn't—ah—compatible with this country. Fact
is, I've decided to drop the title. If Harry's a howling
success and decides to revive it later on, he can, but
an English barony stuck on a few sections of Saskatchewan land is, to say the least—ah—incongruous."

Billy scratched his head in acute disappointment.
" Hell, Tom, you don't want to drop that there handle.
Why, it makes you stick up like a sore thumb among
all these here plain misters around."

" Sorry I can't oblige you, old man, but I've always
been a commoner. With two elder brothers in the
line of descent, I never had the slightest expectation of
inheriting. I'm perfectly satisfied to remain a commoner."

' Yes, but what does Mrs. Kent say ? "

" She always had the right to call herself Lady Lucilla Kent if she chose. Only a courtesy title, of course, but she had a right to it. She quite agrees with me."

Billy shrugged his shoulders resignedly. " Well, I see I can't do nothin' with you. But I must say you're the most peculiarest lord I ever heard tell of. A real live lord, an' won't put on no dog at all. Maybe I wouldn't show some style if I was a lord ! I'd just like to get the chance."

There was a slight constraint on Billy's part for a few days thereafter. He had a disinclination to call Kent by his name, lest he should seem too familiar. But that soon wore off.

After the first nine days' wonder the settlement quieted down also, though strangers were invariably informed that Lord Mountalban owned the Cloam Stock Farms and lived in the district.

Mrs. Petworthy had the superb audacity to call on Mrs. Kent. Her reception was frigid enough to discourage even her, but not to keep her from writing to all her friends and relatives in England about " my best friend out here, Lady Mountalban."

The only person the new dignity much affected was Mrs. Kent. Not that it moved her to arrogance toward her neighbours, but she seemed to consider it absolved her from her self-imposed resolution not to speak of England. She began to talk wistfully of " Home," and home with a capital H means only one thing to English folk the world over.

Another thing that contributed to her desire to revisit the land of her birth was the removal of the slight coolness that had subsisted between herself and her family since she had had the bad taste to marry the hopelessly younger son of an impoverished peer.

Nellie Kent had shown herself a not incapable manager, and so, not without dubiety, Mrs. Kent entrusted to her the care of the house and dairy during her absence.

Her plans were indefinite : she said she might stay six months or a year. She was back in thirteen weeks.

" I never knew the English climate was so positively loathsome," she said on her return. " It never did anything but rain the whole time I was there. All the people are as poor as rats, and all my old girlhood friends are either frumps or trying to pretend they're sixteen. Carrie Mountmorris thinks she's overdressed in a string of beads."

There were no delicate half-tones in Mrs. Kent's view of men and things—nothing but ebony black and snow white.

She made no allowance for the fact that she had left England with Queen Victoria newly dead and the Boer War won. Change was coming, but only the most prevenient realized it. Life still seemed grounded on adamantine Victorian rock.

She returned to find that apparently irrefragable foundation cracked in a thousand places and terrible fires bursting up from the infernal regions. The débris of the war lay strewn about her. Of those who had ruled the destinies of the Empire in her day hardly one remained. An upstart Welshman swayed the sceptre of Salisbury and faced a Labour Opposition that awaited confidently the day when it would snatch it from his hand.

Society was shattered. Peerage after peerage had

died with its last heir in Flanders. Huge and ancient estates were being broken up daily under the burden of taxes, or passing into the hands of a hateful new race known as profiteers.

The duchy of Cloamshire had suffered as heavily as any. Her ninety-year-old father sat mourning for his only son, in straitened circumstances. At his death the title would pass to another branch of the family and the great estate would be broken up.

Last and worst, all her acquaintances had grown old. Moreover, in the years between, she and they had moved in diverging paths. They could not meet across the abyss of mutual misunderstanding.

The new generation was worse still. They had scant respect for her—or for anything else, it seemed. They spoke a language she hardly understood, and looked at life from another angle. It was not given to her to understand that all life is one, and that fate and circumstance bind man as they have ever bound him, no matter what fantastic gambols he may play for the laughter of the gods.

And the weather during the whole time of her visit was bad. Used to the clear skies and infrequent rains of Saskatchewan, she had forgotten that grey skies are commoner than blue in England and that people there habitually carry umbrellas for use.

England was beautiful, as England must ever be: it is sad that her loveliness is so often veiled in tears.

CHAPTER XXVIII

KENT was now a comparatively wealthy man. He had been fortunate in many ways, particularly in having some capital to start with, but the greater part of his success had been due to hard and intelligent work. That quality of doggedness, a certain ponderous inflexibility that allowed no obstacle to daunt him, and a clear idea at all times of his own interests, had carried him from the ownership of a quarter-section of wild land to the ownership of over four sections.

Two sections of this had been bought cheap from impoverished Swedes. The land was fit only for grazing and for growing hay, but he had utilized it well, so that he now had the largest herd of pure-bred stock in the district. But the Normandin place, the quarters originally owned by the Collins brothers, and a half-section lying towards Cloam, were mostly arable land. Another half-section of swamp land, bought cheap, would be profitable as soon as it was drained.

Even when the war began he was firmly upon his feet, and the rapidly rising prices had soon wiped out the indebtedness he incurred in buying out Madame Normandin and the Collinses.

True enough, the prices of everything he had had to buy rose also even more swiftly, and he was forced to pay very high wages for indifferent help. But even those things did not cut down his profits materially.

His final and greatest coup was due in equal measure to sagacity and mere good fortune. He had the wit to see, when prices were at their height just after the war, that such a state of things could not endure.

He made haste to sell—a little this side of the crest of the wave perhaps, but who can judge just when the wave is about to break ? He sold everything but his seed grain and the nucleus of his herd, a score of young heifers.

With the money he bought the certificates issued by the Wheat Board, in whose hands the entire crop of the country lay that year. They paid a certain sum per bushel to the farmer on delivery of his wheat, handing him at the same time a certificate to be redeemed later. Many farmers, thinking a bird in the hand worth two in the bush, or hard pressed for cash, sold their certificates for what they would fetch. Kent cleared seven thousand dollars on the transaction.

Then followed the winter of 1919-20, which Western farmers will not soon forget. That year the first snow fell early in October, a month before time. Cattle had to be fed instead of running at grass. The haying season had been wet and hay was scarce and poor in consequence. By midwinter most of the stock owners were in difficulties.

Oat straw will just keep cattle alive, wheat straw will not, and the beards make barley straw as deadly as strychnine. But there was not even enough oat straw that winter : everybody had grown wheat because of its higher price.

Kent, with his herd reduced to a handful and his well-drained marshes, had plenty of feed. All his oat straw was also for sale.

Hay had never been such a price. It was even imported two thousand miles from Eastern Canada and sold at a profit at forty-five and fifty dollars a ton. Hay had seldom risen as high as fifteen dollars a ton. Even oat straw sold at twelve dollars a load to men who hauled it themselves.

And spring was late. It was mid-April before the pastures were free of snow. Only a few feeble racks of bones survived to graze upon them. Thousands of rotting carcasses were strewn across the prairie provinces that spring. Stock breeders with tears in their eyes offered their herds to anyone who would keep them alive. Old Squatter Banks died that year of grief as much as old age, haunted by the pleading eyes of the animals whose sufferings he could do nothing to alleviate.

None of this touched Kent. All his feed not absolutely required for his own stock was sold long before that ghastly spring. He flung open his meadows to farmers who cut upon the ice, wading through snowdrifts, the long brown grass that had been growing in water out of reach of the mowers.

Spring found him with fat stock, horses in perfect condition, and a bank account that made the Cloam bank manager inclined to take off his hat in reverence every time they met.

For Billy the dream had ended. The march of events during the war had put out of his head all thought of moving. November 1918 dropped him into a pit of boredom. The peace negotiations were beyond his understanding and aroused no interest.

His own financial position was sounder than he had ever known it. He was not in debt to anyone, but the money that had come his way seemed to have vanished mysteriously. He had a little farm, a few head of stock, some worn-out farm implements, and six growing children. And everywhere the walls of a settled society were closing in upon him.

He roused up to take some interest in the wedding of his favourite child.

Ted had refused to take up farming. There was a garage business for sale in Riverton, and he suggested that his father advance him the necessary capital to purchase it.

Kent acted with his usual fairness and generosity. He said that Ted had been a partner in the Cloam Stock Farms ever since his majority, that his share of the profits would be placed to his account, and that he and Harry would buy out his share between them.

The business was bought and Ted returned from Riverton to claim his bride. Billy gave her away, joked at the wedding breakfast, but sank into a brooding silence that endured for days. He felt the dark cloud drawing nearer, and knew that his work was not yet done.

He lost four head of cattle during the hard winter, despite Kent's help, and Maggie braced herself for the annual outburst.

" If we was in a country that wasn't lousy with neighbours we'd have plenty feed," he grumbled. " Never had to worry about hay when we first come in this

country.   Now half the cattle dies of hunger every
winter."

" We didn't ought to keep so many head," said Maggie.

" An' how're we goin' to live ?   Think four or five
head of cattle'll keep a gang like this ?   I tell you the time
to pull out is right now.   Land values are high right
now :   they'll be goin' down.   We can pull out with
cash in our pockets an' go to Peace River."

" We're doin' well enough where we are," said Maggie.

" Like a chunk of hell !   How do you get like that ?
Think the whole gang can live on this place until king-
dom come ?   The girls is all right :   likely they'll get
married :   but what about the boys ?   Here's Billy just
about old enough to take up land for himself.   Where's
he goin' to get land ?   What do you think about it, Bill ? "

The boy lifted shining eyes to his father.   Maggie
sighed.   She knew that look.   The Clovelly strain ran
true.   Here was another fated to be a wanderer in the
waste places, a horizon-hunter.

" I'm fed up stickin' around here," said Billy, Junior.
" No fun.   I like to go places.   This country's all fenced
up."

The voice was like an echo coming down the ages
from Clovelly to Clovelly.

" Hear that ? " cried Billy exultantly.   " He's got
the idea.   He's just like me.   To hell with fences, he
says.   Wouldn't you like to set afire to every fence post
in the country, an' let them damn ploughed fields go
back to pasture ?   Sure you would.   An' what about
Charlie an' Donald ?   It won't be long before they need
land too."

" I won't stick around here," piped up Donald.   " I

want to go where I can ride my pony right across the prairie. I want to be a cowboy an' punch big herds of cattle, an' go huntin' an' shoot bears and mooses, an' not just go to school."

"You see," said Billy. "He knows what he wants. He don't want to slug around in the mud trailin' a damn plough. That ain't life. What about you, Charlie?"

But Charlie was a disappointment. ."Oh, I don't know. I don't like to farm, but I'd like to be a engine-driver, like what pulls the trains, you know, or maybe have a garage business like Ted."

"Well, if you'd like to go an' live in a stinkin' town go to it," growled Billy. "You got that from your mother. She's got no get to her neither. All she wants is take root here an' grow moss on her back."

Maggie said nothing.

"Well, how about sellin' the farm while chances is good?" said Billy with a brisk confidence he did not feel. "Let's get to blazes out of this dump an' go to a good country."

Maggie shook her head.

"Go on, say it," he snapped at her. "I might know you'd crab the works."

"I won't let you sell the farm, nor I won't sell my cattle," she said resolutely.

Though he stormed at her for days, when he was not sulkily silent, from that position she would not budge. It was an unhappy household that summer; Billy with his eldest and youngest son at feud with all the rest. Though little Myrtle, the baby of the family, gave her father moral support, the odds were unequal, and the year's campaign was another victory for Maggie.

In midsummer of that year Billy had his last sight
of another pioneer.

He had to take a young bull from Kent's to a farmer
in the northern part of the settlement. Three of them
lifted the animal into a double wagon box, secured him
with ropes, and chained his head to a crossbar.

By the time Billy had delivered the bull at its desti-
nation it was late afternoon. The farmer kindly pointed
out to him an alleged short cut which he said would
bring him out on the old Beaver Island trail.

The main roads of the district ran east and west,
there being comparatively little traffic north and south.
Billy, though an unexcelled trail maker in an unsettled
wilderness, had the not uncommon peculiarity among
pioneers of becoming confused in a network of roads.
After following the short cut until it split up into a maze
of faint trails, one ending in a hay slough and another
in a pasture, he had to admit to himself that he did not
know where he was. In an unsettled country he would
have headed due south and made his way home without
the slightest trouble. But here he found every piece of
open land blocked by fences.

Musing bitterly on the subject of fences and the
pleonasm of neighbours, he worked down along some
enclosed land on a cow-path, among stumps and tangled
willows through which he had at times to cut a way with
his axe, and emerged quite suddenly upon a cluster of
log buildings.

It was a warm evening and a very old man with a
black cap on his head sat on a bench by the door of one
of the shacks, watching several brown-skinned children
at play.

But what made Billy stare was that the old man was singing in a thin quaver, and the song he sang was one that Billy had never heard south of Swan Lake. It was the song John Crawford sang when he was in his happiest mood, on the out trail with dangers and difficulties multiplying around him :—

"Oh, bury me deep in a hole in the ground, a ground hog's hole is best;
Oh, bury me deep in a ground hog's hole an' leave me there to rest."

Billy stood up in his wagon, cupped his hands and bawled, " Hey, there, you old ground hof ! Hey, John Crawford ! "

The old man got up, shading his eyes against the level beams of the setting sun, as Billy drove up.

" Why, if it ain't Billy Clovelly. Where you been all these dog years, you old mossback ? Come on down outer that 'fore I fetch you by the neck. You ain't goin' away from this dump to-night, no sir. Put your horses in the barn, damn you, an' come on in an' eat."

" I'll just take you up on that, you old mudhen. Think you can bluff me. I been bushed all afternoon in this here damn country of yours, an' got so turned around with fences an' bum trails I don't know which end of me's up."

John Crawford began to issue commands in a ghostly echo of his old hectoring bellow, " Hey, there, Joe, show a leg, now. Get a wiggle on, somebody. Here's a old friend of mine come to see me. My God, do I have to stick around here all night ? "

" All right, Grandpop, all right," answered a well-grown, lemon-coloured youth, coming out of the barn.

He helped Billy put up the horses and then they went into the house. The place was pervaded by the indefinable Indian smell, but was kept with that speckless, whitewashed cleanliness so often found in halfbreed houses.

A very dark young woman, whom Crawford introduced as one of his numerous daughters-in-law, prepared Billy a bountiful supper of eggs and breadand-butter.

A number of people of all ages from infancy to decreptitude, but most of them children, and of all shades of colour from light yellow to burnt sienna, filled the large room. They were all related in some measure to John Crawford; his sons and their wives and children.

He beamed round upon them patriarchally. "This ain't only the half of 'em—ain't no room for more. Four of my boys got places of their own, an' my three eldest girls is married. Yes sir, I'm proud of my family. I figure there's enough Crawfords kickin' around the country to keep the good old name goin' for quite a while."

In appearance the oldest person present was a squaw, an old, old woman, bent like a bow, who squatted on the floor in a corner and paid no attention to anything.

"That's my woman," said Crawford with a jerk of the head. "She's gettin' pretty old an' feeble now. She ain't strong like me, though maybe I'm five or six years older'n what she is. I'm seventy-four. She don't pay no 'tention to nothin' no more, just only me."

He spoke to the poor old creature in Cree, and she lifted herself upright with her hands and turned her head in the direction of the voice. Billy saw by her white eyeballs that she was quite blind. She dwelt in a darkness not only mental but physical, responsive only to the voice of her mate. She mumbled a few words and sank back into apathy.

" It's too bad," said Crawford with a sad shake of the head. " It wasn't until just lately she commenced to go that way. She ain't strong like me. I'm around seventy-five now. But I'm gettin' old too—soon be eighty. But she's a good woman, Billy, she's a good woman."

Billy was much struck by the change in his old friend. He had not seen Crawford since they last met on the freight trail, the winter before the war. At that time the sturdy old pioneer had borne his sixty-odd winters upon erect shoulders and sturdy legs. But now the wide shoulders curved forward and his knees rubbed together when he walked.

There had been an even greater change in his disposition. Of old he had been cheerful only at the greatest possible distance from civilization. The nearer he came to the common haunts of man the more gloomy and morose was his outlook on life. But to-day he radiated a quiet happiness. He smiled and nodded and chuckled softly over old mishaps recalled and perils shared.

After all the others had retired for the night, the pair sat talking and smoking for a long time.

" Well, old-timer," said Billy at last, " it looks to
me like you worked off your old grouch. How come ? "

" It's a fact," admitted Crawford. " Some way
things don't get me het up like they used to did. I
guess it's because I'm commencin' to get old an' ain't
got so much time to enjoy life. What's the use of fussin',
anyway ? I used to be worryin' all the time about
how I'd feed all them hungry kids of mine an' where
I'd get a few clothes to put on their backs—oh, an' one
thing an' another. But that's all past an' done."

He sucked at his pipe reflectively for half a minute.

" Yes, that's done. I ain't able to keep the gang
any more. But what do they do ? They turn right
around an' keep me. Them's the kind of kids to have.
Nothin's too good for the old man. An' look at my
bunch of grandchildren—seventeen of 'em. I'd have
more only a good few died in the influenzy. That was
a bad thing. I lost three of my own. Oh, it was bad
around here. But the old man went through it all—yes,
sir, he was tough."

Billy made sympathetic noises, and the garrulous old
man went on happily.

" Yes, sir, I sure been lucky. All my boys, every
last one of 'em, turned out good straight lads. That's
the old New England blood. It ain't so many can say
that."

He fumbled in his pocket and drew out a little case.

" See, that's what my boy Art, my second boy, got
in the war. It's the Military Medal. Poor Art didn't
come back, but I guess it won't be so long now till I
see him again. Anyway, he died game. They tell me
there wasn't a sniper on the front could touch him.

He always was a great hunter, that lad. Got his first moose when he was only twelve year old, yes sir. It was the Indian blood he got from his mother, I guess. I had five boys in that there war, but they all come back safe but Art."

"Your family sure done pretty good," said Billy.

"Well, sir, I believe you. Five of 'em; all that was old enough. I'd been along too, but they wouldn't take the old man. I wasn't such a slouch of a scrapper in my old days, neither. Remember the time I trimmed that horse-killin' shyster on Swan Lake, eh?."

"Well, I should say, John. Ain't liable to forget it, neither. Dandiest scrap I ever see in my life."

The daughter-in-law came in and dragged the old man off to bed, despite a querulous protest. Billy rolled himself in a couple of blankets on the floor. In the morning he bade John Crawford good-bye for the last time, and young Joe Crawford put him upon the right road home.

CHAPTER XXIX

THAT summer relations grew somewhat strained between Mrs. Kent and her daughter-in-law. Both were women of decisive character, and their mere propinquity generated friction. Kent and Harry took counsel.

As a result they bought out three farmers adjoining the half-section of swamp land north of Billy's place. Harry moved his wife to one of the places, and undertook the task of building a unified farm out of the properties and draining the swamp.

With the arrival of a granddaughter, the incipient feud betwen Nellie and Mrs. Kent was healed. Now that they didn't see each other too often they came almost to have a regard for one another.

Ted was prospering in the after-the-war boom in Riverton, and in the early winter Lucy presented him with a son. Billy was jubilant, far more so than he had been about any of his own children. He had greeted the last four or five with pessimistic prophecies of starvation.

But that was for him the dreariest winter he had ever spent. His crop was fair, nothing to boast of either in yield or in quality, and the price of wheat was falling. Cattle prices were already as low as before the war.

When he had hauled it to the Cloam elevator, he had nothing to do. A branch railway had pushed north from Riverton to Swan Lake, and it was the settlers now pushing into that country who carried the freight forward from the end of the steel.

He and his eldest son took a hunting trip, and were away five weeks in the forest country north-west of Beaver Island. The pair had long talks over their camp-fires and found themselves very much at one.

" Well, even if the family don't move," said the boy, " I'm goin' up in the Peace River country an' take up land next year."

" You hold your horses, boy," said Billy. " It ain't so much of a snap. You got to have some money to start, even if it ain't very much. Now I got none to give you the way I am now, but if I can get your ma to let me sell the farm—why, we'll all go together. We'll go way out, where there's room to turn around. Then me an' you can take up land right next each other, and when the other boys gets old enough they can file close in too. That way we'll have a real chunk of land we can do something with. We'll have it so that, even if the country does settle up, we won't have a bunch of neighbours settin' right on our necks."

" That's right, Dad. We can get a whole section, anyway. Let's start in the spring."

" Hm," said Billy grimly. " Your ma'll raise hell. I don't know how we'll handle her."

" We'll do it," said the boy confidently.

But Billy shook his head doubtfully.

The boy had the joy of bringing down his first moose, a tough old bull with a fine spread of horns. Billy, more practical, picked up two bad-land caribou, which are much better eating. Moose meat, even young cow moose, tastes like inferior beef, but bad-land caribou is better than most mutton.

They returned with a superfluity of meat, and all the family were thoroughly weary of moose before the spring came. Billy hauled a little firewood, and did some freighting for Kent, but during most of the winter he spent his time in moody loafing.

The snow began to drip. Once more the winds waked the sere grass, long silent under the drifts. Cocks crowed on every fence and dunghill, scratching hens advertised eggs in strident tones ; grave and elderly cows, remembering their calfish youth, gambolled ele-phantinely in the mild sunlight.

The birds began to come north and the skies were full of water birds on their way to the Arctic. Billy heard once more the frogs, and his old friend the loon dropped him a word one dark evening from high up in the sky.

Maggie watched her man with the keenest anxiety. She felt her hold upon him slipping. He would hardly speak to her now, and often he would not answer when she spoke to him. A settled frown lay upon his forehead and his mouth drooped sullenly. She saw that only a little thing now would bring an open break, but she was stubborner even than he, and she prepared for the battle.

It was a broken seeder that precipitated the conflict. The thing had been used and misused for years. It had lain out in all weathers, for Billy had the true pioneer carelessness with possessions. All the paint had flaked off, and rain and melting snow had soaked into the woodwork and rotted it : the metal parts were eaten up with rust.

He was seeding wheat one afternoon when the machine languidly shed a wheel. The full weight fell upon the drills. The rusty metal crumpled like paper. In a moment the whole thing was a total wreck, past repair.

The only thing to do was to buy a new machine, and he had no money and would have to go into debt again. Nearly all the machinery on the farm was in much the same condition.

Billy did not break into furious curses, as was his excitable wont at each small mishap : the matter had gone too deep for that by now. In grim silence he unhitched his horses and drove them to the barn, leaving the wreck standing in the field.

Then he went into the house and sat down in brooding silence by the stove. Maggie, after one glance at his face, wisely forbore to ask him why he had stopped work so early.

Presently he got up and loafed about the yard, casually examining his machinery. Several of the castings on his mower had been cracked and wired together ; his hayrake was a tottering ruin ; the binder, under its flimsy shed, looked like the survivor of a remote age. His buildings were rotting away, sinking into the piles of manure that rose about them. His fences sagged, for the posts had rotted off at the ground level. Poverty and decay had everywhere set their stamp. Even the stovepipe leaned askew on the roof of his house.

Still in a silence nobody dared to break, he ate his supper, filled his pipe, and took the slough path for Kent's.

On the top of the slope stood a shelter belt of the quick-growing Russian poplar. A neat iron gate admitted him to a big kitchen garden, wherein two rows of crab-apple trees were putting forth tiny leaves and pink-tipped buds. Beyond was a well-grown caragana hedge, and then a small and well-kept lawn.

He stopped for a moment to look at the house, square and substantial and comfortable-looking, with a broad, screened verandah facing south. He shook his head and clucked his tongue at the contrast it presented to his own crumbling log home.

" He done better'n me," he admitted. Yet there was little envy in his tone.

Behind the house another belt of poplars shut off the brutal north wind. To the east he could see the big cattle corrals, dominated by the huge red barn, and beyond a hundred-acre field of black plough, newly seeded.

He crossed the verandah and knocked gently.

Getting no answer, he opened the door and hailed, " Anybody home ? "

" Yes, Mr. Clovelly," came Mrs. Kent's voice.

He entered a spacious hall, patterned after that of an English manor, even to the fireplace at the far end, in which a cheerful fire of logs crackled softly. Rooms opened out of it to right and left, and a broad stairway led to a wide gallery upon which the bedrooms opened.

Softly shaded electric lights hung from the high ceiling, and the floor was of polished hardwood with skin rugs upon it. There were a few good pictures on the walls, which, with some old silver, comprised all that remained of the ancient barony of Mountalban.

The furniture was all good, not too obviously modern, and harmonizing well with its surroundings.

The whole spoke of the genius of the Kents for comfort, and the moving spirit in its creations sat at a businesslike desk near the fireplace, tapping away busily on a portable typewriter.

Mrs. Kent was chairwoman of the woman's branch of the Grain Growers' local, a position that gave full scope for her love of organization and management.

From the rear came muffled squeals and swiftly suppressed guffaws, indicating that the two Swedish maids were entertaining their swains in the kitchen.

The years had changed Mrs. Kent very little. She was one of those slender women who wither with age like an apple, retaining their soft bright tints to the last. Her once brown hair was now pure silver, but her eyes were remarkably bright behind her glasses and her teeth were still beautiful. She was as erect and quick-moving as she had ever been.

She gave Billy a nod and a smile. " Tom's in his den, Mr. Clovelly, if you want to see him. You know the way."

" That's right, Mrs. Kent. I'll leave you to your coffee mill," he answered with a grin.

He entered a small room on the right and found Kent deep in an armchair and the pedigree of the Countess of Cloverdale. The Countess's blood was of the very bluest and all her connections were born aristocrats. She had won many prizes for Kent in the Shorthorn class at various stock shows.

Kent, in Norfolk jacket, riding breeches, and leggings, looked very English, every inch a Cloamshire gentleman farmer. He had put on weight in recent years, the whole top of his head was bald and pink, and his heavy moustache shot with grey.

Billy had grown leaner, but his tall spare body was as tough and elastic as whalebone. Physically he was very much the superior of his friend, though Kent had been by far the stronger man twenty years earlier. Hard work and a spare diet confer a few blessings.

Time and change of scene leave few marks upon men like Kent. All his years in Canada had not changed his accent a whit, though he had picked up a few Western words and expressions.

" Ah, Clovelly," he said, " sit down and help yourself to the cigars."

But Billy preferred the rank tobacco, whittled from a plug, that he had smoked all his life. He sat down opposite his host in another comfortable chair and the two smoked for some moments in friendly silence.

" Will you buy my place, Tom ? " said Billy suddenly.

" Hm." A pause. " Thinking again of pulling out ? "

" This country's all shot to hell," answered Billy gloomily. " Look where the price of wheat is. An' you just about got to give your cattle away. An' taxes —my God, it takes all a man makes to pay 'em ! "

" I don't know that you're likely to better yourself by going away," said Kent. " It seems to me the whole world is in a state of—ah—financial chaos. Things will pick up again."

" Aw, hell, Tom, you know I was just talkin'. I don't give a damn what the price of wheat is, nor whether

cattle is fifty cents a head. They can raise the taxes to
a million dollars a acre for all me. I'm fed up with the
country—too many neighbours—I feel like a bull in
a corral. I got to have room to turn around in—want
to go where I can spit without decoratin' another feller's
land."

Kent smiled without speaking.

"Now, see here, Tom," Billy went on. "My place
is stuck right in the middle of your land like a cow in
a bog. You got to go around me to get to Harry's ;
you got to go across my place to get to Dahl's old place.
Everything'd be handier for you if I was out of there.
You could clear a little land along my east line an' get
a three-hundred-acre field by joinin' mine with Dahl's
and Watson's. They both belong to you, but you got
to make two fields of 'em account of the runway from
Grout's slough."

"I know all that, Clovelly. I'd like to have your
place, but I don't like to lose a good neighbour, and
I don't want Mrs. Clovelly to hate me the rest of her
days. I don't think she wants to go."

"Damn her, she don't," admitted Billy. "She
raises the devil every time I open my head about it."

"You can't sell without her permission, you know."

"I guess she's told me that eighty million times,
Tom. But, see here, what about my boys ? Billy's
old enough to take up land, an' it won't be so long before
Charlie an' Donald'll be lookin' for places. Now I
ask you, where in hell is a young feller goin' to get a
homestead around here ? "

"That's the soundest argument you've given me yet,
Clovelly. I hadn't thought of it."

" Well, now, Tom, if I get the woman around, will
you buy my place ? "

Kent puffed at his cigar for several minutes. At
last he said slowly, " If you've really made up your mind
that you must go, and if you can get your wife to see
it that way, I'll give you two thousand cash for your
land."

" Hm," grunted Billy, with a farmer's usual ex-
aggerated ideas of the value of his property. " I thought
you'd do better than that."

" It's a fair price," said Kent. " I bought Albert
Magnusson out last month for sixteen hundred. I only
want the land ; you can sell everything on it, right
down to the buildings."

In his heart Billy knew that he was being offered even
a generous price, and he said no more. They talked
for another hour. It was one of Kent's finest traits
that he never tendered uncalled-for advice. He listened
patiently, if only with vague comprehension, while
Billy tried to put his vision of the Desirable Land into
stumbling words.

CHAPTER XXX

IT was late when Billy marched into the house. The younger children were in bed in the room behind. Billy was working at a neighbour's for seeding. Maggie was sitting up for him, filled with rage and dread.

" Tom's offered me two thousand for the place," blurted Billy. " What you got say about it ? "

" Just the same as I always said : I won't let you sell. I don't care who offers you how much for it. I'm here an' I'm goin' to stay here. You can just cut out all that wild talk an' come to bed ; I ain't listenin' to any-- thing you say. I heard it all before."

They stood and glared at each other. The antagonism at the base of every marriage blazed up in bitter hatred.

" I'll say no more to you," said Billy between his teeth. " Never."

They went to bed in silence and rose in silence. Billy borrowed a seeder from Kent and finished sowing his field.

Though Kent looked at him inquiringly, neither spoke again of that evening's conference. With Maggie, Billy hardly exchanged a word all week.

She imagined that he walked about hating her, and the thought distressed her. She would have been still more distressed if she had known the truth.

Actually, when she was not immediately before him,

she passed completely out of his mind. When he saw
her he felt vaguely that he was confronting a stranger
who was evidently hostile and therefore best let alone,
unless and until a movement of aggression was made.

He finished his seeding one noon, had his dinner in
the usual constrained silence, and then climbed the
hill behind his house to meditate. It was a favourite
habit of his. When any difference cropped up between
him and his wife, or when the feeling of insufferable
bondage weighed too heavily on his spirit, he sat down
on the brow of the hill, as now, and let the winds lull
his feverish soul to rest.

He looked out over the landscape as he and Maggie
had done that spring day so many years ago. There
had been astounding changes in that time : the very
contours of the country had altered.

His first view had shown him a land of bald hills
and wooded hollows, of tall, serrated spruce bluffs
and innumerable sloughs. No sign showed that the
eye of man had ever rested upon it. It was a land virgin
and unpolluted.

Nothing of that remained. The spruce bluffs had
been ruthlessly levelled, and the second growth struggled
despairingly against an army of invading poplars and
balm of Gileads.

The hollows, where the richest land lay, had been
cleared and ploughed, but on the lighter land of the hill-
tops, abandoned chiefly to pasture, white poplar, hazel,
willow, and birch had sprung up thickly. Fires no
longer swept thousands of acres bare of trees and
shrubs.

At first glance the land seemed far more thickly

wooded than of yore. The sloughs had shrunk until only a gleam of blue water was to be seen here and there.

The work of man was everywhere. Close at hand stood the big house of the Kents, set in its lawn and garden, with its background of tall silo, great barn, sheds, outhouses, and corrals.

Farther off lay the roofs and elevators of Cloam, and to east and west along the line of the railway other elevators raised their tall red towers in dwindling perspective. Northward he looked out over a rich farming country, pasture and fallow and newly seeded plough.

And wherever his eye rested were those symbols of his captivity, the roads and the fences.

The Army Without Banners had made good its conquest. It lay encamped on the subjugated land. The wild had been driven back into the forests of the north, there to linger yet a little while before the invincible army took the field again and hurled it yet farther back into the frozen wastes about the Pole.

Man had changed everything. The native beasts, all but the cunning coyote and the nauseous skunk, had fled or been ruthlessly killed out. The quarrelsome English sparrow, following the railroad, had driven many of the shyer native birds away; weeds and pasturing cattle introduced by man had destroyed numbers of the sweetest and fairest flowers of the prairie garden.

Only the pure sparkling air and the glorious blue of the sky had escaped, though man would have polluted them also with foul smoke if he had been able.

It was still a beautiful land, a rich, fruitful, smiling land, but it was the beauty of maturity, of motherhood, not that of wild, shy, unconquered virginity.

To Billy it was like the face of a woman loved twenty years since.   Sentiment might play delicately about it, but the love it had inspired lay dead among the years.

He let his memories crowd about him.   He thought of Kent and the formidable man, and of poor Pierre, of Hank Berry, and Willy Croker, and old John Crawford.   Now that he had definitely made up his mind to leave them all, he felt he could afford to indulge a little regret.

He had not prospered in this place, but he had made many friends and known much happiness.

But he could not stay.   The spirits of his ancestors called him to arise and seek what lay beyond the horizon, to leave the haunts of man and pitch his tent in the waste places.

It was his destiny.   He was not made for civilization, but appointed by fate a scout, a spyer-out of the land.   It was written that he should not tarry long in one place, and that none of his seed should lay his head in the sepulchre of his fathers.   He did not say these things to himself, but he knew that it was so : once more the trumpet had sounded for him and he might not linger.

He could not stay.   He had loved Maggie, and he still loved her.   He felt no bitterness toward her : she had obeyed her instincts as he his.   They were but dice thrown by the hand of the mocking god who rules the world.

It would be hard to part from her, but if she would not come with him he must go alone. He could live without her, but without his vision he could not live.

The quest of the Desirable Land was greater than the love of woman, and he must make haste to set out upon that quest before his muscles stiffened and his eyes dimmed.

He rose slowly, shook himself, and sighed deeply. Now Maggie must be told, and she would be angry. The resulting argument would doubtless be long and bitter, but this time he would not be turned from his purpose. He would leave the farm to her and set out alone. And there was even a little joy in the fact that he would be once more a free man, absolutely free to go whithersoever he would and render account to none for any trail whereon he chose to set his wayward feet.

He came slowly down the hill. He saw her out in the yard, hanging some washing upon the line. He approached her with an impassive face.

She was a little brown woman now, burned by years of toil in the sun about the yard. There were a few streaks of grey, a very few, in her luxuriant brown hair. She had lost some teeth and her cheeks had fallen in somewhat. But she was still strong and active and good for many years of hard work.

She came to meet him. There was a mysterious smile upon her lips that he found far more daunting than a tight mouth and angry eyes. He knew of old that she was a woman dangerously capable of getting her own way, and he wondered uneasily of what stratagem he was about to be made the victim.

" Still figurin' on pullin' out ? " she inquired.

" Uh· huh."

" Old sour-face," she mocked. " Goin' to ask me to sell the place again ? "

" No."

" O-oh. You must have got it bad. I never seen you so cranky before."

She lifted a hand to his shoulder. He stiffened suspiciously, waiting for the dangerous attack he would have to repel.

But she only gave him a little shake and laughed gently.

" All right, Billy boy, all right. No need to look so scared. I been thinkin' it over, an' I ain't goin' to scrap with you no more about it. If you got to pull out, go ahead, but I'm comin' too. Now give me a kiss for not startin' another fight."

With tears in his eyes he bent and kissed her.

Printed in Canada